IN SILENCE SEALED

KATHRYN PTACEK

For Bob Booth, the first to see the link and who has always proved enthusiastic about August.

NOTES:

While this is a work of fiction, many of the events concerning Keats, Shelley, and Byron described within the pages of this book are indeed incidents which actually occurred. Still others have been deleted in order to advance the story.

PREFACE

In 1985 Kathryn Ptacek's fine novel *Blood Autumn* appeared. I read it and admired it greatly. Her monster was August, a lamia. Sort of half-vampire and half-succubus, August first seduced men and then drained them. In the novel she off-handedly mentioned August's friendship with John Keats.

In 1987 Kathy was our guest of honor at Necon, a small horror convention held annually in Portsmouth, RI. We talked and I told her how clever it was to mention Keats. It had prompted me to ponder the strange deaths of all three of the darker Romantic poets—Keats, Shelley and Byron.

Like any good writer Kathy was curious and followed through with an incredible amount of research on the period. The result was *In Silence Sealed*. Here August is joined by her sisters and the strange deaths are explained. It is at once sensual, creepy, and historically accurate.

—*Bob Booth*

And mighty poets in their misery dead.
     —William Wordsworth, *Resolution and Independence*

Her lips were red, her looks were free,
Her locks were yellow as gold;
Her skin was white as leprosy,
The nightmare Life-in-Death was she,
Who thicks men's blood with cold.
     —Samuel Taylor Coleridge, *The Ancient Mariner*

Was it a vision, or a waking dream?
     —John Keats, *Ode to a Nightingale*

A solitary shriek
     —Byron, *Don Juan*

How wonderful is Death,
Death and his brother sleep!
     —Shelley, *Queen Mab*

The human heart has hidden treasures,
In secret kept, in silence sealed.

     —Charlotte Bronte, *Everting Solace*

PART I
WINSTON—GREECE: 1824

CHAPTER 1

Winston Early gazed eagerly across the vivid blue of the Ionian Sea at the land which lay ahead.

Greece.

Or rather, he corrected himself as he looked longingly at the slate blue mountains in the distance, the mainland of that country. Technically, he had arrived in Greece two days ago, when the ship docked at the Ionian isle of Cephalonia.

But he couldn't count that, not really, not until he actually reached the mainland, and had actually stepped down onto the soil of the birthplace of art.

Home of Aristotle, Socrates, Homer, Sappho, Pindar, Euripides, Herodotus, Sophocles, democracy, logic, mathematics, art, theatre, the *Iliad*, the *Odyssey*, the mighty gods and goddesses of Mt. Olympus.

Greece. The perfect end to his year-long European Grand Tour.

Originally, he hadn't planned on coming here at all, but a few months ago, while living in Rome, he realized he didn't want to return home quite yet. He was having a good time traveling, and he sat down to decide where he might go next.

What better place to go than where Western civilization virtually began? Even as he considered the notion, an intense excitement grew in him, and he knew he could not stay away. Just prior to his departure, then, he posted a brief letter to his father, telling him of the change in plans. He knew his father wouldn't be pleased, but he knew, too, that he couldn't stay away from Greece; and the more he considered it, the more captivated he became.

He sighed deeply, thinking of his father's likely displeasure. Yet, the entire idea of a Grand Tour was the elder Early's suggestion, although Winston knew full well that the European trip had not produced the results his father hoped for.

When Winston had turned twenty-three a year and a half ago, Richard Early, a wealthy attorney with a large country home and a prosperous practice in London, had declared that he wanted his son to travel abroad so that he might expand his education. Winston had recently earned a degree from Cambridge, but, his father said, more could be learned from travel than from books.

The real reason for this generous offer, however, was the intense hope that the extensive journey would rid his son of an "odd" notion the young man had had for the past few years—that he did not wish to carry on the family's tradition in law.

But Winston did not want to be a barrister. In fact, he hated the law. His only passion in life since he had been a lad was art, and he wanted nothing more than to be an artist.

Not surprisingly, his father deplored this caprice, declaring it was no occupation for a gentleman. Yet Winston's dream was hardly whimsical. At an early age, when he was barely out of skirts, he had begun sketching, first in charcoal, then later in pencil. He had persuaded his tutors to teach him the basics of composition and painting, and over the years had painstakingly refined his technique. At home an immense trunk contained hundreds of sketchbooks he had filled as a child, then as a young boy, then as a young man.

He would be an artist. His father could not dissuade him.

Then Richard had suggested the Grand Tour. A bribe, Winston knew, because his father was also aware of how he yearned to travel. *I will give you a trip through Europe, and I expect you to repay me by giving up your art.* That was the unspoken gist.

4

Only it hadn't worked, and not for the first time he contemplated his father disowning him. In his mind he had tried preparing himself for that contingency, but he wondered if he would be strong when, and if, that moment came.

His father was right about one thing, because he had learned a lot this past year, much of it not found in any of his textbooks. The educational benefit of the trip was undeniable.

During the last twelve months he had journeyed from the English countryside to France, and then down to Spain; north again, this time to Bavaria, Austria, across the Alps into Italy, where he had lingered longer than any other place because of the incomparable art and churches.

Now he was on the last leg of the journey. His visit to Greece. He had left Naples nearly a month ago, and passed through the Strait of Messina into the Ionian Sea. Now the boat was preparing to sail through the waters between Cephalonia, largest of the Ionian Islands, and Zante, a rounded verdant hump.

And now I'm in the world alone,/Upon the wide, wide sea:

The remembered lines from Byron's *Childe Harold* made him smile at their truth.

However, these were risky times in Greece since civil war had begun a few years ago when the Greeks rebelled against their Turkish masters. Much travel by foreigners was curtailed, although the country was hardly cut off from the rest of Europe.

Still, the strife added a dollop of excitement—and of romance. Vividly he imagined himself at the site of a battle, quickly sketching the virtuous rebels as they charged their oppressors. Possibly he might persuade a few of the newspapers back in London to publish some of his sketches. Provided he ever reached a front. He grinned at such an obvious dream.

He inhaled deeply the brisk sea air, feeling its salty tang invigorate him. The current of excitement, with him for weeks, increased the closer he drew to his destination. Even though the day was not yet half over, he was surprised that he had neither seen nor heard any signs of civil battles. The man at the British Embassy in Rome had tried dissuading him from going across to Greece for this very reason, saying that it was quite dangerous, but Winston had been adamant.

How could an artist, on his Grand Tour, be denied the sights of Greece, the very beginnings of true art? He would go, no matter what, he civilly informed the man, and that was that.

It was during the initial moments of dusk that Winston first set foot upon the soil of Greece.

His excitement was such that his hands trembled slightly, and nothing could dampen his spirits, not even the drizzle of rain falling on this eighth day of January; and for a single wild moment, he considered flinging himself upon the ground and kissing it, but with a chagrined blush, he did not. That was a wildly emotional gesture, which only a very passionate man, and a genius such as the great poet Lord Byron, might do. Not a novice artist such as Winston Early.

Rather, he stepped forward, grinned broadly, and thanked whatever gods guided his destiny that he had made it at last.

His Greek guide oversaw the loading of Winston's few pieces of baggage onto the backs of several placid burros. Finally they mounted their own beasts. Winston's legs dangled comically on either side of the sturdy creature as he glanced about the countryside. The land was much flatter than he'd expected, nor was this area as green as Cephalonia, and he tried to suppress a slight disappointment. But the islands, he reminded himself, were like paradise, and the mountains he had seen from the boat must be farther inland.

As the final grey light fled the sky and the land was plunged into darkness, the burros began plodding forward, and Winston vowed to rise early the next morning and venture out sketching.

CHAPTER 2

Sometime after midnight Winston and his elderly Greek guide reached Missolonghi, the small town where he planned to stay a few days before he left for the interior. The burro ride had taken far longer than he had anticipated, and he was exhausted. He paid his silent guide, then dismissed him.

Inside the inn, the innkeeper greeted him, while a sleepy boy of twelve or so showed Winston to his room, where he managed to unpack only some of his clothing before falling straight into bed without undressing.

He slept, his night's rest disturbed only by one dream, whose contents fled with the rising sun.

He rose, yawning and aching from the day before, and glanced about the room. Along one wall, his narrow and uncomfortable bed with its thin sheet and blanket; a low chest pushed up against another. A pitcher and basin of pale yellow china sat atop the chest, and a mirror, framed in tin, hung on the whitewashed wall above them. A rickety-looking chair sat by the door. There was a brightly colored rag rug by the bed, and a gaudily painted icon hung above the bed. Opposite the door was a window, which was open. Through it came a slight breeze that stirred the blue curtains and brought with it the scents of fish and salt and sludge.

Not the most welcome of places, he observed, then shrugged. He wasn't staying here very long, so what did it matter?

He crossed to the chest to wash and stared at himself in the mirror, almost not recognizing the image there. He had tanned and grown leaner during his travels, so that he looked like a young man accustomed to a rugged life, not one exhausted from the trip across the Ionian Sea, with deep circles under his large grey eyes.

His light brown hair, worn slightly longer than was fashionable, brushed his shirt collar, and he ran his hand through it, rumpling it even more. He was fairly tall at an inch over six feet, and he was too aware of his size and, because of it, was slightly awkward at times. His face wasn't particularly handsome, or so he had been told often enough by his father when he'd been caught looking in the mirror. His chin was faintly square, his eyebrows heavy and dark.

He smiled at himself. He had his father's own perfect teeth, or so the man alleged, and his mother's own smile, a gracious smile, he'd been told. He wouldn't mind being more like her, for she had been even-tempered and unselfish. Or so the servants claimed. He had those qualities, he thought without pride, and he'd added a trait of insatiable curiosity, something his father appeared incapable of understanding.

He glanced down at his hands. Long capable fingers, hands that were not soft, like others of his class. He smiled, thinking of how often they were stained with ink or paint, and how his father looked with disfavor at those reminders of his son's aberrant pursuit.

He pushed back the curtains and faint light poured into the room. Instantly he felt better. He looked out to see the view, but unfortunately, another building stood there, not more than twenty feet away.

He disrobed and dressed in fresh nankeen trousers and shirt, hastily tied his white scarf into a bow at his neck, pulled on his boots, sadly neglected in this last leg of the journey, then buttoned his coat of grey broadcloth. He passed a silver-backed brush through his hair, and when he was finished with his morning toilette, he hurried down the hall.

The innkeeper, a bony elderly fellow, greeted Winston upon his entrance into the dining room. The sleepy boy from the night before darted about the room, sweeping the floor and straightening tablecloths.

"Good morning, sir, to you." A slight bow followed, along with a big smile. Athanasios Mavronikis's English was nearly as perfect as his white teeth, with only a slight accent deepening his voice from time to time. His deep-set eyes were black and sparkled with good humor. He wore a thin jet-black moustache under a jutting nose; his hair was nearly all white. A long scar, and not very old by its red color, angled down from his eyebrow along one side of his face, and Winston wondered how he'd received it.

"Good day, Mr. Mavronikis." He restrained a yawn, then looked about, taking a table by a window.

The sun struggled to shine through grey clouds promising afternoon rain as they scudded across the sky. The spacious windows of the dining room overlooked the salt lagoon upon whose edge Missolonghi had unfolded. Delicate green reeds that trembled with the breeze fringed the otherwise barren shores. The inn was located at one end of the town and from there he had a good view of it.

Standing on a flat, marshy promontory sticking out into the lagoon which was navigable only by small flat-bottomed boats, the village did not look like those he'd seen on Cephalonia. Here and there he saw fishermen's huts built on stakes in the water, and long red fishing nets hanging from the stakes or drying on the pebbles.

It was extremely picturesque, although not at all the image of Greece which Winston had held in his mind for so long. Perhaps if he hadn't arrived in the winter. Spring was bound to bring color to the land.

Some three miles offshore, the lagoon was separated from the waters of the gulf by "islets," or rather a low line of sand pits and mud dunes that reached nearly the base of the cloud-capped Varassora Mountains, those he had seen from the boat yesterday.

Near the end of the promontory stood a large sprawling house. It caught his attention because it stood three stories high, while almost all of the village houses were one-story structures.

Though the town was without any visible defenses, he knew they were safe from Turkish attack by sea—the lagoon's very shallowness insured that.

Suddenly the sun broke through the grayness, the room filled with dazzling light, and Winston squinted so that he could see.

"Ah, the sun. We have not often seen it recently, for it has been raining day and night for a week now. I must caution you when you go out later, Mr. Early, that there is much water and mud in the streets, and you must take care. Now, you must eat."

Without further ceremony, he brought Winston a large pot of tea. He snapped his fingers at the boy, who hurried over with silverware for Winston. The boy smiled shyly, then left.

"You see, Mr. Early, I know the customs of your people already. There are many Englishmen visiting in the village of Missolonghi."

"Indeed?" he inquired politely as he poured the steaming tea into a white porcelain cup. The brew looked a bit darker than what he was accustomed to, but no doubt it was simply a different variety. "A rasher of bacon and toast, if you would, Mr. Mavronikis."

"Indeed." The man bowed and left the dining room. He ate the bacon and the toast, and the eggs fried in olive oil that Mavronikis volunteered, then topped it off with the tea.

The beverage tasted somewhat oily, as if some liqueur had been added, but overall he enjoyed the meal. He had traveled too far—and too often—on an empty stomach in the past year to be particularly fussy about his food. And this meal wasn't bad, not really. He had suffered through far worse in the backwater towns and villages of the continent. As he ate, he studied the landscape he saw out the window. He could hardly wait to get his things together and start sketching.

Later, he carefully folded his napkin and with a wave of his hand bid Mavronikis join him as he finished his tea. The man seemed only too happy to do so, for the man had never sat still for a moment. He had been constantly on his feet, every few minutes inquiring if Winston needed anything, flicking dust off the various chairs and tables, straightening a picture here and there, and always watching his solitary guest.

"Now, Mr. Mavronikis, what about those other Englishmen you mentioned?" Winston asked. He was always glad to hear about his fellow countrymen. It might have indicated he was more than a little home sick, but he preferred thinking that it was one way of keeping up with news from home.

"There are many English here."

"Tea?"

"No, thank you, I will have some ouzo. You will join me?"

What the devil was that? Winston wondered. Well, better not be rude, particularly to his host. "Of course, I will."

The man jumped up to fetch a bottle and two tiny glasses. He poured equal amounts of the clear liqueur into each, then watched with an amused smile as Winston raised his to his lips and sipped—and coughed harshly as he slapped the glass down, aware that his vision was blurring slightly. The drink had an anise like flavor, but was unexpectedly potent. "Good God, that's strong. What is it?"

"Ouzo. A popular drink around here." Mavronikis tilted his head back and poured his drink down, then filled his glass again. "Now, for your fellow countrymen. Some have come to fight in the war. Others travel for pleasure, as you do."

"Do you know any of their names?" It was fairly inconceivable that he would meet up with anyone with whom he was already acquainted, but one never knew. Too, the possibility existed of their having a mutual acquaintance. He had already discovered that more than once in Austria and Italy.

He tapped his fingers on his glass. "Let me think. Ah yes, there is a Lord and Lady St. John, a very attractive couple and so in love. This is their second visit to my little village. You know them?"

"No, I'm afraid not." He took another sip, cautiously this time. The ouzo still burned the entire length of his throat.

"Mr. Thomas Cameron of Scotland. He is a fine fellow, always full of mirth, that man, and the only one who cannot be drunk under the table by me." Mavronikis grinned broadly. "I have tried often to see that, believe me, Mr. Early."

Winston chuckled. "I don't doubt that, Mr. Mavronikis. I don't believe I know the gentleman, as admirable as he sounds."

11

"There are two sisters," the innkeeper began, "but they are only half-English." Winston looked inquiringly at him. There was something about the tone of his voice. Something that he could not pin down.

"But they live on the outskirts of town, and you will not see them, I think."

Was that distrust that he heard? Or was it fear? Fear of what? Two sisters? But since the man was so decidedly ill at ease, he decided not to pursue the matter, asking instead about other guests in the inn.

The innkeeper shook his head sorrowfully, and one hand went to the scar on his cheek. "Times are bad for my business. In the old days I had twenty, thirty guests staying here at one time. Now I am fortunate to see one or two or three."

Winston sincerely doubted that ten guests, much less twenty or thirty as the innkeeper boasted, could be accommodated at the small inn at one time, but prudently he kept silent.

"Bad, bad times, Mr. Early." He shook his head, poured himself another glass and drank that one just as rapidly as he'd finished the others. He named a dozen more men and women, all English, who had come through the village in the past months.

Unfortunately, Winston recognized none as acquaintances.

"And then there is Lord Byron."

"Lord Byron?" Gaping at Mavronikis, Winston sat up. "The English poet?"

Mavronikis seemed delighted at the recognition, as if it were his own reputation. "The very same, the very same. You know him?"

What Englishman didn't know Lord Byron, the greatest living poet! Winston whistled softly. "I know of him, Mr. Mavronikis, but I have never met him. That is. I saw him once at a party in London, but the opportunity for conversation never arose. You say he is staying here? How perfectly marvelous!"

Vividly Winston recalled his brief glimpse of George Gordon, sixth Lord Byron, years before. The poet's curling dark hair with its chestnut glint had straggled over his broad forehead into his eyes giving him a casual look. Those gleaming sardonic eyes might have been hazel or brown, but he couldn't be sure; too, he suspected they changed color with the poet's mood.

Byron had a well-defined cleft in his chin—a feature, it was whispered to Winston, that all the women adored—a long aristocratic nose, and much less height than Winston had expected. Surely a man with such a reputation should stand like a giant, and yet Winston towered over him some five or six inches. He had smiled at Winston, who knew he had seen Greatness.

If only he could be as dedicated to his art as Byron was to his poetry!

"Of course. Every time he comes to Greece, he come to my inn, although this time, he not stay here. Instead, he have a house."

"Indeed! A house in this very village? And he's here now? Is it possible that he might visit you sometime, Mr. Mavronikis?"

The Greek shrugged as he drank more ouzo. "Well, he might, he might not. It is hard to say, yes, what he does. He is a very popular man and has much work. I tell you, Mr. Early, if tonight he comes here, then I introduce you. You like that?"

Winston grinned. "Yes, I like that very much."

CHAPTER 3

Winston left the Inn in the early afternoon and went to sightsee at the black-walled fortress guarding the harbor on the islet of Vassilidi, just outside the village. He spent some time sketching the fortress.

How forbidding it must look to a potential invader, he thought, and was comforted by that. The innkeeper's advice had been good. The narrow and winding streets of irregular paving stones were muddy, sometimes even impassable, while many lanes were nothing but one puddle after another. Deep ruts from the enormous wheels of carts cut through the mire, often leaving gaping holes, and Winston was surprised not to see wagons and cattle caught in the mud as well. But then the inhabitants must be accustomed to this, he reasoned, as it rained so frequently.

Mavronikis said that it dried out quickly when the sun came out for a' few hours, and Winston hoped that would happen while he was staying there.

He had brought along two notebooks and several times paused to sketch some of the hovels and their wizened inhabitants. Such suffering in those faces and eyes, he thought sadly, as he tucked the notebook under his arm and strode on.

Toward dusk he returned to the inn to dine heartily on eggplant stuffed with lamb and raisins, a loaf of freshly baked bread, and dried figs.

He lingered over his meal, and drank more glasses of wine than he knew he should, for wine often made him light-headed. But as long as he waited in the dining room, Lord Byron did not put in an appearance.

As the night wore on, and Byron had still not shown up, Mavronikis directed Winston to the newly renamed Freedom Tavern, located at the opposite end of the village. It was about a quarter of a mile away, and sometimes, the Greek said, Byron visited there.

"Be sure," the innkeeper added, his voice dropping to a whisper, "to return before midnight and always stay on the main street. Do not stray from it."

Winston thanked him for the directions and the rather curious advice, and as the young artist made his way cautiously through the narrow dirt streets, he remembered Mavronikis calling after him that there was no way that he could get lost. He didn't know about that … not on a night as dark as this.

No welcome moon hung above in the stark black sky to light his way, and all the windows of the lean houses facing the street were darkened, too, as if the inhabitants were in bed already, even though it was not yet nine o'clock. He had never seen such an unwelcoming place as Missolonghi at night. A shudder ran through his body, and frowning slightly, he walked faster.

A few minutes later he thought he heard the echo of a footstep behind him, but when he paused, and listened, he heard nothing but the mewing of a cat in the distance. He waited a little longer, but when the sound did not repeat itself, he resumed walking.

Almost immediately something not-quite tangible swept across his left cheek like a cold breath, and with a shriek forming on his lips, he jumped backward, pressing his body against the front wall of a house, still warm from the afternoon sunlight.

He trembled, but didn't understand why, and even as he looked around in the darkness, he saw nothing. He cursed himself for not bringing a lantern. Whatever had touched him must have been a bird or a bat; or a moth, he reassured himself. His heart would not slow its

15

erratic pace, no matter how he tried calming himself. He must be more tired than he'd thought earlier; now his mind was inventing footsteps and soft breaths that weren't there. He tried smiling, but failed. And yet over the smell of mud and salt, he caught another scent, a sweeter one, and he pulled his brows together in a frown.

The tavern seemed much farther away than the quarter of a mile that Mavronikis had originally indicated, and Winston's pace quickened until he was half trotting down the street. Finally, though, he stumbled upon the Freedom Tavern. Slightly out of breath, he welcomed the light and spirited music and conversation spilling out onto the lonely street.

What a hospitable sight it was! Winston thought, feeling a strange prickling across the back of his neck, as if he were being watched by unseen eyes. Quickly, as if pursued by demons, he stepped across the threshold of the open door and stared around the large smoky room of the tavern.

Abandoned fishing nets draped across the unfinished beams overhead, while slender lanterns were suspended from the ceiling, providing pools of yellow light. Square tables were scattered across the wide plank floor, and every one of the mismatched chairs and stools was occupied.

A handful of musicians occupied the very back of the room and continued playing, regardless of any attention given them. The fish smell present in the village was more pronounced here, perhaps because the tavern lay close to the lagoon or because half of its customers wore the dingy clothing of fishermen. There was just the single room, and Winston noticed that the windows were all covered with dark curtains. Only the door was left open, as if guiding lost souls like himself to the tavern.

Winston hesitated, smiling shakily, hoping to exude more self-assurance than he felt. Of the nonfishing customers, most wore embroidered tunics, and he guessed they must be Greek soldiers. There were no women here. One or two men looked his way, then turned back to their drinks and friends. Relieved that no one was challenging him, he relaxed a little. His glance swept left and right, as he looked throughout the room for Lord Byron.

16

And there he was, toward one side, away from the enthusiastic musicians. The man glanced up, and for the briefest moment Winston thought he saw a look of terror pass across the poet's face, but the expression faded quickly. Winston started across the room toward the poet.

He paused by the table while Byron finished his conversation with another man; a Greek, he supposed from the man's dark complexion and costume. There were several empty bottles in front of the two men, and it looked as though they were doing some sort of business. For a moment Winston wished he hadn't intruded, but it was too late to turn back now. Byron was stirring.

"Yes? May I help you?" He stood a little awkwardly and gazed at Winston. His voice was well modulated, that of an educated gentleman.

Byron's right foot and ankle had been deformed at birth, and Winston knew that in spite of Byron's lameness. or perhaps because of it, he had become a powerful swimmer and successful cricketer in school. Winston kept his eyes away from the foot.

Byron was at once the great melancholy poet, the icily reserved aristocrat, the irreligious rake, and the charmingly shy boy, and Winston didn't know which was the man, and which was the persona he had created for the splendid outpouring of his romantic nature.

Such an incredible vital force emanated from the poet that Winston could scarcely find his tongue to speak, and yet in those few seconds he saw there was something else corning from the poet tonight, too.

For some strange reason the man seemed haunted, and while he was still handsome, Byron had aged considerably since Winston had seen him in London. Although Byron was only thirty-six, he looked far older. Grey now streaked the once-dark hair. He was far heavier, too, no longer a slender youth. Shadows lay under Byron's expressive eyes and an unhealthy shade tinged his skin; and he trembled, as if cold, or in fear. Winston wondered if the poet had been ill recently.

Still, Winston admired the very casual nature of Byron's attire—his collar was open in the almost oppressive heat of the room and he had discarded his coat, now hanging across the back of his chair. He wished he could look so at ease, so tousled, but when he tried, he merely looked unkempt.

Byron raised one perfectly arched eyebrow at Winston's continuing silence.

Then Winston's words tumbled out. "My name is Early Winston, my lord, I mean, Winston Early. I'm from England, and the innkeeper told me I might find you here, and so I came here tonight."

Byron's lips quirked into a smile. He was not entirely without a sense of humor. "As if I couldn't tell your country from the moment you entered the tavern, Mr. Early, is it? Please, sit down." He had a soft Scots accent, quite pleasant to the ear.

"I couldn't intrude, my lord," he murmured without hesitation, and yet it was the very reason he had come to the tavern, he realized ironically. He had been a fool to so brazenly present himself. Whatever would Lord Byron think?

The Greek at the table muttered something to Byron, rose and nodded briefly to Winston, then left to join others across the room.

"I'm sorry, I didn't mean to—"

"You didn't," the poet said, his tone ironic. He indicated the vacant chair. "Here now—Mr. Winston, was it?—you must sit with me for a while. I abhor drinking by myself."

Trying hard not to blush, Winston sat, then clasped his hands together in his lap. He didn't want them to betray how nervous he was in this man's presence. "Thank you, my lord."

"Where did you say you were staying?"

"I'm at the inn—at the upper end of the street—and when I was talking with Mr. Mavronikis earlier, he told me I might find you here."

"Ah, I see. The inevitable connection between the English, of course. And how is dear old England?" Byron poured wine from a bottle in front of him into two glasses and shoved one toward Winston.

Winston smiled slightly. He had once heard that while a student at Cambridge, Byron had used as a drinking cup the skull from a long-dead monk. Only a rumor; or was it? "Well, you see, I haven't been there in some time. I've been traveling for a year now."

"The Grand Tour." Byron sipped his wine. "An enchanting occasion."

18

"Er, yes. Sir, I would like to say how much I enjoy your—"

"Yes, yes." Startled, Winston fell silent. Byron gazed distractedly into the distance. "From what little town do you hail, Early Winston?"

Winston colored at Byron's slight mocking. "My family's home is in Royal Tunbridge Wells, although sometimes my father and I live in London, where he is a barrister. I am an artist," he added shyly, and proudly, a moment later.

Byron peered at him. "Are you a good one?"

"I think so, sir, at least for what I have done thus far, and I admit that isn't all that much as of yet. My father doesn't believe I'm very good, though," he confided. "He claims art is for children, not men."

"Your father is an ignorant man, then. I suppose he was opposed to this year-long trip?" Byron poured himself another drink.

"Well, no, my lord. Actually, he suggested it, but I think only to disabuse me of my 'odd' notions. I know that he's hoping I'll come home soon and settle into the family business."

"How utterly boring."

"Yes."

"Didn't he realize how much art you'd see, and how your experiences would only serve to inspire you in your choice?"

"I don't think he saw it that way."

"I suppose not. Fathers can be notoriously shortsighted." He smiled somewhat wryly. "Have another drink, Mr. Early."

"Thank you." The wine, although resinous, was more tolerable than the ouzo he'd tasted earlier in the day.

Byron was staring off into the distance now, and a shudder passed through his body. He grimaced, then drank some more wine.

Winston set his glass down. "Excuse me, my lord, for my presumption, but you aren't ill, are you?"

"No, I am not … ill, but thank you for your concern, all the same."

Although he had every reason to believe Lord Byron, Winston suspected that the man was lying because his eyes shifted when he spoke. But why lie about this? It made no sense.

He decided trying another topic. "The war has brought you to Greece then, my lord?"

"Yes, I returned only a week ago—I was here once before, you know-to help the Greeks against the tyranny of the Turks. For four centuries the Greeks have been ruthlessly enslaved. At present the chains are broken indeed, but the links are still clanking. Theirs is a terrible struggle, and much remains to be done yet, Mr. Winston. So very much."

Once more Byron's eyes strayed into the distance, and it seemed that whatever he saw there he did not like. He gazed down at his glass gripped tightly in his hand, and for a moment Winston thought the glass would break.

Not knowing what else to do, Winston murmured sympathetically.

"However, despite that struggle, I still have some time to myself, and I believe that tomorrow I might well be free."

Byron finished his glass of wine and poured himself another. Winston was amazed that the poet wasn't drunk by now. He had drunk many glasses in Winston's presence, and doubtless before that as well. Yet the wine seemed to invigorate him.

"So, if I find I have free time, I would like to show you something of the village and surrounding countryside, Mr. Early, and tell you a little of its long history. I think you will find Missolonghi fascinating, despite its dreary appearance."

Winston protested at once. "Dreary the town may be now, my lord, but there's still so much here to catch an artist's eye!"

"You needn't flatter me, sir. I know the town is hardly like those on Cephalonia. What do you say of my offer?"

"I would be honored to meet with you tomorrow, sir." The poet was offering to escort him through the village? He could scarcely credit it.

Byron chuckled. "You needn't be so formal, I'm not a god, just a great poet." They fell silent for a few minutes, then Winston shifted. He didn't want to bore the other man.

"Well, my lord. I shouldn't take any more of your time then. I should return to the inn, I suppose. I'm feeling somewhat tired yet from my journey. I arrived on a burro last night, and I'd never ridden one before," he confided. "And I still ache."

Byron only smiled.

Winston rose somewhat unsteadily and thanked Byron for the wine and the conversation, and as he was leaving, he heard Byron call to him.

"Yes?"

"Be careful, and do not tarry, Mr. Early. The night is very dark here."

With that cryptic message echoing the innkeeper's, Byron dismissed him with a nod.

CHAPTER 4

The following day Winston punctually met the other man. As they walked, Byron talked about Missolonghi.

"The village has a long history of freedom fighting, which is one of the reasons I chose it. Too, it is such an unappealing place that no one—especially the Turks—can believe that anything of value could come from it."

Winston smiled.

"Still, there is much left to do here yet. Look over there, Mr. Early. The ramparts are in bad repair and should be rebuilt. You see those old Turkish cannon? Over there? To the left; farther left now. Yes? Good. We can remove them, and put them to use. And I must see to it that the islet—it commands the entrance to the lagoon—is more heavily guarded. That, I believe, is our vulnerable spot, and I fear the Sultan and his men will learn of it all too soon. I am currently enlisting money from England—as a temporary loan to the Greeks, you understand—so that I will be able to organize a new artillery brigade and an infantry corps." He paused to take a breath; his face was slightly flushed, but he looked less ill than the night before. His voice was strong and firm, his gaze level as he looked around. "Greece cannot continue under this yoke of tyranny."

Winston, who had never been overfond of politics but was interested now because Byron was so devoted to it, nodded from time to time in what he hoped was an intelligent manner. He found the rapid succession of Greek names and skirmish sites and the discussion of strategy confusing, but he refused to interrupt and ask Byron to explain. He knew he was ignorant; he simply didn't wish the other man to know it.

As the day wore on, Winston found himself being outdistanced by Byron. The poet never let his lameness slow him, even though he was obviously quite conscious of his clubfoot. Several times Byron referred to it as his "little friend," and too embarrassed to say anything, or even to know what to say, Winston remained silent.

Although limping severely as the afternoon hours passed, Byron moved quite speedily and at times Winston hurried to keep up.

Byron was fascinating. The young artist realized he could watch and listen to the poet for hours, even days, and that probably the man could talk freely and knowledgeably on any given subject, not just on freedom, Greece, and the purpose of art. Byron had an opinion on everything, and if he didn't like a particular subject, it was at the mercy of his scalding humor. It was apparent from Byron's conversation that he had known most everyone of importance in London, and in Italy and Greece as well—perhaps the entire civilized world. He was especially well pleased when Byron suggested they meet again.

Over the next few days the two men met often, sometimes at the inn or tavern in the afternoon or early evening, and then finally at Byron's house, which Winston considered an honor.

With surprise, Winston discovered that the three story house he saw that first morning from the inn's window was the house given Byron upon his arrival in Missolonghi. It was decidedly Turkish-looking with projecting balconies, outside staircases, smallish oblong windows, and several open turrets. Several sheds were attached around a large dirt-floored courtyard, and behind was an open space. On rainy days the ground about the house became a morass and could be approached only by water.

The house possessed only a single pleasing aspect, Byron remarked casually, and that was the marvelous view southward toward the open waters of the gulf which lay beyond the lagoon. From his window on the top floor, and only if it was a clear Day—and that was not frequent—he could see the mountains of the Morea and the dim outlines of some I of the Ionian Islands.

"I spend many hours staring out that window," Byron said dreamily, and Winston could not but think that the poet's eyes seemed to be looking far beyond the view, as if he were trying to look into his own future.

Albanian mercenaries, in Byron's pay and acting as guards, lived on the ground floor, while Colonel Leicester Stanhope, a representative of the London Greek Committee, had the second floor, with Byron on the third. The poet's living quarters included his bedroom and sitting room facing the lagoon, and three rooms for his servants: a Venetian gondolier with a fierce countenance; an English valet, William Fletcher; a steward: a black American servant recently acquired from a friend as cook and groom; and a handsome young Greek boy as a page.

The rooms were simply furnished with beds and a few tables and chairs and several shelves filled with Byron's books. But his sitting room looked more like an arsenal than a receiving room, the artist thought, immediately intrigued. Old and more recent swords, Turkish sabers, rifles, Albanian bayonets, pistols, silver trumpets and helmets, and other implements of war decorated the walls so thickly that hardly an inch of plain white wall could be detected.

In the Turkish fashion, they sat upon cushions on a kind of mattress laid out on the floor. The poet's Newfoundland dog, Lion, lay with his massive head on his master's knee and watched Winston out of mournful brown eyes.

Winston quickly became a frequent visitor. Often Byron's house was filled with Albanian mercenaries and Greek soldiers, their silver trappings flashing in the candlelight, their rough conversation and raucous laughter booming through the small apartment. Winston had never seen anything like it, and he was thrilled with it.

Winston listened to the conversations that flowed and ebbed through the rooms, and sometimes he walked from one group of men to another, simply watching. Occasionally he perched upon a stool and deftly sketched, catching the glinting eye of one, the sad countenance of another. Sometimes he would unobtrusively draw his host. But mostly he listened.

Stanhope wished to establish a post office and schools in Greece. Byron smiled wryly.

"The only school which I will support would be a gunnery school," he declared. Stanhope glared at him.

Byron continued, unaffected by the other. "All the stories of the Greek victories by sea and land are exaggerated or untrue."

"Not at all, sir!"

"Indeed, they are, Colonel Stanhope. I neither despond nor despair of the Cause. But it is my business to state things as they are to the Committee." Stanhope said no more to this, and that was the end of the discussion.

Often Winston and his host discussed art and poetry when they were alone.

"Passion—that of the heart and of the mind, my dear boy—is the only true reason for living. God knows, but I have had my share of passion these past years." His lips quirked into an ironic smile.

Winston wondered which of Byron's many affairs he was thinking of, for there had been many. And some gossips alluded to a love for his half-sister as well. Winston could scarcely give credence to that.

"Am I passionate enough to be a great artist?" Winston asked suddenly, then blushed when he realized what he had blurted.

Byron chuckled. "Yes, I think that you are, or will be, Mr. Early. But I warn you"—and here the poet leaned forward and lowered his voice—"passion also can bring the end of life."

Winston said nothing, but remained puzzled about that odd declaration.

Occasionally the two Englishmen were joined by the young Italian physician, Dr. Francesco Bruno, Byron had brought with him as his doctor. The doctor was not highly experienced, but he seemed genuinely worried about the health of his famous patient.

At times, Dr. Bruno, in a hesitant voice, would remind the poet that he must rest, while Byron would simply wave away his concerned words with an airy gesture. And Byron would continue talking as before. Dr. Bruno would look close to tears, then wring his hands and walk away, as if he realized he could do no more.

Sometimes Byron read poetry to Winston.

"'O'er the glad waters of the dark blue sea/Our thoughts are boundless, and our souls as free/Far as the breeze can bear, the billows foam/Survey our empire, and behold our home!'"

Byron's voice was strong, musical, and it hypnotized Winston. He saw everything so clearly when Byron read aloud his poetry that he almost felt as if he were living the poem.

However, the longer Winston spent with Byron the more he realized something was definitely wrong with the man. It must be illness—although Byron denied it—that caused Byron's hands to tremble so badly at times that he was forced to keep them clasped, the knuckles white, for hours.

Too, the extra weight Winston had seen on Byron was now dissolving daily, and while he knew the poet dieted, he thought there was another reason for the sudden weight loss. Still, Byron refused to give in to his strange unnamed ailment and continued his life as usual. But he always seemed worse in the late afternoon.

"When are you going to bring your sketches so that I might see them?"

"Oh, you don't want to do that," Winston demurred, his voice low.

Byron arched an eyebrow. "Of course, I do, dear boy. Otherwise I would not have mentioned them. And don't think I haven't seen you sneaking about sketching me or the others when you thought we weren't looking."

"I wasn't sneaking!" Winston protested, then relaxed with a smile when he realized the other man was simply teasing.

Winston thought Byron sounded sincere, but could this great man truly wish to look at the drawings of a young artist? He could scarcely credit it. Nearly a week later, though, Byron coaxed him into bringing his notebooks, and shyly he showed Byron the sketches he had drawn during his European travels of the past year.

"They're excellent, truly brilliant, Mr. Early!" Byron exclaimed as he studied each one intently. "I've never seen such detail! Simple lines used so very boldly, and you've captured the true spirit of the Roman

26

ruins. And these"—he jabbed at several sketches with a forefinger—"who are they?"

"Swiss shepherds I encountered on a walk one day," Winston replied.

"This boy's face is so innocent; he's almost an angel. Look at those wide eyes, that small mouth." Byron gazed a while longer at the boy, then studied each of the sketches. Finally, he set the sketchbook down, then looked at Winston. "I have friends in London who must see these as soon as possible. When you return home, you must go to them—I will write a letter for you, explaining our friendship—and see what they can do for you."

"Oh, but, I couldn't—" Winston began.

"Of course, you could, my dear boy. Your brilliance cannot be left to mere chance. Never turn down an offer of patronage. It is not a word to be scorned, you must understand."

But before the astonished—and incredibly pleased—Winston could thank the man, Byron was flinging the sketchbooks aside and verbally skipping on to another altogether different subject. At the same time a haunted expression crept across his face. The shadows of afternoon were lengthening outside.

It was as if Byron's fear—or his illness worsened as daylight decreased.

Why this was, Winston didn't understand, and he wanted to. He sensed that Byron bore a secret, and the thought intrigued him all the more.

He must find out what frightened Byron so much.

CHAPTER S

Shortly before sunset, one wet day in late January, the chilly winter rain finally stopped, and the two men decided to go walking.

Originally, Winston hadn't planned on staying beyond a few days in Missoionghi, and now, to his surprise, he found he'd been there nearly two weeks.

And yet, when else, he reasoned with himself, would he have another opportunity to talk with a man as great as Lord Byron? Never, and thus, his tour of the remainder of Greece could wait for a while. He knew Byron planned leaving the village in a week or two, and he would leave then, too. Their direction shifted slowly toward the lagoon, which was difficult avoiding on a casual stroll around the town. Winston wrinkled his nose at the strong odor wafting through the air.

Byron smiled. "You get used to it, after a while. And there are far worse things, believe me."

Winston swallowed. "Truly? I find that difficult to believe, my lord."

The other man chuckled. "You're young yet, Mr. Early, and many things are difficult to believe. When you are as old as I—"

"But you're not old!" Winston protested.

"But I feel old, and so it is all the same," the other man said quietly.

And as Winston glanced sidelong at his companion he saw in a rare moment of insight just how much the poet had aged in the past fortnight. Faint new lines marred the delicate skin at the outer corners of his eyes, and a deep wrinkle slashed across his forehead, almost like the scar of a saber blade. And the faint trembling—it was ever present in his hands and even now in his voice. Winston, unnerved, said nothing.

The afternoon light was rapidly fading from the now cloudless sky, leaving it a deep leaden grey, and a brisk cold breeze—reminding Winston it was still winter—had sprung up. They had just rested a moment by a large outcropping of rock and were once more walking when Winston noticed two others out for fresh air during this rare and unexpected interval between rains.

The two were some distance ahead of them yet, coming toward them at a sedate, though steady, pace; already the figures were fairly shadowy in the twilight.

Byron, whose head was bent down with his gaze fixed on the rocky ground before them, did not notice.

As the others approached slowly, Winston saw that the two pedestrians were both women, one dark-haired, one blonde, and fairly attractive, he ascertained, even from this great distance.

Grinning to himself, Winston adopted his most jocular tone.

"Why, look here, my lord, we've been sent some companionship on this cold, cold night." He nodded with his chin in their direction. He hadn't seen many women in the village, certainly not English ones, and every one of the Greek wives and daughters he'd glimpsed had been wrapped in concealing robes and veils. And he wasn't opposed to a little flirtation with an Englishwoman; God knows he hadn't met many on his tour.

"What, Mr. Early?" As if he'd been lost within his own thoughts, Byron jerked up his head, and in that moment, even though virtually no light lingered in the sky, Winston could see that the poet had gone deathly pale.

The two continued walking toward them.

Winston smiled and waved in return.

Byron grabbed Winston, his fingers pressing like claws into the young man's arm, and ran as quickly as his lame foot would allow back to his house. Too startled to protest, Winston followed.

Byron led Winston upstairs, slammed the door, barred it, then sat heavily on a stool at the dining table. He dropped his head in his hands.

"What is it, my lord? What's wrong?" Winston was still astounded by Byron's reaction. He knew that Byron sometimes acted outlandishly, but surely this was bizarre behavior. He had simply called Byron's attention to the ladies with whom they might have stopped and chatted for a while, and perhaps even flirted. He had heard of Byron's great power over women, and had wanted to witness it. And yet Byron had raced back to his house, as if Death were at his heels.

"Nothing, nothing."

Byron was still out of breath from his retreat, and gulped for air, as if on the verge of choking. In the past few moments he had grown even paler, despite the two spots of high color in his cheeks. But, Winston realized, the red wasn't the color of health.

Something's not right here, he thought uneasily, but what could it be? He knew that if he pressed Byron about the matter tonight, the man would refuse to answer; he was far too agitated to talk about it. Too, Byron was forever disinclined to explain his actions to anyone, and he would talk only when he was completely ready. So, despite the questions that jumbled through his mind, Winston prudently kept his silence.

From time to time Byron glanced at the window, as if expecting to see something out there in the darkness. And yet this was the third floor. Nothing could reach these windows.

Finally, he caught his breath and seemed to calm himself. He poured some wine, and when he had downed that, his hand far from steady, he began talking about the rigors of Italian society. The topic was so far from Winston's expectations that he could do nothing but listen, his mouth slightly agape.

Sometime later when Winston rose to return to the inn for dinner, Byron begged him not to leave.

"Please, Mr. Early, stay and have dinner with me. Stay the night. It isn't safe outside."

"What? What's out there?" Winston peered out the window, as if expecting to find the house under siege by the Turks, but Byron pulled him away from the dirt-streaked window.

"No, don't stand so close there, please, I beg you, Mr. Early." Byron shook himself, then continued, his Scots accent more pronounced now. "You see, sometimes Turkish soldiers sneak into the village to get supplies. It's dangerous. You might run across some of them and be shot mistakenly for a Greek patriot. At times like these, it's best to stay inside until morning."

Surely the poet didn't expect him to believe such a feeble excuse? Yet Byron seemed earnest. "I see, my lord. Well ..."

"Please, Mr. Early, stay. I would be most pleased if you stayed to dine with me. My cook is excellent, by the way, and will prepare anything you wish. And I'll have Fletcher open a room for you. It won't be any bother at all, if that's what you're worried about."

Winston stared at Byron, then glanced out the window. Still nothing but darkness. It was hard to refuse. The man was positively frantic. He reminded Winston of a bird he had once seen. It had flown into a parlor at home and, confused, darted about the room. It had struck mirrors and walls and the ceiling, until it had finally beat itself to death against a heavy leaded window. He thought about walking back to the inn in the darkness, and remembered that time on his way to the inn when he thought he was being followed.

"Very well, my lord."

"Good." He paused, not looking at Winston.

For a moment Winston thought Byron was about to confess what preyed upon his mind.

"One thing, Mr. Early."

"Yes?"

"Do not have anything to do with those women we saw earlier."

"What? I don't—"

"You don't need to know or understand—not yet anyway. Please believe me when I say that I will tell you in good time."

"Very well." He could do nothing but trust his agitated host.

CHAPTER 6

Do not have anything to do with those women.

Byron's warning remained with Winston, even when he was unable to see the poet. Byron had left town to meet with an important Greek about the war and would not be back for some time. Winston decided to stay until the poet returned so he could talk with him again, and so he was left on his own. He wandered about the village, sketching the buildings and those who lived there.

Because he was a recent arrival, the townspeople were curious about him, and so he was sought out by the villagers. He could not communicate very well with them, because few spoke English, and his vocabulary in their language was equally limited. Still, he bought them drinks, and they toasted each other round after round, and they sang songs for him, and he and the villagers smiled much at one another.

He found that he was completely enjoying himself and had not thought of his father—or his father's displeasure—in a long time. He arranged to draw one old grizzled sheepherder who claimed, through his nephew, to be well over a hundred years old. Whether it was true, Winston didn't care. The man's seamed face was a study, and he wanted to capture it in pencil.

Each morning Winston rose as early as he could manage so that he could take a brisk walk before breakfast, and then immediately afterward, he began working. More and more the Greeks, having lost their initial reserve, came to him to show him various locations outside the village they thought he would be interested in drawing. He enjoyed scrabbling along the rocky, almost barren, slopes beyond Missolonghi to find a perch where he could be comfortable as he sketched the vista of mountains, sea and land spread panoramically below him.

His only complaint was that for the past few nights he hadn't slept as well as he would have hoped; certainly he was receiving enough exercise. But despite that, dreams constantly interrupted his sleep, and when he woke in the morning, he couldn't remember their content, and only knew that something within them had frightened him. And because he did not sleep through the night, he was growing more tired.

A week after Byron's departure, Winston walked over to the poet's house to see if the poet was home yet. He wasn't, and Fletcher didn't expect him for some days. Winston left, then decided he wouldn't return to the inn yet.

It was one of the most pleasant afternoons since his arrival, and he was glad to he out. As he strolled along the beach, he watched the play of flickering light against the clouds. The air was cooling quickly, despite the sun's presence all day, and a shiver ran along his back. He continued walking, and only when the sky darkened to a slate grey did he consider turning back.

As he turned, he spotted two women in English dress. One waved, and ignoring Byron's warning, he walked steadily toward them.

Avoid them? How could Byron, the libertine, the great advocate of freedom, suggest that he not do something? It was unthinkable; besides, Winston was far from home and his father, and wanted to be daring.

When only a few feet away, he sketched a formal bow. He saw them only faintly now because the last of the light had fled the sky.

"Good evening, ladies."

"Good evening."

The woman with black hair smiled at him, and her teeth gleamed white in the darkness. Her slightly husky voice sent an unexpected thrill through him. He thought he detected a slight accent, but could not place it. The other woman merely smiled.

"I saw you the other night, but before we could greet you, my friend … experienced a momentary illness, and we were forced to leave." How smoothly the lie slipped off his tongue, he thought uneasily, and yet he could hardly confess that his friend feared these women. He knew his checks must be burning from the untruth.

"I understand that that sort of thing happens." She glanced at her companion. "Pray forgive me, sir, but I've quite forgotten my manners. I am August Kristonosos, and this is my younger sister, Athina."

"How do you do," Athina Kristonosos murmured, her eyes downcast. The other sister, he thought, suffered from no such shyness.

Her voice was higher than her sister's, and it, too, sent a thrill through him. Winston mentally shook himself. What was the matter? He was acting as if he'd never before spoken to two attractive women.

"My name is Winston Early, and I am English, as you might have gathered already. I'm relieved that you both speak English, and I must compliment you on your facility with it. My Greek isn't what it could be, y'know. I can read it fairly well, but speaking is altogether another matter."

He was aware that he was chattering like a magpie, but he couldn't help himself. The only sound beyond his voice was the crashing of the sea upon the rocks beyond the lagoon. Only that, and the darkness around them. The three of them might as well have been the only humans on the earth.

The older sister answered for them. "Thank you for your very pretty compliment, Mr. Early. The reason we speak English so well is that while our father was Greek, our mother hailed from your land."

"How delightful!" he said, and they all laughed comfortably, as if friends for many years. "Where is your mother from? You know, I might he familiar with her people."

"Oh, I don't think so, Mr. Early. You see, she left England a long time ago, and few of her family remain there."

"Well, no matter then, I suppose. Are you growing cold, Miss Athina?" he asked the younger sister, who had spoken so little. "I'm afraid the beach does chill rapidly." Indeed, within the past few minutes he had chilled as if standing in ice water, and he was shivering, unable to keep his teeth from chattering.

"I am comfortable, sir, but if you wish to leave, do not feel compelled to stay."

"Not at all," he responded gallantly. "Rather, I was thinking of building a fire."

The sisters glanced at each other strangely, then August Kristonosos spoke. "Go ahead, Mr. Early, if you so wish. Warmth would be welcome."

"Thank you." He stepped away and started looking for driftwood. He sensed a slight movement by his side and saw Athina had joined him in the search.

"Do you mind?" she murmured.

"Not at all," he replied, and it was all he could do not to stutter from the cold.

Together they found enough wood, and when it was heaped into a pile, he struck the tinder he always carried in his pocket to iron. A small blue spark appeared in the wood's center, then caught, and he stepped back quickly as the fire grew steadily. He noted that Athina had rejoined her sister at a fair distance from the flames. Perhaps they were afraid that an errant spark might be blown their way and ignite their hair or clothing.

"Ladies, please." He indicated a nearby outcropping of rocks. The women sat so that they did not look into the fire, and he thought that odd, for fire had always held a fascination for him, but perhaps the light was too bright for their eyes. Or perhaps simply they were afraid of fire. Many women were, he knew. Well, he didn't know that from personal experience, but his father had told him that once long ago.

The fire grew and his chill eased; now he could study them more closely.

August wore her black tresses free. Several white star-shaped flowers, no doubt a souvenir of her evening stroll, were set in her hair, and he thought them enchanting. Her chin was slightly pointed, her cheekbones wide, and her high forehead indicated great intelligence. Her flawless skin was nearly alabaster white, while her lips, contrasting

35

with the paleness of her skin, were full and red. They glistened in the firelight as if she had licked them a moment before.

She smiled now, a strange expression into which he could read no meaning; it was not a smile of amusement, or was it? Elegant dark eyebrows arched over her eyes which sparkled like polished jet. Thick lush lashes fringed those eyes, lined expertly with kohl.

She was clad in a mulberry-colored velvet gown with a bodice cut low; cloth leaves trimmed the puffed shoulders of the long sleeves. The gown was belted beneath her bosom with black velvet, while three scalloped rows of the same material trimmed the skirt's hem. An English *Thibet* square shawl with embroidered corners was tossed lightly about her shoulders. A double strand of tiny garnets was clasped around her throat, while delicate garnet earrings graced her earlobes.

The gown's narrow fit accented her hour-glass figure. What he could see of her breasts was remarkable: They were full and high, the skin flawless. He had never seen breasts like those before, and he wondered what they looked like, those wonderful breasts, completely stripped of concealing cloth. Were her nipples as red as her lips? Would they be as sweet? He blushed, painfully aware that he had never been given to such thoughts until that moment.

Athina was attired in lavender velvet that perfectly offset her blonde coloring. White satin bows decorated the short puffed sleeves and the neckline, while twin rows of pearls paraded down the length of the skirt.

She, too, had a shawl, of peach silk, draped about her arms. She wore a simple necklace of moonstones, and a moonstone ring upon her slender right hand.

Her figure was not as lush as her sister's, and yet he could not keep his eyes from it, either. Her waist was so tiny that he suspected he could easily span it with his two hands, and he doubted that its smallness owed anything to a confining corset.

Again, he found himself staring at the curve of her breasts above the bodice and wondering what lay beneath the cloth. How he wished to touch her breasts, and those of her sister's, and feel the warmth there, nestle his head against the softness. He wanted to kiss the pliant flesh, mouth the taut nipple—

With a jerk he raised his eyes to Athina's face. She was as fair as the other was dark, although her skin was pale, too. Her face was more delicately shaped, her eyes the shade of a summer sky. Her mouth wasn't as wide, yet her lips were hued a deep rose and just as pouting. Just as kissable. Her fair eyebrows tilted upward, giving her an almost startled expression he found quite appealing. She wore an air of innocence, while her sister—older by some years—was very much a woman of the world. A woman of experience, and as he thought that, a warmness responded in his groin.

Embarrassed at his body's betrayal, he turned away slightly so that the women would not see his shame. He did not wish them to be disgusted.

The young man could not keep his eyes away. He found the sisters the most seductive women he'd ever met, although they appeared totally unconscious of their dizzying effect upon him. They were the most natural beauties he'd ever seen, and he thought that the loveliest woman of London society would suffer in comparison. Not even those dark-eyed ladies he had seen in Florence and Rome were as attractive.

And Winston knew, too, that he would like—no, he was *compelled*—to sketch them. But he must ask for their permission. Surely they wouldn't refuse.

"I'm sorry if I've fallen into a brown study," he said ruefully. "I'm not a very talkative chap, you see. I suppose it comes from having been an only child and raised in fairly solitary circumstances in the country." He shrugged casually.

"It's quite all right, Mr. Early. Your silences are most refreshing after the tiresome chatter of the Greeks. I fear they are a talkative race, as are those Italians we've met."

"Am I to understand, then, that you do not live in the village?"

"No, we've rented a house on the outskirts and plan to stay there several more weeks," the older sister replied. "We have several homes located throughout Europe and travel frequently from one to the next."

Obviously, the sisters had a generous income. Perhaps both their father and mother were dead.

"Where were you last?" he asked, reluctant to end their conversation, even though the bonfire was dying steadily, and occasionally the thrust of the breeze cut icily into him.

"Most recently in Genoa."

"How incredible! So was I! In Italy, that is. What cities did you visit?"

"We stayed at Pisa before that," Athina replied, "and Rome and Milan."

"Ah," he said, sadly shaking his head, "our paths might have crossed earlier, for I also was in Pisa and Rome a short time ago."

"How remarkable," August Kristonosos murmured. "Perhaps it was not our fate to meet earlier." Once again the mysterious half smile appeared, lifting her lips slightly.

"Yes. A shame, too."

"What are you doing in this small town now, Mr. Early, if I may ask?"

"Certainly, Miss Kristonosos. I am on a Grand Tour. My father sent me traveling to disabuse me of a persistent notion I've taken into my head. He hopes that I will forget it, and yet my trip has done more to make me desire it than anything else."

"And this notion?" August Kristonosos asked. She leaned forward, and he caught the scent of her perfume, a musky odor that made him light-headed. He licked his lips. Her thighs ... how firm and soft and white they must be under that heavy cloth, how fragrant that dark warmth between them. He blinked rapidly and looked away, appalled. No gentleman entertained such thoughts of a lady whose acquaintance he'd just made.

With some effort he spoke, as if his tongue and lips had grown so thick he could scarcely move them. "I am an artist."

"How enchanting," Athina said. "In what medium do you work?"

"Mostly pencil and charcoal, although I do an occasional pastel. I was wondering." He paused. August Kristonosos raised an elegant eyebrow. "Would you ladies sit for me? I would so enjoy for you to do so, and I think that I might even paint your portraits rather than simply sketching."

"I would be quite delighted, Mr. Early, and I know that my sister agrees." Athina nodded. "You have only to name the date—and the time."

"Excellent!" He felt himself grinning and wondered if they thought him a fool. Again August leaned toward him; he forced his eyes to stay on her face. "I fear, though, sir, that the daytime hours would not be the most convenient for us, because we are usually occupied then, and too, alas, we are both late risers."

He was disappointed, because the best light for sketching or painting was in the day. He thought rapidly, then smiled.

"We do have the evenings, Miss Kristonosos, in which I can work. Would that be all right?"

"Yes, actually, it would. When would you wish to begin?"

The sooner he could start the sketches the better, he thought with anticipation. "Tomorrow then, at say, eight in the evening?"

"That would be fine. And where, Mr. Early?"

"I'm staying at Mavronikis's inn, and that would prove somewhat inconvenient, I think. Hmm." He could scarcely have these two women come to his room at night; it would appear unseemly to others, even though they were simply his models.

"Perhaps Mr. Early could come to our house," Athina suggested.

"An excellent notion, dear," August said. "Shall I send my carriage around?"

"Thank you, no, but I prefer walking. It can't be too far, now can it?" He smiled at her. "All I need is the directions."

"It's just a short distance out of town. You'll have no difficulty in finding it." The rented house was less than a quarter mile north of the village, and was the only habitation in those lonely hills.

He smiled. "Then it's settled. Thank you very much for your great kindness, and I shall see you next evening, ladies."

"I fear we must go now," August said. "Our dinner is waiting."

"I'm sorry. I hadn't realized you had not yet dined. Would you care to join me?"

"Thank you, Mr. Early, but we are already committed. Perhaps another night?"

"Yes, I'd like that."

39

He bowed, then watched as the two sisters picked their way carefully over the rocks and sand and faded into the darkness. Within minutes even the faint echoes of their footsteps died away, and all that he heard was the soft sighing of the wind.

As he sat on a flat rock and stared into the dying flames, he realized that he was jealous of whomever they were meeting for dinner tonight. What utter nonsense, he told himself. How could he be that way when he had just met them?

Tomorrow night, though, he would visit their house and begin his sketches. He suspected these might well be among some of his best. Wouldn't Lord Byron be surprised when he showed him the drawings?

CHAPTER 7

Promptly at eight the following evening Winston arrived at the Kristonosos house, where a small wizened-faced Greek man opened the thick wooden door and wordlessly showed him in.

The house was a narrow two-story whitewashed structure, practically identical to the others in the town. It lay at the base of the hills, some distance from Missolonghi, and Winston had found the walk to the house very dark and very lonely. He wondered why the sisters would want to live this remotely from the village; perhaps they enjoyed their privacy.

Inside and out, the wooden sashes around the windows and doors had once been a bright blue, but the paint was now faded and chipping. Bright flowers in simple ceramic vases abounded on the wide sills.

The dampness was not as noticeable as in Byron's house, but then this house was located far from the lagoon. At least, he thought ruefully, it has a chance to dry out between rainstorms.

There wasn't much furniture in the small parlor with its stark white walls, and most of the pieces looked as if they'd come with the rented house. Some were interesting, though.

He crossed over to study an ornately carved teakwood chest, about six feet in length, four in height, pushed against one wall. He regarded it thoughtfully.

The box, a piece of remarkable craftsmanship, looked almost Oriental to his untrained eyes, and certainly was not of Greek origin. Obviously, the sisters had brought it with them; it probably contained linens or something like that, he decided.

Against an adjacent wall he found another similar box, constructed this time of fragrant sandalwood. He was about to lift the top when he saw a small metal lock on the outside; his hand dropped to his side. He would ask the sisters about them. He thought the boxes were beautiful, and perhaps he could use them in the background of his portraits.

Alongside a brocaded settee stood a needlepoint stand, upon which was a nearly completed tapestry of intertwined flowers and leaves. He was sure he recognized the lovely purple blossoms of foxglove and the dark blue helmets of monkshood, but he didn't know about the others. What an unusual floral combination, he thought. Before he could further study the canvas, he heard the swish of skirts. He turned.

August and Athina had entered the room.

"Good evening, ladies."

"Mr. Early." August nodded to him, while Athina smiled. "You are prompt, I see."

"An unusual trait among artists, I believe," he said with a half-smile.

August chuckled.

On his way here tonight he had vowed that he would regard the two women only as artist's subjects; he would keep his mind strictly on business and not their beautiful faces and bodies. But now that he was here, he was finding it difficult to honor his promise.

Tonight Athina was attired in a jonquil-colored gown, and he thought she looked fetching. Once more August wore dark colors, shades that suited her equally well. Her gown was just as revealing as the one she had worn the previous night.

He turned away and ran his tongue across his suddenly dry lips.

The room in which they stood wasn't very bright, and although he saw oil lamps and candles scattered about on shelves and low tables, only a few tapers were lit. If he were to start his work in this room, that would have to change.

On a wall between two windows he suddenly noticed several small watercolors of tall mountains and thunderous cataracts. He went over to them.

"Who did these?"

"Athina did, on one of our many journeys."

"You're quite talented," he said to the young woman now standing at his side. Her paintings were accomplished, albeit quite simple in style. Definitely, she possessed skill, although she needed some polishing. Perhaps he would be permitted to give her some lessons. The paintings were very dark, though, for she had not painted much light into them. He was even more intrigued; the style differed from that used by other women painters he'd seen.

"Thank you," Athina murmured. "I've only been painting a short time. My sister works the needlepoint and is a remarkable needlewoman."

Momentarily her eyes met his, and he felt as if his breath had been whipped away by a sudden cold wind. He could scarcely breathe and, momentarily panicked at his lack of air, he looked around to see if the windows were closed, but every last one of them was flung wide open. He forced himself to relax and to inhale deeply.

"Are you all right, Mr. Early?" August Kristonosos asked with concern.

He took another deep breath. "Yes, thank you. Do you wish to start now?"

"Yes, why don't we, Mr. Early." She crossed the room to pour wine for each of them, and when she returned, she asked, "Now, how will this work?"

"I thought I would make preliminary sketches tonight. Just pencil, or perhaps even charcoal. I'll do this for several nights, trying different poses, then I'll begin the serious work. Is that all right with you?"

They both nodded, and he smiled, then opened his notebook and selected a pencil from the small box he had brought with him.

"Which one first?" the older woman asked.

"Miss Athina, I think. Miss Kristonosos," he said pleasantly, and a smiling August motioned for her sister to come forward. "I think you should sit on the stool by the settee. Oh, and, Miss Kristonosos, I will have to have more light for my work."

"Very well." She called for the servant to light more candles. When it was sufficiently bright, Winston nodded, and the man, who still had not spoken, left.

Winston balanced the pad upon his knee and quickly roughed in an oval that would be the young woman's face. He would do head and shoulder studies first, then later full figures, if time permitted.

Briefly the thought of Athina naked before him flashed through his mind, and his fingers trembled. He gripped his pencil more tightly. He worked quickly, and at one point he found his fingers cramping. He tried not looking at August, but it was almost impossible. She sat apart from her sister and watched, wearing that slight smile again.

He reasoned that the trembling and shortness of breath came because he hadn't had much sleep last night. Even though he'd gone straight to bed, he had awakened time and again, fighting his way out of some nightmare that he couldn't remember longer than a few seconds. Still, even though he was tired, he would do the best that he could tonight. Concentrate, he told himself, and forced his eyes to look objectively at Athina.

He sketched until well after midnight, then, pleading exhaustion despite their pleas for him to remain, he walked back to the inn where he fell into a deep slumber. Once more he dreamed.

He couldn't figure where he was; sometimes it was like the narrow dusty streets he had seen in Italian towns. Sometimes it was the muddy streets of Missolonghi. On either side of him were house fronts, their windows and doors all closed, like shuttered eyes. He walked along the unpaved street as it gradually climbed up a small hill. The odors of fish and salt—and something else, something he couldn't identify, but which seemed faintly familiar—assailed him.

No one stirred. It was close to nightfall, and he knew he had to get inside before the last of the light fled from the sky. He began walking rapidly and once in a while glanced over his shoulder. He didn't see anything, but that didn't mean he was alone. Finally, feeling the panic rise inexplicably in him, he broke into a slow trot, then an extended lope. His heart pounded and his breath was whipped away by the wind. He would have screamed had he seen anyone behind him at that moment.

Still no one.

He ran up the incline, sometimes falling to one knee and nearly pitching forward onto his face, but he was always able to scramble up somehow and keep running. He had to get away from whatever caused his panic. He stopped before one door and tugged at it. Locked. He crossed to another; it, too, was locked. He kicked at the door, but it wouldn't budge.

The light faded to grey and lingered, taunting him at his failure to get inside, and then it seeped away within a moment and left him, alone, in the darkness.

He ran.

The sound of his harsh panting filled his ears, mocked his attempt to run away, and he sobbed in fear.

Even though it was now dark, he could still see clearly, and ahead was a grove of trees. As he drew closer, he recognized the dusty green-grey leaves, the gnarled trunks, the black fruit. Olive trees. He would be safe there. The trees stood thick; he could hide in the boughs of one.

Behind him he heard faint laughter, a musical sound that teased him.

He must get away.

He ran into the grove, then paused as he looked around. He selected a tree with branches low enough for him to grab, and he swung himself up and crouched on the limb, pressing his mouth against his arm to quiet his breathing. He was afraid his gasping for air would give him away.

Something passed underneath the tree. He couldn't see it, but he knew it was there, and he could smell a new odor now, one that was almost musky. Making no sound, he twisted carefully on the branch and peered down into the darkness. But still he saw no one.

"Winston."

Someone called his name, lingering on the last syllable. Without thinking, he opened his mouth to respond, but then abruptly clamped his lips together. He mustn't let them … it … know where he was.

It? No, he knew somehow that more than one pursuer followed. There were two of them, to be precise, even though he still couldn't see them. They passed beneath his tree, their footsteps soft on the spongy ground, searched through the grove, and then came back again, softly calling his name.

The sound of their voices was seductive, and he wanted to call out that he was in the tree just above their heads. He almost laughed aloud at the joke. How clever he had been! How much more clever were they!

Flecks of silver and gold appeared, and danced in front of his eyes. The colors whirled and coalesced, then caressed him, and he gave in to them. The pursuers lured him away from the tree, downward, downward, and he knew he was failing, but he didn't care. He didn't land on the ground, but rather on something soft, something that cushioned him, and two pairs of hands stroked his face, his chest, his thighs.

The colors swirled faster until he could no longer distinguish them, and he reclined against the softness, and was kissed.

"Winston," the voice said again.

And he smiled.

CHAPTER 8

The following night Winston again sketched the sisters, and once again after he returned to the inn, he was bothered by dreams. For two nights he had suffered from these uneasy dreams, yet when he woke in the morning, he felt fine, although a little tired.

The sessions advanced well. Athina was an ideal model: she sat perfectly still, without moving or even speaking until he indicated she could. It was almost as if she were a statue carved of alabaster. Sometimes he had to lean close to make sure she was breathing. But, of course, she was.

Within a few days he finished the studies of Athina, and then it was August's turn. Despite the distraction of her unusual beauty, he managed to finish her sketches within a few nights, also.

When they were done, August smoothed back a stray wisp of hair, then gazed over his shoulder at the collection of sketches. She stood very close to him, and he shivered involuntarily.

"Now what do you do, Mr. Early?"

"I'd like to study these for a few days and think about the preparation of the paintings, Miss Kristonosos. Then I will come by to tell you when I'm ready for you to sit once more."

Athina looked disappointed, but then perhaps he was reading too much into her expression.

"Very good, Mr. Early," August replied, almost briskly, as she turned around. "Then we shall wait patiently to hear from you again."

"Thank you. You've both been splendid subjects—I don't think any artist has ever had as easy a time as I did these past evenings." He blushed suddenly, thinking he sounded so young. "I mean, you both are excellent models, and ..." He stammered to a halt, and forced his eyes to the floor.

"Well," August said, linking her arm with his and escorting him to the door, "it was the artist who made all the difference."

He blushed again, and was grateful that the darkness kept her from seeing his face.

Athina handed him his pads and box; he smiled at her, then walked away into the darkness.

Tired, but not sleepy, he went for a walk along the lagoon. The night was very still, broken only by the soft cry of a night bird and the occasional splash of a fish in the lagoon. He was tired, but pleased with his efforts, and now, away from the women, he felt a little lonely. He wanted one of them with him ... he wanted to run his hands through her unbound hair ... brush her lips, her breast with his lips, push her down in the sand, rip off her dress and—

Winston stopped. What was he thinking of? Certainly his thoughts were not those of a gentleman. Disgusted with himself, he returned to the inn and, setting his sketchpad aside, splashed cold water upon his face and neck. Then he undressed carefully, slipped into bed, and fell right to sleep.

He dreamed.

When he awoke early the following morning, he was shaking. He had dreamed of the Kristonosos sisters; lewd dreams that brought a blush to his cheeks even now as he recalled them.

He had been with Athina, coupled on his bed, and he had been kissing and nipping her, savoring her fragrant flesh, and then August had slipped up behind him, and pressed her naked body against his. He had become even more inflamed then, and had twisted around and pulled her down on top of him. She had straddled him, all the while her sister continued kissing and caressing his face.

And then—

No, he could think about it no longer.

A brisk walk, he told himself, was very much in order, and perhaps he should avoid the sisters, for at least a day or two.

But that decision did not make him happy.

Winston delayed beginning the portraits, and after a few days, he knew the sisters were growing impatient with the postponement.

He wasn't sure why he hadn't started on them; he only knew that he must wait.

He spread the sketches across his bed and stared critically at each one in turn.

They were good-even excellent, he thought, and he wasn't being conceited. Far better than those Byron had seen, and he was pleased that even in this short time he had improved.

But. … But somehow as skilled as these drawings were, they did not represent the true spirit of the sisters. Certainly the beauty of the women was actually captured on the paper, yes, and that alone might be sufficient for most artists, but something … something crucial he *felt* while in their presence was lacking.

He had been unable to present the very essence of the two women on paper. Perhaps he wasn't proficient enough; but after some reflection, he knew that wasn't it. What could it be? It was almost as if his hand had somehow shied away from capturing their substance.

Curious.

He shivered, and glanced around his room, as if expecting to see something in the shadows. But sunlight poured through the window, and there was nothing but Winston and the curious sketches. Carefully he gathered them up and placed them in his pad.

Perhaps it was time he thought about leaving Missolonghi now and traveling deeper in Greece; there he could do more landscape studies. And then he could eventually turn toward home to face the inevitable wrath of his father.

But he knew Byron would be back soon, and he did want to see the poet once more. So, he would wait. Just a little bit longer, he told himself; after all, that couldn't hurt.

CHAPTER 9

Toward the end of the month, Byron had returned to Missolonghi. Winston waited a day or two then went calling.

One of Byron's servants showed Winston into the sitting room. Eagerly he strode across to shake Byron's hand, but he stopped just a few feet short and, unable to help himself, stared.

The man looked terrible.

He forced himself to smile, to hide his horror at the drastic change in his friend's appearance.

"Lord Byron, 'tis a pleasure to see you again!" Winston offered his hand.

Byron's lips barely moved. "And you, Mr. Early. Come, sit here and tell me what you've been doing while I've been away."

Was this the magnificent voice that had read grand poetry for Winston, painting pictures of corsairs and journeys through classical lands? The voice that could easily have been that of a Shakespearean actor upon the London stage? No, not this. The voice he heard now had the timbre of an old man's; it was quavering and weak, almost reedy.

Gone too was the last shred of youthfulness that Byron had possessed; he looked tired and old, and Winston could feel the sting of tears in his eyes. He cleared his throat and forced another smile.

"I'm more eager to hear what you've been doing, too, my lord."

"In a moment, in a moment. All of that can wait, Mr. Early."

"No, please."

Byron smiled, his eves had dulled. and were without life. Winston saw new streaks of silver in the poet's hair.

"Very well. Let me see." Byron leaned back in the chair and Winston saw that his hands trembled as they rested in his lap. "I took some of the Greek troops to Lepanto, as I am sure Fletcher informed you." Winston nodded. "I trained with them several days, and in fact, while I was there they captured some Turkish troops."

"Bravo."

Byron's lips quirked slightly. "Yes, bravo, Mr. Early, although I fear the Greeks' training is far from complete, and they may well suffer in the future for that very thing. Unfortunately, I had to ... I was called back to Missolonghi."

Prudently Winston did not ask why; presumably Byron had found it impossible to continue with the soldiers. At least he had the sense to return before it was ... was what? Too late?

"And then my birthday was the twenty-second."

"Oh?"

"You see, the important matter is that I have survived the bane of my life." He smiled at Winston's puzzled look. "This was my thirty-sixth birthday. My father died when he was that age, and I have greatly feared it for some years. Now that is past, and I have been able to write some verses, you know. I call it 'On This Day I Complete My Thirty-sixth year.'" Byron's eyes scarcely focused, as if he were about to faint.

"May I hear the poem, my lord?" Winston wondered if he should call Fletcher to help his master to bed.

"Another time, Mr. Early, perhaps. I am weary and have much on my mind at present. There is still the siege on Lepanto to consider."

For some time they discussed politics and the war which Byron thought would escalate greatly within the year, then Byron shifted, almost as if he had just awakened.

"That is enough of that." Winston protested but Byron held up a thin hand. "Now, how have you occupied your time since I left?"

"I have been sketching nearly every day, my lord. The villagers were very eager to sit for me, once they saw what I was doing." It was the truth. Not the whole truth, though, and he was reluctant to say any more. He remembered all too well how adamant Byron had been about staying away from the sisters.

"Excellent, my dear boy! I'm glad to hear that—the more you sketch and paint, the better you will become, and believe me, my friend, you are already quite good. Perhaps later you will show me some of the work. I would like to see it."

Apparently Byron saw something in Winston's face that bothered him, and sitting forward, he stared intently at the young man. "What is wrong? Have you been seeing those two women?" he demanded, his voice harsh. "Well, have you?" he asked when Winston did not reply at once.

"Lord Byron—"

"I warned you about them, Mr. Early. Did I not make myself clear?"

With effort, Byron struggled to his feet and moved about the long room with such agitation, Winston thought he would collapse. The poet's eyes burned feverishly in the dim light.

"I warned you, did I not? You can't say that I didn't! I told you not to see them! I told you—I insisted—and yet you deliberately flouted my word, Mr. Early. You could not believe me. No! You must go about sneaking behind my back to see those … women … and now, now, you have no one to blame but yourself!"

Byron's voice rose higher and higher as he berated Winston. Was the poet suffering from a fever of the brain? Winston wondered. Should he send for Dr. Bruno?

Byron acted like a madman, at times striking a hand against the wall, at others sweeping books and papers from tables. Each time Winston flinched as if he had been struck.

Byron tottered as he whirled around. His color was high, his eyes bright, and sweat trickled down the sides of his face.

"Did I not warn you for your own good?" He dropped his hands, and his voice softened a little. "You should have listened, truly you should have, dear boy. How many times have you seen them?"

Carefully Winston licked his lips and cleared his throat, then took a deep breath. He was shocked by Byron's passionate outburst, and it scared him a little, too. But, then, he told himself, Byron was only concerned for his well-being.

Or was it something else? Something less altruistic? Could the poet be jealous? Could it be that the Kristonosos sisters had spurned Byron, the notorious woman's man, the man all women, or so it was said, longed for? Yet as he gazed at the poet, he realized that jealousy played no part in this strange matter. Fear was in Byron's face and voice, and hatred, as well.

"I went there ... a few ... perhaps half a dozen evenings. I don't really remember how many." He was reluctant to admit the actual number of times he'd visited the sisters. It was none of Byron's business, he told himself.

"You are lost, lost," Byron moaned as he dropped heavily into a chair. A spasm of pain creased his face, and he shuddered. "I have waited too long, I see. I was stupid. I should have spoken to you before I left, and then I should never have come back." With some effort, he pulled himself together, and when he spoke once more, his voice was steadier. "I need to speak seriously to you now, Mr. Early, before it's too late, although I already suspect all may be lost."

"Surely, my lord, you exaggerate."

He shook his head. "God knows. I wish that I did, but I do not." He leaned back, his arms resting lightly on the chair arms. "I have a strange story to relate, Mr. Early, one far more fantastic than any gothic tale you will have read. You must believe it. You know of John Keats and Percy Bysshe Shelley?"

Winston was astounded at this-sudden irrelevance. "Yes, I've read much of their poetry. While I was in Rome, I visited the very rooms where Keats died. Next to the Steps."

The look Byron gave Winston was both ironic and sad. "Yes. Well, I knew them, too. Both were young men—younger than I—and now they are dead. Gone too early to their graves, gone years before their time. And, Mr. Early"—here he leaned forward to stare intensely at Winston—"they are dead because of the Kristonosos sisters."

Winston smiled skeptically. Was this some fever dream of Byron's?

Byron gazed at him. "You must listen to my tale, Mr. Early, as it is a matter of life and death to you. And you must believe me."

Winston's smile faltered as he saw the passion on the other's face. Mad or not, Byron believed what he was saying.

"And now I will tell you how these two great poets died."

Byron began his story.

PART II
KEATS—LONDON: 1819

CHAPTER 10

His soul shall taste the sadness of her might,
And be among her cloudy trophies hung.

—Ode to Melancholy

O, what can all thee, knight-at-arms,
Alone and palely loitering?

—La Belle Dame Sans Merci

"Tom, I'm home!" John Keats's voice rang through his rooms in the house in Hampstead Heath; silence met his cheerful greeting.

He paused. The only sound he could hear was the faint chatter and tumbling of the children on the next floor. Otherwise, an eeriness pervaded the rooms, as if no one was there.

No one was, he remembered.

Tom was dead.

His hands trembled. Quickly, he thrust them into his pockets, leaned against the door to close out the terrible cold of the January afternoon.

When he no longer shook, he took a deep breath, then removed his gloves and set them carefully on the small table by the door.

How could he have forgotten? he asked himself. He was overly tired, and the day had been long. He had just returned from the funeral of a friend who had died unexpectedly, and had meant to tell his brother about it. But he couldn't. Tom was dead, and had been since December 1, only a few weeks after his nineteenth birthday. The doctor had ruled consumption as the cause of Tom's slowly debilitating illness, and all through the second half of the year Keats, powerless to do anything, had watched his brother decline. Tom had rallied for a while, and at his urging and against his own better judgment, Keats had gone on a journey to Scotland, leaving Tom in their brother George's care. But when he returned, he had found George gone to America and Tom much worse.

The wraithlike figure in the bed was not recognizable as Keats's brother. Tom had aged so much in a few weeks that he looked like an old man. His face, no longer smooth but lined, had grown as white as new snow, and yet his dark eyes, with great grey pouches beneath them, shone as though a fever raged within him. His long dark hair had lain limply across his forehead and cheeks, and in some strands silver gleamed. Keats was angry at George's desertion, but Tom said he had urged George to leave as he was feeling better.

After Tom's death, Keats had stayed in the house, seeing no one until friends forced their way in and insisted he come out with them. He knew they had been thinking of his own welfare, and he was grateful. And so the slow process of healing his grief had begun.

But today's funeral had only served to bring back the sorrows.

And this was supposed to have been the best of their homes, he thought wryly.

In March of the previous year he had rented the first floor of the house at No. 1 Well Walk so that he might have quiet to work, and shortly after that his two brothers had moved in with him. The area, north of the city, was a far better place to live than London with its crowded and noisy streets, and smoke-filled skies.

The pleasant lime-lined avenue of Well Walk led to the spring which had been a fashionable spa over a century ago and was only a brisk five-minute walk from the Vale of Health, that singular place that had somehow managed to escape completely the plague of a hundred and fifty years past. Keats had thought that there could be no healthier place for his younger brother, but how pitifully wrong he had been.

When Keats returned from Scotland, there had been much for the two brothers to talk about, because each knew the boy was dying. Hour after hour Keats spent by his brother's side, remembering times that had been happier, times when they had been a whole family, when their father had been alive, before their mother had deserted them all.

Sometimes Tom was too weak to talk, so he listened to his brother. Keats read his newest verses to the boy, who had always loved his work. He said nothing of the reviews he had received in the past few months, the reviews that were an agony to him. He did not want to burden Tom with that.

One cold night before he died, Tom opened his eyes and stared at his brother. The room was awash with yellow light from the candles, and momentarily the flames wavered, as though a draft had swept across them.

"Tended me," Tom murmured.

Keats, who had been drowsing, stirred. "Yes, Tom, what is it?"

"Tended," the boy repeated.

Keats shook his head to indicate he didn't fully understand, but he wasn't sure Tom saw the gesture. Tom seemed to be staring beyond him, and when Keats turned his head around, he thought he saw a shadow on the wall. He blinked, and it was gone. Or more rightly, he thought, it was never there.

"Each night she came and tended me ... the beautiful angel."

His brother was out of his head with a fever, Keats thought sadly.

"That's all right now, Tom." He smoothed the covers, placed a palm on the forehead. The skin was cool. Keats frowned.

Even though Tom was in great pain, he was making a determined effort to speak. "The woman ... George and I met her one night while we walked. We talked often after that. And when he left, she came to me one night and helped."

"What did she look like, Tom?"

"An angel, as fair as an angel. So beautiful." A shudder ran through Tom's body, and his eyes closed gradually. Tom was dead.

Keats swallowed quickly, trying to keep the tears back, and yet he couldn't.

All his life he had swung from one emotional extreme to the other. One moment he could be laughing, the next crying, then raging a second after that. George, and even Tom, were much more even in disposition. They took after their late father in that respect, who had been a kind and solid man, a man firmly in grip of his emotions. Their mother had been quite the opposite, however, and although some had told John Keats that he looked like his father, Thomas, in temperament he favored his mother, Frances.

Seeing his brother fail day by day had not been easy, and often he had spent hours weeping. Yet weeping did not help, and finally, feeling drained, he would rise and wash his face and go sit with Tom.

Now, his vigil was over, and yet the emotions within him still roiled.

He had other concerns, too, that would not go away. The money from Tom's estate, which was owed to Keats, would not be coming to him now-it could not be touched until his sister, only fifteen, came of age. And then the sales of his poems had virtually stopped now, after the fury of the attack by the *Quarterly*.

He had just enough money to pay for Tom's funeral, the simplest ceremony at best, and the rest he must save until he received his next allowance, from the estates of his mother and grandmother.

He rubbed his hand across his face and eyes, and his fingers came away wet. The funeral today had brought back too many memories. He was tired; he should rest, and perhaps tomorrow he could work.

On his way to his room, he passed a gilt mirror hanging on the far wall. He did not pause, did not have to see his reflection.

Red hair lay in gentle waves, while hazel eyes, claimed by his friends to be his best feature, stared calmly out at him. They were of such a shade and quality that strangers passing him in the street turned around to look at him, a circumstance which never failed to bring a blush to his cheeks. His complexion was bright, and he had a large mouth with a jutting upper lip. Some of his friends called it a pugnacious mouth. He smiled at the thought.

He wasn't handsome, or at least he would not have described himself as that. But his features were pleasant, and even more so when he smiled.

He stood barely three-quarters of an inch over five feet, but he seemed taller, due in large part to the erect carriage of his limbs and head and the perfect proportion of his body. Only when he was deep in thought or reading was his tiny stature noticeable.

He glanced out the window and saw that the afternoon light had faded, and that evening was here. It was perfectly quiet upstairs now, and he wondered if the family who lived there had left for an evening stroll.

He sighed. He must find something to eat; he hadn't dined since the night before, and his stomach ached from hunger. He paused to light a candle, then went into the small dingy kitchen and rummaged through the cabinets until he found a few stale biscuits. He nibbled at them without interest, then poured himself a stiff whiskey and quickly downed it. The warmth of the alcohol spread through him, numbing his body and his mind.

Keats went out into the hall, and in the near darkness, he sensed another presence. The hairs along the back of his neck prickled, and momentarily he felt—or thought he felt—something touch his sleeve. He jerked his arm away, then puzzled, peered down the corridor, but he saw no one.

"Hello?"

No one answered him.

Of course, no one did, he told himself, no one had been there. He was imagining things. Hunger and grief, and strong drink, would do that.

He headed toward his bedroom. He lit a second candle, then washed his face and hands. Afterward, he sat at his table, with quill in his hand, unblemished paper in front of him.

He stared at its whiteness, almost the color of his brother's skin, of the skin of his friend to whom he had bade farewell this afternoon. He tried erasing the haunting image of those faces from his mind. He couldn't work … not tonight. He crossed his arms on the desk, and then, too tired to think further, he rested his head on his arms, and within moments was asleep.

CHAPTER 11

She seem'd, at once, some penanced lady elf,
Some demon's mistress, or the demon's self

—Lamia, Part I

On the fourteenth Keats had a visitor. Before his brother had died, Keats had begun a poem, *Hyperion*, and he had continued it after Tom's death, but the lines had not flowed smoothly and his mind kept wandering from the theme, and so he had stopped working on it and had gone on to *The Eve of St. Agnes*.

The poem was going well, for which he was thankful.

But no—already had his deathbell rung:
The joys of all his life were said and sung:
His was harsh penance on St. Agnes' Eve.

There was a soft knock upon the front door.

Startled, he looked up. It had grown dark since He'd begun hours before, and he took up a candle, then passed into the sitting room and opened the door. Who could be calling at this hour?

"Good evening, sir." The sound of the woman's slightly husky voice thrilled him in a curious manner. He shivered slightly.

"Come in, please, madam." He closed the door, then stared at her in the dim light.

She wore a rather simple gown of peach silk, and a paisley shawl around her shoulders because of the cold, but he did not notice any further details of her costume. He could not take his gaze from her face.

Her skin was the palest he'd ever seen on any living woman; she could almost have been sculpted from pure white marble, he thought. Her oval face was delicately shaped with a gently rounded chin, a petite and straight nose, and eyes tinted a vibrant blue under blonde arched brows. Her mouth was neither too wide nor rich, yet neither were the lips thin. They were a deep rose, those lips, pouting and eminently kissable.

Her long, slightly curling hair was the color of honey, and one curl caressed her shoulder. He wished he could put his lips to that spot.

Then slowly, almost reluctantly, his gaze traveled downward. The gown was trimmed with lace about the bodice, and he could see the swell of her breasts above the pale material. White breasts, soft and inviting. Lush and beautiful. Ripe; breasts to be touched reverently, kissed with awe and respect.

Hers was a voluptuous figure, one to be noticed by any man, despite the current slender style for women without breasts or hips. Hers was a figure not to be ignored, the body of a goddess, of a Helen, he thought with admiration. She was not tall. Hardly more than an inch or so above his height, which pleased him, and she was truly the most beautiful woman he had ever seen.

He realized then how rude he had been these past few moments, and saw to his amazement that she was appraising him as openly as he had her.

Surely she was simply politely waiting for him to speak. Whatever could he have been thinking of? He blushed slightly.

"To what do I owe the honor of this unexpected visit, madam?"

"You are Mr. John Keats? I am Athina Kristonosos," she said. Her voice was like a caress upon his arm; again he shivered.

He bowed over her hand, so very cool to his touch. Once more he thought of marble. "I am happy to make your acquaintance, Miss Kristonosos."

"I came at once to offer you my condolences, Mr. Keats. I have been out of the city for some time, and have only recently learned of poor Tom's death. He was such a splendid boy."

"Thank you, but at least Tom is no longer suffering as he did those past few months."

"Yes."

Was that a slight smile on her lips? He must be mistaken, tricked by the dim light. Tom's dying words came back to him. "Is it possible that you … that it is you that I must thank for taking care of my brother?" He spoke formally, confused by the tumult of emotions she raised within him.

She dimpled. "Why, thank you, Mr. Keats. It's true that I visited Tom upon occasion, and I did try to make him more comfortable, although I did little other than plump up his pillows and fix him a meal or two. It is no more than any other would have done."

"I am sure that you did far more than that. And I want to thank you for the care you did give." She inclined her head, and the curl shifted. "Won't you please sit down, Miss Kristonosos."

She did so, and he sat opposite her on an old, nearly threadbare chair.

"Did you enjoy your stay outside the city, Miss Kristonosos?"

"Yes, I did, Mr. Keats. I traveled northward to Scotland."

"Scotland! Why, I was there in the autumn."

"What a coincidence," she murmured. "Were you able to work there? Your brother spoke often of your writing. I should like, if you don't mind, to read one of your poems sometime."

"I will provide you with a copy of my latest volume." Latest volume. He tried not to smile. So far, he had only the one, which had been savaged by the critics.

"Thank you. I must leave now. Good evening, Mr. Keats."

He watched as she walked away from the house and down the street, disappearing into the night. He had asked when he might see her again, and she had said she would be out walking the next evening. Keats promised himself that he would make sure he encountered her.

He returned to his work, scribbled a few more lines, then set his pen down, stretched and went into his bedroom. Once in bed, with the covers pulled up around him to guard against icy drafts, he opened a book and read until at last his eyelids felt heavy, then set the volume down and blew out the candle. He fell asleep.

A curious purple light awakened him, and when he rose, he saw that he stood in a small boat and not his bed, as he had imagined. It was neither day nor night, and he wore a cloak of soft blue material.

Beneath the waters of the river, he saw schools of large fish, golden and rainbow-sided, vermilion tailed, finned with silvery gauze.

The boat nudged to a gentle stop along the riverbank, and he climbed out onto bright golden sands, and beyond that gold rocks covered with golden moss.

Farther away he saw a great forest, and he walked rapidly toward it. Above him in the woods hung silvery oak apples and brown fir cones, and the air was awash with the smell of wild thyme and poppies. From the dark depths of the woodlands came the lilting song of a lark. The air was not very cool now, and he pushed the cloak from his shoulders, and left it where it slipped off, like a puddle of water.

Past jasmine and weeping trees he went, and finally he came to a palace carved from rosy-veined marble, its supporting columns. inlaid with coral, pebble, and pearl, and standing so tall that their tips were lost in mist. He wanted to enter this glorious place, but suddenly he was afraid. Fear stripped him of his reason, and yet he could not turn and flee. His feet felt riveted into the ground, as if they had become rock, and he knew he had no choice but to go forward.

He went through the door of gold, and inside, the marble palace was cold, and he shivered, wishing that he had kept his cloak. The cold seeped through his skin, into the depths of his bones, and as he gazed down at his hand, he saw it was white, like that of a dead man's.

He looked around in the light which had now faded to silver, but saw no one. Once he heard the low laughter of a woman, and its entrancing sound inflamed him. The floor was turquoise, the balustrade carved of diamond. He walked slowly, gazing around, and saw a thousand fountains, caves, and chasms.

He quickened his pace, and ahead glimpsed the hem of a garment as someone—the woman?—disappeared around an ebony pillar. He was running now, his breath laboriously loud, and still he couldn't catch up with her.

"Come back," he called.

Only her laughter, more faint and echoing this time, answered him. He stopped momentarily; his side ached, and he could barely breathe. He couldn't run any longer. The light had dimmed until he saw the outlines of the columns only faintly.

Exhausted, he sunk onto the floor, his head on his knees, and closed his eyes.

A hand as cold as the grave touched his cheek, and when he looked up, he screamed.

Keats awoke suddenly out of the depths of the dream, with a chill passing through his body. He couldn't remember what he'd seen, only that the vision had terrified him greatly.

Now he sat up abruptly. Surely someone was in the room. He looked around, but all he glimpsed were shadows, and when he strained, listening, he heard only the rasp of his own breathing. Momentarily he thought he heard the faint rustle of cloth, then nothing.

Still uneasy, he pushed the covers back and padded out of the room. Out of habit, he looked into Tom's old bedroom, and for an instance thought he saw the outline of his brother's body under the coverlet. He moved, and the illusion disappeared.

There was no one in the rooms, except him and his imagination, he told himself, and he returned to his bed and to an uneasy sleep.

CHAPTER 12

How is it, Shadows, that I knew ye not?

—Ode to Indolence

A few days later Keats was interrupted by yet another visitor.
"I thought I'd come by and see how you are doing," Joseph Severn said as he entered the house. "Haven't seen you in a dog's age, Johnny."

"Thank you, Joseph. I truly appreciate your concern." Keats tried smiling, but realized he was too tired to command his facial muscles to move. He indicated for the other to sit, then followed suit.

"You don't look well" Severn said, peering at the other man.

Little light filtered through the windows into the room, and it was difficult to see Keats clearly. And even now he kept his head down. as if he didn't wish to show his face.

Keats shook his head. "It's nothing, and I'm feeling all right. Really."

"Hmm."

The two friends had met in the spring of 1816. While Severn was some two years older than Keats, he looked and acted younger than his years. He was thin with delicately chiseled features, large brown eyes, fair hair worn in straggling curls, and a mouth almost girlish. He towered some inches over his friend, a subject which provided them with much teasing from their acquaintances.

Severn was exceptionally good-humored, but always anxious to please. Sometimes this very quality made him clumsy, but although he might be irritating at times, he was also endearing. His father, a music master, had bitterly opposed his son's desire to be a printer and had apprenticed him to a copper engraver.

Severn hated this work, and at night, in defiance of his father, attended classes at the Royal Academy. To earn the money to buy the oils he needed he painted watercolor portraits at half a guinea each. Luckily he could do them quickly and with very little effort, and so far he had managed quite well.

"What does that 'hmm' mean?" Keats demanded.

Severn blushed a little. "I just mean that I don't think you're telling the whole truth. You know that I'm your friend," he said, a pleading tone in his voice. "You can tell me."

"Well, you're right, of course. Things aren't going the way they should. I have debts, and little money, and the inheritance I was depending upon from Tom has been denied me."

"Is there anything I can do for you?"

Keats smiled, a sweet expression filled with great sadness. It was a generous offer, but Severn had little more money than he did. "Thank you, but I think not. I miss Tom, too. A few days ago when I came home, I called out to him-then remembered."

Severn made a sympathetic noise and nodded, his eyes suddenly moist. He could not trust his voice to speak. He cleared his throat.

"It cheers me considerably, though, to see you. We have been too long apart for old friends."

"I agree," Severn said solemnly.

Keats poured them both cups of tea, and when he returned to his chair, he frowned thoughtfully at his friend.

"Tell me, Joseph, when you visited here while I was in Scotland, did you ever meet a young lady who was attending Tom?"

"What? No, not at all. I never saw a young lady-or anyone else for that matter. Sometimes I stayed with him for a few hours, but Tom always protested that he was all right, and he wouldn't rest until I had left. I didn't want to, you know."

"I understand. Enough of this! I trust you have some good news for me. Come, Joseph, tell me how your painting fares."

For the next half an hour Severn talked animatedly about the series of watercolor landscapes he was doing presently.

"I thought I'd show them around before I finish -find out what you and the others have to say. What do you say, Johnny?"

"It sounds like a good idea to me, although you must remember not everyone knows art the way you do. And not everyone will be laudatory." He hoped the bitterness he felt toward the critics' attack on his work didn't reflect in his voice.

"Well, I'll try to remember that." Severn munched on the biscuit Keats had offered him. He didn't like to eat too many of them, because he knew that Keats didn't have much food in the house.

"How is Champion?" Keats asked. "Haven't seen him since before I went to Scotland." Henry Champion was a long-time friend, who had encouraged him many years ago to write poetry. Champion had no such talent himself, and although he admired the ability in others, he was never envious. Henry did enjoy sketching, and while he would never be great, his caricatures of the London elite were highly sought after.

The expression shifted on Severn's face, alerting Keats at once.

"What's wrong?"

Severn coughed gently, then looked away. Clearly he was uncomfortable.

"Joseph?"

Severn met his eyes. "I am afraid that Henry Champion is dead, John."

"Dead!" Good God, Henry was barely two and twenty! "What happened?" Henry gone? It was impossible; he couldn't believe it. No more nights of long discussions of poetry and art and music, no more, no more.

"I don't know precisely. Just after you left for the north, he was found dead, just a few steps away from his house. It looked like he had been running away from someone. He had the most terrible expression of fear on his face." Severn shuddered. "You see, they asked me to identify the body. It was horrible."

"Why didn't you write me?"

"I didn't want to disturb you. I knew you went there to rest, and …"

"I see." Keats sipped his now-cool tea, then released a great sigh. "Someone murdered him, then." His voice was barely above a whisper.

"So it looks."

"Don't the Runners know?"

Severn hesitated. "Not precisely."

Keats looked puzzled. "I don't understand. Either poor Henry was sick and died, or he was murdered, and from what you said it looked like he was murdered. After all, he was found outside his home and looked as if he'd been pursued."

"It's not all that simple, John. You see, there wasn't a mark on his body, beyond a curious-looking rash on his belly. Damned strange."

"A what?"

"A rash, or at least the doctors think it was a rash. They aren't sure about that, either."

"Well, then it was a disease."

"No."

"I don't understand!" Keats cried out in frustration.

"What do they know about poor Henry's death?"

"Very little," Severn whispered. Keats said nothing. All too vividly could he imagine a frantic Henry running and stumbling away from someone, something … something chasing him in the dark, and then just within reach of his home …. Alone, and in the dark. He felt tears well up in his eyes and quickly changed the subject.

"What about Robert Mattison?" He was a fellow poet of Keats who had not yet published, and was a fairly recently acquaintance.

"Oh, right as rain," Severn announced sunnily, glad to be away from the other topic. "He's busy at work on an epic about Hippolyte, or so he claims, but no one's seen a word of it yet. I think the poem only exists in his head as yet."

"Could be." Keats could barely keep his mind on what the other man was saying. He was still upset by the news of his friend's death.

"Last month Jessup and I -" Severn stopped; his cheeks colored.

"Yes?"

"Er, nothing."

"Come, Joseph," Keats said, somewhat irritably, "you've begun a thought, so you might as well finish it. What about you and Richard Jessup?"

"I was just going to say that Jessup and I went to the Royal Academy, and I was showing him some of my work. I know he did not think it very good, although he said kind things."

"You know you'll improve with your lessons and with experience." Why would Severn not wish to tell that to him? "How is Richard? What's he doing these days? Has he a show planned?"

Severn pressed his lips together and stared down at the teacup balanced on his knee.

"Joseph?" Something tightened oddly deep within his chest, making it difficult for him to speak. Slowly the words came out. "Joseph, what is it? What's the matter with Richard?"

Severn raised his head and looked at Keats; his expression was agonized. "I'm afraid that Richard Jessup is dead, too."

Stunned, Keats rocked backward, his teacup dropping from his hands. Neither man noticed the crash of the porcelain against the floor. First, Champion, and now Jessup. Both had been in perfect health when he'd seen them in the early summer.

"How?"

"He burned away in a sudden fever. Caught it one night, and within a week he was dead. Had the most frightful dreams, he told me."

Fever and dreams. Like Tom, Keats thought, but then those symptoms were fairly common to many illnesses. But healthy and vigorous young men did not weaken and die within a week. Not usually. His medical training of years ago told him that.

"Do the doctors know what it was?"

"Not yet."

Keats said nothing. Only then did he notice the broken cup. He stooped to pick it up with numb fingers, not caring if he cut himself.

And then there had been Tommy Fitch's funeral. Poor Tommy. Keats had met the other young man when he was studying to be a doctor at the hospital.

Tommy was planning to go into medicine, too, but actually his great love was the theatre. The two young men had found much to talk about. And Tommy, Keats remembered with a faint smile, had always threatened to run away and become an actor, an announcement which never failed to horrify his parents.

Three of his friends gone in such a short time. Dead, like his little brother. One chased by someone, hounded to his death; another cut down by a fever; the third-he didn't know what Tommy had died of. Well, at this point, it didn't matter.

"I'm sorry, John, for bringing all this bad news to you in one day; I didn't mean to, you know. Perhaps I should go."

Keats spoke almost mechanically. "You don't have to, Joseph."

"No, I should. You're tired, I can tell, and I'm not making it any better."

Severn leaped to his feet and took his cup out to the small kitchen. He returned and helped Keats pick up his own broken cup. He helped Keats to his feet.

"I'll be back in a few days, John, and then perhaps we can go for a walk or even a ride. And I can show you my latest sketches. Perhaps you'd sit for one?"

"Yes, I'd like that."

Severn smiled shyly, pumped his friend's hand, then hastily left.

Keats stared at the closed door, then eased himself into the chair. The silence of the house was too intense for him. The tears spilled over, and he wept for his lost friends.

CHAPTER 13

I see a lily on thy brow,
With anguish moist and fever dew;
And on thy cheeks a fading rose
Fast withereth too.

                        —La Belle Dame Sans Merci

Keats often took long walks upon the heath through Caen Woods and out into open fields. Here, he had always found contentment as he passed through land yet untouched by man. Now his feet sought the familiar path he often traveled, and he found himself once more upon the heath. And to think that only a century before highwaymen had been common on the heath, and it had been dangerous to self and possessions to pass along this way.

It was much safer these days, he reflected, although perhaps not as exciting.

And Athina Kristonosos had not appeared.

He was enchanted by her, and he was lonely.

He had strolled the well-worn paths, enjoying the moonlit trees and bushes turned silver, and the expanse of long grass that shimmered with the slight breeze. It was quiet, with only an occasional sharp sound as a bird stirred somewhere in its nest. He was warm inside his thick coat, his hands thrust into the pockets.

He tired more easily than he would have months before, and so sat upon a wide flat rock. She had said he might see her out walking occasionally, but every evening he'd been out, and yet he'd failed to come across her. He was disappointed. He wanted to talk with her, watch her, simply be with her. He rested for some time, and then had the curious feeling that someone was watching him. Yet, when he shifted and looked around, he saw nothing out of the ordinary—nothing but trees and grass and shrubbery in the darkness.

After a while he rose again, deciding to go home. He headed back into the woods again and ducked under a low hanging branch, then stopped as his feet encountered something just in front of him, half hidden under a bush with long thorns.

It was darker here than out in the open, and something made him pause momentarily. Then he stooped to see what object he had nearly tripped over.

His hands groped along the contours, then quickly withdrew. A man's body.

And the skin was cold.

Resolutely he pushed the man over so that he might see his face, and squinted.

Keats recoiled and, standing, rubbed his hands down his thighs. It was Carl Osterly, a young writer who had just moved to Hampstead from the north.

Carl dead? He had had tea with the man shortly after Tom's death when Carl had called to offer his condolences. They had talked about their work for some time, and how much better Hampstead was than the cities they'd both lived in previously.

Carl with his fresh complexion and wide hazel eyes had been so alive.

But now, he was dead, alone on the heath.

Shuddering, Keats turned away. He started back toward the village to report the man's death.

Over the next few days he was unable to forget the look that had been on Carl's face; it had been twisted with sheer terror.

What could have produced such fear in a man who stood a few inches over six feet and was huskily built? Who-or what-could have killed him?

The Runners had no leads as yet, and the doctors were unsure as to the cause of death, only that it had not been natural.

At night, he lay awake and wondered if the something or someone he had sensed watching him earlier had been the man's killer. The deed must have been done by then, for surely he would have heard Carl's struggles or cries. Keats shivered. If he stayed there a few moments longer, or left just a minute or two earlier. What if he had been stalked … like his other friend. He could not bear to think of it.

As soon as possible, Joseph Severn came calling again. This time he brought with him Leigh Hunt, another friend of Keats's.

James Henry Leigh Hunt, eleven years Keats's senior, was dark-eyed and dark-haired, with a slight cleft in his chin. His face was plain, but totally engaging, and he rarely frowned; generally, he was in a good mood. A poet, too, he also edited the *Examiner*, and had published some of Keats's earliest poems. It was through him that Keats had first met Percy Bysshe Shelley.

"It's good to see you, John," Hunt said at once, as he pumped Keats's hand.

"You're looking tired, though. Are you getting enough sleep?"

"Yes …" His voice trailed off.

"I heard about your finding the body on the heath. Bad luck that, although it could have been worse-it could have been you lying there."

Severn shot a sharp glance at Hunt. Sometimes Hunt was just a little too blunt for Severn's taste.

As Keats seated his guests and sat down, he closed his eyes. He could still see the man's body too clearly. And that horrible look-the eyes open wide, the lips pulled back in what must have been a scream. He shuddered. He wondered if he would ever forget that expression.

"I'm sorry you went through such an ordeal when you were already tired."

"Well, thank you, but I'll be all right." He tried to sound cheerful, but knew he failed.

"Tell me, Johnny, why in blazes have you got all the curtains shut when it's sunny as summer outside?" Severn demanded as he glanced around the darkened room. He scratched his head.

"The light hurts my eyes, Joseph. I haven't been sleeping too well recently … what with finding poor Carl the other night … and so I closed them."

"Well, I think the light would do you more good than moping around in the darkness."

"Not now, please, Joseph."

Severn shrugged and sat back down.

"You aren't ill, are you?"

"No. I just need some rest."

Hunt glanced at Severn, but didn't speak.

"Did you ever locate the woman who tended Tom while you were gone?"

"Yes, I did. She visited me one evening to offer her condolences-she had been out of the country when Tom died. We chatted for a while, but I haven't seen her in some time." There was a wistful, almost longing, tone to his voice.

"Well, perhaps she'll turn up again," Hunt responded cheerfully. "Now, John, I wanted to talk to you about some poems."

"Please, Leigh, not now. I'm not really fit to talk about work."

"Because of your lack of sleep?"

"It's more than that, I think. You see, I dream all the time now."

"That's not unusual," Hunt said.

"No, but my dreams are."

"Why?" Severn asked, sitting forward.

Suddenly Keats seemed more cautious. "They just are; I don't know why nor can I explain. I can't remember any of them right now."

Severn sensed more than Keats would admit, but he knew, too, that he couldn't push his friend. Keats would simply turn mulish, and nothing would be accomplished, no matter how much Severn pushed him. When Keats was ready, he would tell Severn what was bothering him.

"You know," Hunt said thoughtfully, "a change of scene might do you good, John. I have some good friends in Chichester. I would like to include some new poems of yours in another volume-with your permission, of course-and you could work there, or you could simply stroll through the countryside. Either way, I think it would be an excellent tonic."

"Well ..."

"No, do say you will go, John, I insist. There's been too much death around here recently, and it's preying on your mind. You need to get away. Do say you will go and work."

Keats smiled slowly. Was there any way he could refuse Leigh Hunt? "Oh, all right, I'll go. Under protest, of course."

Severn chuckled, as did Hunt.

"I'll write to my friends at once, and I know they will be delighted to see you. It's not a long journey, which is good, and the lovely couple enjoy all my friends, which shows, I might add, their incredibly good taste."

Severn laughed again. "And the only thing you'll dream about, Johnny, is the bucolic life."

It was Hunt's turn to chuckle, but while Keats smiled, he remained silent. He wondered if the dreams would stop if he left Hampstead. And he wondered if he really wanted them to stop.

CHAPTER 14

Where youth grows pale, and spectre-thin, and dies.

—Ode to a Nightingale

In March, when Keats returned to Hampstead, his first visitor was Athina Kristonosos.

She then began dropping in several nights a week for just a few minutes, then she would leave to continue her walk.

His nightly dreams had taken on a physical nature, and in them he knew the young woman figured greatly. He was too embarrassed to meet her eyes, afraid that she would know about his dreams. He was aware, too, of how much more beautiful she had become since he last saw her. She had bloomed; her skin was more vibrant, her hair brighter, her lips redder, her eyes a deeper shade of blue.

His body throbbed with desire.

As he turned away, she caught him by the arm. He trembled ever so slightly and silently cursed himself for being such a fool.

"Mr. Keats, what is the matter?" she asked, her voice soft. She was standing close now, her musky perfume captivating him. He could see

81

the rounded skin of her breasts, and he wanted to brush that perfect smoothness with his tongue. He colored.

"Have I somehow offended you? I hope that I have not."

"No, Miss Kristonosos, you haven't offended me-far from that!"

"Then what is it?' She stepped even closer, and the muskiness enveloped him in its strong net.

"It's n-nothing," he managed to stammer. At his side, his hands clenched and unclenched as the stirrings began within his groin. He groaned softly. "I have just been working very hard recently, and am still tired from my journey. That's all."

"If you say so, Mr. Keats." She released his arm, and instantly he regretted it. He liked having her hand on him, enjoyed her softness against him, and, again embarrassed, he pressed his lips together.

"Perhaps I should leave," she said.

"No!" He blushed. "I'm sorry that I'm not the best of company now."

"That's all right," she said with a sweet smile, and ran one hand along his arm.

He trembled. After she left, he fled to the table where his papers and books spread in comfortable clutter. What was the matter with him? It wasn't as if he had never had a woman. God knows he had. Several, in fact. What was wrong?

The answer was simple. He wanted her. Each time he saw her, the wanting grew. One night, he feared, he would simply grab her and-No! Yet he'd never met a woman who possessed such allurement. And now his dreams were about her. No doubt they mirrored his body's hunger. He put his head in his hands.

Several times, he had caught himself flirting with Athina, and he thought she responded. At least, she hadn't turned a disapproving look his way. He liked her. Truly he did. He had never seen such a beautiful and intelligent-and caring-woman as Athina. And he wanted her.

He had never felt as comfortable around a woman as he did her, even though her visits were never as long as he wished them to be; and he wondered if he should ask her to marry him. It wasn't such an absurd idea, he told himself; others had married for far less.

But he didn't have the courage to propose. He couldn't offer her much of a life. After all, he was only a poet, and perhaps a failure at that, and certainly one with too little money.

Enough of this. He straightened and pulled out paper and dipped his quill into the inkwell. He would work tonight, and in the morning, he would rise early and take a brisk walk. He would walk until tired, and then perhaps he would no longer dream.

The following day Severn bustled in. "Are you ready, Johnny?"

"Ready for what?"

"Don't you recall? I promised to take you to meet my sculptor friend? Robin's ever so clever."

"Oh, yes, I remember."

He rubbed his hands across his face. The dreams had been present all night, and he felt as if he'd slept little. His eyelids were gritty, his mouth dry, and his hands trembled ever so slightly. He thrust them into his pocket so that his friend wouldn't notice.

Severn's friend's studio was on the outskirts of London. Keats paid little attention to the houses or buildings around them, and concentrated on climbing the steps up to the third-floor study.

"Well, we're here, Robin!" Severn called out cheerfully after he perfunctorily knocked, then opened the door and strode in.

"Good!" exclaimed a small figure standing on a small footstool.

Unblinking, Keats stared. Severn's sculptor friend was a woman.

"Good afternoon. I am Robin Morrow. It's very pleasant to meet you after hearing all that Joseph says." The woman was wiping her clay-streaked hands on a towel. Keats shook hands with her, then glanced at an amused Severn.

"You didn't tell me."

"Oh, he didn't warn you, did he?" She grinned at Severn. "He's a rascal, isn't he?"

Keats, still numb, nodded. She was just about as tall as he, but where he was slender, she was plump, although not unpleasantly so. Her hair was dark brown and had grey streaks in it. At first he thought it was silver hairs, then he realized as she brushed back her hair with her fingers that she'd left streaks of clay there. Her eyes were wide-set and the blackest he'd ever seen. She wore a stained apron over already stained clothing, and she was one of the most unaffected people Keats had ever had the pleasure to meet.

"Well, I suppose you want to see my work."

"Yes, please."

They stood in an immense room, which had large windows all along one side. Cloths were scattered across the floor, and here and there draped over figures he imagined were sculptures.

Robin led them to the clay figure she'd been working on when they entered.

"It's just a rough model," she said. "I work it in clay, and then when I'm satisfied with it, I start the real one-that one's done in marble."

The clay figure was nearly life-size. He watched as she smoothed one side, pinched the clay underneath, then swept her hands across the face to quickly sharpen the features.

"That face ... it seems somewhat familiar. That isn't-"

"Yes, you're right," she responded cheerfully, "it is Lord Byron. You see," she said, leaning close and lowering her voice, "his current paramour has commissioned a full-length study of her lover. She has willingly provided all details of his lordship's body."

Keats blinked, then chuckled. Severn joined them, and then Robin brought them back to a small sofa and two chairs in the center of the room. She poured them wine, and they sat down.

"I'd like to see some of your other work, too, if it's possible. I know that some artists don't like to show their work in progress."

"Oh, well, I'm not like Joseph," she said with an impish grin. "It does me no good for them to lurk, unseen, under cloths."

Robin rose and stretched and said she would begin by showing Keats what she'd just finished. The statue was across the room in the shadows, and when Robin pulled the cloth from it, Keats gasped.

He stared in wonder at the full breasts, the slender waist, those smooth hips and thighs. All of that nude beauty caught so magnificently in marble, cold stone as cool as her touch.

"Do you like it?" Robin asked, pride on her face and in her tone.

"Yes, very much."

The woman's face was that of Athina's.

In April, Keats began a new ballad, which had come to him one night in a dream.

La Belle Dame Sans Merci he called it. The beautiful woman without mercy.

Full beautiful—a faery's child,
Her hair was long, her foot was light,
And her eyes were wild …
And sure in language strange she said—
'I love thee true.'
And there she lulled me asleep
And there I dream'd—Ah! woe betide!
La Belle Dame sans Merci
Hath thee in thrall!

As he glanced through the lines, he wondered if this was his unconscious image of Athina. Yet, he did not consider her a cruel woman toying with his affections. Or did he?

Not completely … and yet … he didn't know. He didn't know if she had deliberately entranced him, or if he had simply been weak and fallen completely under her spell. No matter what he did. he thought of her, saw her face, even when he closed his eyes. And waiting for her to return each night was agony. She was his muse, he thought suddenly, and liked the idea.

And he wanted her very badly.

In July he began another poem, and the words seemed to pour from him.

She was a Gordian shape of dazzling hue.

Were not his own feelings a Gordian knot? He could not think of Athina without desire, or without disgust coming quick upon the heels of his desire, and yet even the disgust could not quench the desire.

With brighter eyes and slow amenity,/Put her new lips to his, and gave afresh/The life she had so tangled in her mesh.

85

Night after night he wrote, and rewrote feverishly, and when he was done he called the poem *Lamia*. He was satisfied because he knew it was good. Now let the reviews tear this one apart. He was ready.

Memories of that afternoon in Robin's studio returned, and he recalled Lord Byron's likeness. What would Byron think of Keats's latest poem, he wondered. Perhaps, he might like it, and if he did-that would be all the better for Keats. He would write Lord Byron, and he would enclose a copy of his poem, and he would wait to hear what the great man had to say.

Yet, even as productive as these months were, the nightly visions took their toll upon him. He slept little, and during the long black hours he wandered through the house aimlessly. Often he thought he heard Tom calling his name, or the lilting laugh of Athina. And sometimes he would sit down, in the midst of his wanderings, and write until the sun was coming up. It was the best of his work, he knew, but it was taking its toll of him. How long he could continue, he didn't know.

Often, exhausted of body and mind, he would fall into bed to sleep. One night, though, he sat up and realized he was screaming. He rose, his trembling legs scarcely able to hold him, and lit a candle. Then he glanced down at his nightshirt.

The linen was red with his own blood.

CHAPTER 15

When the Night doth meet the Noon
In a dark conspiracy.

—Fancy

For several weeks now Joseph Severn had posted daily notes to Keats, but all he'd received in response was a hasty scrawl—"too busy to receive anyone."

With each successive note, the handwriting became less distinctive and clear. Severn knew that his friend was working. but still …. He glanced over the latest note and frowned.

Something was wrong, and he wanted to see his friend without further delay. He had already waited too long to visit. Summer had already come and left, and now autumn was fully upon them.

When he reached the house at No. 1 Well Walk, he tapped on the door. He knocked again and waited. Still no response. Feeling a growing sense of unquiet, he tried the door. Unlocked. He pushed it open and walked in. The sitting room was silent, with not even the sound of a clock. Was John asleep?

Severn closed the door quietly behind him, then went directly to Keats's bedroom. Perhaps John was so engrossed he hadn't heard the knocks, although toward the end he had been pounding. No one could have slept or worked through that, surely. Somewhat cautiously he poked his head around the corner.

Keats was lying nude on the bed, but half across it, as if he'd just fallen onto it. A corner of the sheet straggled across his body.

"John?"

No answer.

His heart beating faster, Severn crossed to the bed. "John, are you all right?"

His friend was breathing, but shallowly, and flecks of fresh blood stained the pillowcase and sheet. Swallowing heavily, Severn fled from the room. It was time to find a doctor.

Within twenty minutes Severn and the village doctor, a vigorous man in his mid-fifties, returned. Keats was awake then, but unable to rise from the bed, and upon seeing the doctor became agitated. Severn tried calming his friend, but could do little until the doctor finished his examination.

Finally, the doctor clasped his hands firmly behind his back. His expression was grim. "Mr. Keats, it's my opinion that you must leave before the cold season comes. I don't think you will survive another winter here in England, no matter how mild it might be."

"Where should I go?' Keats asked, his face stricken with this prescription.

"I would suggest Italy. In the winter it's sunny and warm, and has the added benefit of beneficial breezes. That should help."

"What is the matter with him?" Severn had finally found his voice.

"Consumption, I think, although not yet an advanced case."

Keats paled, and Severn knew he was thinking of his brother.

"It's as if your life is being squeezed from you, Mr. Keats. I fear that all that will remain soon is a dry husk."

Severn showed him out, then came back to see if Keats needed anything. While the doctor had been there, they'd gotten a nightshirt onto the poet, and Severn had changed the soiled sheets.

"Thank you, Joseph." Keats's voice was low and Severn had to lean forward to catch the words.

"I couldn't just let you lie there." He tried smiling, but the attempt failed.

"Yes, you could have. You should have. And then perhaps I would have been dead soon." Keats pressed his trembling lips together.

"Now, John, don't talk like that! You don't want to be dead."

Keats raised his head for the first time since the doctor left, and the look in his eyes chilled Severn.

"I can't go to Italy," Keats said several days later when he seemed stronger.

"Why not?"

"I just can't."

"But you must, John. The doctor said you must go before winter came."

"No. I can't." Keats was too embarrassed to admit to his friend why he couldn't leave England. But the reason was simple: He had little money left, and although Leigh Hunt had been enthusiastic about a second volume of poems, he didn't know if there would be one.

"But the doctor said you would die," Severn said, a pleading tone in his voice.

"Nonsense, Joseph."

"No!"

"Yes."

Severn had enough sense to not pursue the matter.

With Severn's help. Keats survived the winter in England, as he knew all along he would. And while his health did not completely deteriorate, it did not improve, either. Athina still paid calls upon him, and he looked forward to them more than anything else.

In July Keats received a letter from Percy Bysshe Shelley, presently living in Italy. Shelley, whom he had met some years ago through Hunt, invited Keats to come stay with his family. At first Keats was touched by the offer, then, upon reflection, he saw only pity. Not able to tolerate that, he sat down at once and wrote a reply. He refused the offer.

When Severn learned of this, he stared at his friend in exasperation.

"But you're supposed to go to Italy."

"I told you that I cannot."

"You received an invitation." If he couldn't convince Keats, perhaps Hunt or one of their many friends could succeed. In the past few months he had realized. too, why Keats had refused to go abroad last winter; his friend had little money. Surely, he and Hunt could see about securing a loan for Keats.

"Out of pity only."

"Nonsense! It's not too late to write him another letter, accepting his generous offer."

"No," Keats said, and there was a finality in his voice, "it is too late."

But Keats did not put Shelley's letter out of his mind, and often when alone, he took out the letter and reread it. Not knowing why, he began a correspondence with the other poet, and finally in August Keats made an announcement which flabbergasted Severn.

"I have decided to follow my doctor's advice and go to Italy after all, Joseph."

"What?" Surely he hadn't heard what he'd thought he had.

"I said I want to go. God knows how much longer I have."

"Now, Johnny, don't be talking like that," Severn said soothingly.

He hoped Keats wasn't going into one of his dark moods; he had a devil of a time jollying his friend out of them, and tonight he didn't think he would be able to. Keats looked too remote, too distracted. He would try something else. He smiled shyly.

"Would you care for some company on your trip?" His offer was not altogether altruistic. Severn had long wanted to see Italy, and Italy's great paintings. And now that the Royal Academy had awarded one of his paintings a gold medal, he could afford it.

Keats smiled that wonderful smile of his. "Yes, I would, Joseph." Severn heaved a sigh of relief. Surely things would be better now.

For months Keats had felt weak, listless, and wondered why he should bother to rise at all from his bed each morning. What did it matter? The daylight hours were not real. He would stay there and wait, wait for what came in the night.

But while his thoughts drifted, then faded away, the wonderful dreams came, filling him, and they tasted of a musky odor and the red of blood. And night after night he craved them.

More and more he wanted them; they were his welcome companions. Once long ago, he thought, he might have wanted the dreams to stop; he had been afraid then. But he was no longer.

Each night he waited.

And each night, without fail, the dreams came. Dreams that held and caressed him, that whispered his name, that kissed him deeply.

Now, he lay alone in the darkness, waiting. He could not tell if this was a dream or if he was awake. He thought it was the latter, but couldn't be sure, and it really didn't matter any longer. He tried raising his hand, but his body betrayed him and refused to obey even that simple command.

No matter, he said aloud, although his lips did not move. He tried to lick his lips because they were so dry, but his tongue didn't move. Only his eyes moved, shifting back and forth, staring into the night.

The darkness was alive with unseen things. He sensed them as they brushed past him, slithered across the thin coverlet of his bed, tasted them as they touched his dry lips. And all around him was the scent he so craved, that wonderful balm. The musk.

Across the bedroom a point of light glimmered faintly, then it gathered strength as it fed on the darkness, spinning with an incredible force until its terrible brightness hurt his eyes. From within it a shape was drawn. and in turn that became a form, darker than the night outside.

The form glided toward him, and with it even stronger drifted the musky perfume he knew and loved so well, and as the form bent over him, he could see the pale face of Athina Kristonosos.

This was always how the dream began. Or was this not a dream?

She swept her cold lips across his, almost as cold, then opened her mouth so that her tongue flicked out to touch him, an electrifying sensation that charged his body with a tingling. Her fingers brushed the hair out of his eyes, and he trembled beneath her caress.

"I've been expecting you, my love," he murmured, and with all the strength he could muster he opened his arms to her.

CHAPTER 16

Still so pale? then, dearest, weep.

E arly on the overcast morning of Sunday, September 17, when the light was pale and the air chilly, Keats, waiting on the dock, shivered, although not only from the temperature. He had tried several times to back out of the trip, but neither Severn nor Leigh Hunt would allow him to do so, and now he stood close to the *Maria Crowther*, a small two-masted brig, that would take him and Joseph Severn to Italy.

As usual, Severn was late, and Keats tried not to pace as he waited. Finally, disheveled as usual, the artist arrived, baggage in hand,

"I'm sorry I'm late," he said, slightly out of breath, "but there's been bad news."

"What?"

"You remember Robin Morrow?" Keats nodded.

"She's been found dead."

Keats paled and shivered, "Oh my God. What happened, Joseph?"

"She was murdered, the Runners think. Just outside her studio, too, and she had a fearful expression on her face." He looked away.

"She was so vibrant, so alive:" Keats whispered, "and so very talented." He thought of the full-size statue of Lord Byron and wondered if she had ever finished it. And that remarkable statue of Athina Kristonosos. Where would it go now?

"Yes. Well, we'd best board."

Once aboard, Keats stayed on deck and looked out over the Thames River. He thought about poor Robin, dead at such a young age, and her talent gone to waste. Then he smiled to himself as he thought once more of Athina. He had not had to say farewell to her as he had feared the last time she visited, for she had pressed her fingers to his lips and said she would see him again. But for now, she .whispered, it was their secret, and that filled him with a mixture of fear and elation.

On the eighteenth the brig reached Gravesend. Before they were due to leave the port, Keats sent Severn ashore to purchase some medicines for him, chief among them being laudanum.

Severn never saw Keats use the laudanum during the sea trip, yet it was never out of his mind that the poet possessed such a drug.

Mostly Keats kept to himself, while each day Severn stayed on deck as long as possible, sketching the water or some part of the ship which fascinated him. He found this time by himself restful, and he would put off going to bed until he was so tired he could barely drag himself below deck.

On Tuesday night, Severn woke up, confused. He thought someone was bending over him, another over Keats, but when he opened his eyes all the way, no one was there and he knew he'd been dreaming. Finally, as he lay in the darkness listening to the sound of the water against the creaking hull, he fell asleep again.

As the ship reached open sea that Wednesday afternoon, the water became increasingly choppy, and the weather worsened until they were in the midst of a storm. Keats lay upon his upper bunk in a restless half-sleeping state. Severn watched over him, but it was extremely difficult in his own seasick condition. That night their trunks slipped back and forth across the floor, while water seeped through the planks.

Around October 2, the boat sailed out of the Channel, and the brig turned toward Gibraltar. But in the Bay of Biscay another severe storm struck and raged for three days, nearly capsizing the boat.

Finally, favorable conditions returned. While the ship was off Cape St. Vincent, Keats came on deck and lay in a reclining chair.

As Severn painted a watercolor, he would glance across from time to time at his companion. Keats's skin was nearly transparent in the early morning light, and Severn could see each tiny blood vessel, giving Keats an ethereal look. Too, the haunted expression on his face increased with each step of the journey. Haunted because they had left England behind, Severn wondered, or because they were going to Italy?

They reached Gibraltar by mid-October. Severn sketched the Rock, glowing in the golden sunlight like a giant topaz, while Keats lay nearby and watched. Most of their days passed like this-Keats sleeping or lying still-until the *Maria Crowther* finally reached the Bay of Naples on October 21 at sunrise.

In a great semicircle, flanked by islands, rose the hills of Campania. From where the two men stood on deck, they could see the great white villas of Naples, the ancient and yet still flourishing vineyards and olive orchards rising in tier after tier behind.

Beyond that was the purple cone of Vesuvius, from which drifted a long cloud of smoke. To the southeast they could see the cliffs of Sorrento. With each passing hour, the sea had deepened to an intense blue, the like of which neither Severn nor Keats had ever seen before.

But when they reached port, they weren't allowed to leave the ship. The authorities placed the brig under quarantine, because of a current epidemic of typhus in London.

The *Maria Crowther* anchored off the island of the Castle dell'Ovo, that place where, in Greek legend, the dead siren Parthenope was washed ashore after her song had been heard by Odysseus.

Both Keats and Severn longed to be ashore after the three-week-long voyage, but they could do nothing but remain patient. From the deck, Severn sketched the immense and labyrinthine Norman fortress on the island, as well as the magnificent volcano lying east of them, while Keats paced. Finally, though, rain forced them inside, and the wait became intolerable. At the end of ten days, they were allowed ashore. A cold rain was falling.

The day was October 31, Keats's twenty-fifth birthday.

CHAPTER 17

Souls of Poets dead and gone,

—Lines on the Mermaid Tavern

The two men found rooms at the Villa DiLondra, in the Vieo S. Giuseppi. Although used by Englishmen in Naples, it was little more than a restaurant with a few furnished rooms.

To their delight their room had a splendid view of Vesuvius, but the weather remained cold, wet and foggy, quite unlike what Keats and Severn had expected of the Italian climate. Too, their sleep was disturbed at night by the cries and shouts and songs of beggars, fish peddlers, and ballad singers in the street below.

Sometimes, though, when the noise was at its worst and neither could sleep, Keats would chuckle, saying that he never knew so little rest could be so healthy, and Severn would start laughing, too.

They received another letter from Shelley inviting Keats to come live with his family, but Keats declined this offer as well. He wanted to go on to Rome, where, in the English colony, a doctor, Dr. Clark, was already expecting him.

On the eighth of November the two Englishmen set out for Rome in a *vellura*, a small hired carriage. The progress was slow along the bad roads, and often Severn walked alongside the carriage. The trip which normally took two or three days lengthened to a week.

Halfway there, they reached the desolate area of the Campagna, the large plain around Rome. It was a wasteland, known for its malaria, and by the sides of the road they saw skeletons of horses and, impaled on posts, the withered arms and legs of bandits. Keats closed his eyes and would not look at the stark landscape. He could see all too clearly the dying face of his brother.

When they reached Rome, they entered the ancient city through the Lateran Gate, and immediately came upon the Coliseum, unexpectedly surrounded by ivy-covered cottages, an almost English-looking scene, Severn remarked.

Keats's physician, Dr. James Clark, was a well-read Scot in his early thirties, who liked music, and was familiar with Keats's poetry, which he thoroughly enjoyed. Not for this alone did Keats find himself immediately liking the man.

Dr. Clark had found them an apartment across from where he lived in the Piazza di Spagna at No. 23. No. 26, their new home, was on the right-hand side, at the foot of the broad stone stairs leading up to the tawny-colored Church of Trinita' dei Monti. North of the sixteenth-century church the countryside began, and when the wind blew the glorious scent of wildflowers filled the piazza.

When the carriage drew up outside Clark's door, he hurried out to greet the two travelers.

"Welcome to Rome, gentlemen," he said heartily, and pumped their hands, all the while peering at Keats, whose color was not good. Well, as anxious as he was to examine the man, that would have to wait for now. Keats must rest first. "The piazza is a particular favorite of the English living in Rome," he explained. "The neighborhood is relatively quiet, lying on the very northern edge of the city, and you won't find a more pleasant area."

Keats and Severn stared around; the piazza was filled with the small workshops of engravers, flower vendors, and sculptors. Young women in colorful costumes who longed to be artists' models lounged on the church steps.

"You'll have no trouble finding a willing model here," Keats teased, while Severn only blushed.

In the center of the piazza, opposite the grand steps, was the Fontana della Barcaccia, a marble boat-shaped fountain sculpted by Pietro Bernini with lion heads at prow and stern. The delightful music of water could be heard by those living in the surrounding houses. Keats stopped by the fountain and stared into the water and a smile slowly formed on his lips.

"Let me show you your rooms."

Severn and Keats nodded, and the three men climbed up the steep marble steps to the second floor, with Keats resting often to regain his breath. The front door was on the left of the little landing. Immediately inside they discovered a small lightless hall, but beyond this was the sitting room, which commanded a wonderful view of the piazza. To the right was a narrow bedroom, with two windows, one overlooking the piazza, the other the Steps. This room led into another much smaller bedroom with a window over the Steps.

"This room will be excellent for my painting," Severn declared. That would leave the larger bedroom for Keats. Severn and Dr. Clark looked at one another, and after a moment the doctor nodded his head.

Keats thought the rooms looked comfortable enough, although they weren't as large as he'd hoped. However, the furnishings were all neat, and hardly shabby, and far more welcoming than the uncomfortable inns they had stayed in during the past week.

"You must be tired from your long journey," Clark said some time later. "I'll go now, but perhaps tomorrow or the next day, you will let me examine you, Mr. Keats. And if you need anything, please call upon me."

They thanked him, and before they had even unpacked, they fell into their respective beds, and the night passed uneventfully for them.

The following day Dr. Clark examined Keats. Unlike the doctor in Hampstead, he did not think Keats's illness was consumption. As the days passed, Clark observed a great deal of nervous agitation in the young man, which was not typical of lung disorders; yet it did not suggest any other diagnosis. Treatment for consumption seemed the best Clark could do for the moment.

He forbid Keats to sightsee in the city unless he grew substantially better within the next two weeks, despite Keats's disappointment. But on the other hand he did encourage the poet to take daily, though short, walks around the pleasant neighborhood.

As the weeks passed, Keats seemed in better health. His color was better, and he was sleeping more soundly at night, with few dreams disturbing his rest. And when he rested, Severn rested, too.

Severn rented an old piano and played for hours, the quiet music soothing Keats considerably, and also he read aloud daily from the volumes of Shakespeare Keats had brought with him. For his part, Keats would lie abed, listening, until he fell asleep. Sometimes he would try reading on his own, but that never lasted very long and usually he would fall asleep.

As Keats improved gradually, he and Severn, sometimes with Dr. Clark, saw more of the city, but whenever Keats grew faint, they would return home at once as they didn't wish to tire him out.

Still, Keats saw far more sights than he would have thought possible when he first entered the city, and he carefully stored away the images in his memory for a time when he would begin writing poetry again.

Nearly a month after they arrived in Rome, the two men were spending a quiet evening, when someone knocked upon the door.

Startled from his reading, Severn looked up. He and Keats had had a few visitors since their arrival, but none came in the evening hours, knowing how ill Keats was and how he must rest. Dr. Clark completely discouraged the Englishmen and women he knew in Rome from staying much more than half an hour, and forbade them to arrive after six. His patient needed rest more than conversation, he maintained staunchly.

Severn glanced at Keats. who appeared to be sleeping. Well, he would simply tell the visitor to come back another time.

He rose and quietly opened the door. Outside stood two women, one blonde, one dark-haired. They were two of the most beautiful females he had ever seen, and reminded him of the old fairy tale of the two sisters, Rose Red and Snow White. He thought he recognized the blonde one.

"Yes?" he inquired politely.

The blonde smiled engagingly, almost familiarly at him. For some reason unknown to him Severn found himself blushing.

"Good evening, Mr. Severn. It has been quite some time since we last met."

Now he remembered where he'd met her. At Robin Morrow's studio. She had posed for Robin; she was the model for that magnificent statue.

And the dark-haired one? The sister she had mentioned before.

The dark one smiled, and Severn swallowed quickly.

"Could you please tell Mr. Keats that the Misses Kristonososes are here to see him?"

CHAPTER 18

And feed deep, deep upon her peerless eyes.

—Ode to Melancholy

Surprised, Severn ushered the two women into the room. It was, after all, the polite thing to do. And they were beautiful, and he was not at all unwilling to receive them, no matter that a moment before he had been determined to turn away all callers. Then he went across the room to the daybed where Keats lay.

"John, John," he said softly, "there's someone here to see you. Two someones, as a matter of fact." He glanced back over his shoulder.

Keats's eyes flickered open as he glanced past Severn. For a moment Severn thought he saw fear on the other's face. Then it evaporated-if ever the expression was truly there, he told himself-replaced by one of gladness, and Keats was struggling to sit up as he greeted the ladies.

He smoothed the bedcovers with one hand. "Good evening, Miss Kristonosos." He smiled at the dark-haired beauty.

Severn grinned as he stared at the women. One was so incredibly fair, while the other was so lusciously dark-they were almost like day

101

and night, he thought, and was once more reminded of the fairytale sisters. At first glance, the sisters seemed to little resemble each other, but now he thought he saw some similarity in their exotic mouths and eyes.

The dark-haired woman possessed the most incredible figure Severn had ever seen, and it was difficult for him to keep his eyes from her generous bosom, chastely covered with cloth. He longed to sketch them-the sisters, he quickly amended with a slight blush-and he wondered if he dared ask them to sit for him. Finally, he wrenched his eyes away and looked up to see the sisters regarding him with amusement. His cheeks reddened, and he stammered a bit when he finally spoke.

"Well, Johnny, won't you introduce me to your lovely friends?"

"Of course, please excuse my terrible manners, Joseph." Keats propped himself up on one elbow. "This is Athina Kristonosos" — the blonde, Severn noted — "and I imagine that this is her sister-Miss August Kristonosos. And this," he said, with a trace of his old humor, "is my friend, Joseph Severn, who claims he's an artist and the only reason he's come here with me is so he can meet all the lovely Italian ladies he's heard so much about."

"Now, now, Johnny." Severn's face went red. Keats's jibe had struck too close for comfort. But it wasn't the only reason he'd come.

"Good evening, sir," the blonde said, her voice sending a thrill down his spine again. It was as if she had run one of her slim fingers down his back. He flushed at the thought.

"How do you do, Mr. Severn." August Kristonosos held out her gloved hand. He shook it carefully as if he feared he might accidentally shatter it like glass, thinking how cool her skin was, even through the lavender material. He wanted to hold onto it, but reluctantly he let go of it and sighed.

Both were dressed in the latest Paris fashions, Athina in gold and white, colors that suited her well, while August was attired in shades of amethyst and black, almost as if she were in mourning. Her full lips were far redder than her sister's, and they glistened as if she had momentarily swept her tongue across them. *That* thought made him a little weak in the knees, so he indicated that the two women should sit.

102

Once they did so, he was able to drop into a chair with a suppressed sigh of relief. He waited for someone to speak.

"I am delighted to see you again, Miss Athina," Keats said to the blonde woman. "What has brought you to Italy, and in particular, Rome?"

"My sister wrote to me from the continent some time ago, and I decided to join her there. We traveled through France and Switzerland, and then I remembered that you would soon be in Rome, so we headed toward Italy. We arrived only a few days ago, and I heard from friends that you had already arrived. And I thought it high time my sister finally met you."

Keats smiled at August. "I feel as if I know you already, Miss Kristonosos. Your sister has spoken so warmly of you."

August smiled languidly, her eyelids seductively lowered. "Athina has spoken highly of you, too, Mr. Keats. I am sure that we shall get along rather famously. Don't you agree?"

"Yes."

Severn glanced at his friend, who had replied somewhat woodenly. The lively expression that had been in Keats's eyes a moment ago had faded, and now he thought his friend looked quite exhausted. Their visitors had been there only a few minutes; what could have drained Keats? Maybe he was far weaker than Severn had previously thought.

"John, if you're tired, then perhaps ..." He didn't finish because he didn't wish to be rude to the young women.

Athina Kristonosos took her cue and smiled graciously. "Yes, Mr. Keats, if you are tired, we should leave. We don't want to be nuisances."

Athina began rising, but Keats waved a vague hand, indicating that she should remain seated. He tried to smile, but couldn't find the strength to do so, and momentarily he closed his eyes.

"No, no, please, stay, ladies. I am grateful for your company. I've been in bed all day, isn't that right, Joseph?"

"Yes."

"So you see, I should be well rested."

"Very well, Mr. Keats," Athina said, concern and a certain flirtatiousness mixed in her tone, "but the minute you are feeling fatigued, you really must let us know, and we shall depart. There are other evenings we can visit, you know."

"I will." And his lips curved into that sweet smile that Severn had not seen for so long.

The sisters remained rather late that evening, far longer than Severn had expected, although it didn't seem *wrong* by any means, even though they didn't leave until well after midnight. Once the women had departed, though, Severn smiled at his friend and said it was time for Keats to retire. But Keats was restless, and said he wanted to talk instead.

Suppressing a sigh, Severn urged him to rest, while the poet peevishly replied that he would soon be getting all the rest he would ever want for eternity.

Severn, seeing another spell of morbidity setting in, refused to talk further and bid his friend a quiet good night and then withdrew to his own bedroom. He undressed, blew out the candle and then lay in the bed, listening to the small sounds issuing from the other room. He was comforted that Keats settled down faster than he'd anticipated. Then Severn slept.

Sometime during the night Severn awoke abruptly, his heart racing, his breath harsh, as if he'd just run a long distance. He sat up and thought he heard someone moving about his room.

"Johnny?" he called softly, thinking it was Keats.

But no one answered him. After a moment, he lay back down again and promptly fell asleep.

In the next few days Keats took an unexpected turn for the worse, and when Dr. Clark was called from across the street, he thoroughly examined the patient despite Keats's feeble protests, then solemnly drew Severn into the other room.

"I'm afraid it's only a matter of time for Mr. Keats." Dr. Clark shook his head. "He was doing so well that I had great hopes. But now ..." He shook his head gravely and looked away.

Severn stared down at the tips of his shoes. He was not surprised at Dr. Clark's announcement, and yet one small part of him had entertained the hope that somehow the Italian climate would miraculously heal Keats. Now, he saw bitterly that he had just been dreaming. His friend would never get better; he could only wait.

Severn walked Dr. Clark to the door and thanked him, then returned to sit by his friend's bed, his spirits the lowest they had been since the beginning of the Italian trip.

Keats scarcely moved from the bed any longer, but simply lay there, not quite awake, but not asleep.

Sometimes he would ask Keats if he wanted to work, but Keats would shake his head, and sigh, and Severn would leave the room.

Dr. Clark saw Keats again a few days later and ordered him bled, and Severn retreated from the room at that dismal news. He sat in his studio with tears slipping down his face, his shoulders shaking from his emotion. He had never confronted the thought of his friend's death as he did now. He had no plans for afterward, had no idea whether he would stay in Rome or return home to his father, who in his letters indicated he was still angry with his son's abrupt and unapproved departure. Yet how could he remain in this house, which would be a constant reminder of his own failure to help-to cure-Keats?

Severn kept his feelings to himself, and cared for Keats as best he could.

Yet somehow, against all expectations, Keats managed to hang onto his life, even as it slipped away little by little. Each morning when Severn went into Keats's room, he dreaded discovering his friend dead, and each day he was relieved that Keats still breathed.

Few visitors came to No. 26 any longer on Dr. Clark's strict orders, although the Kristonosos sisters never failed to drop by at least twice a week. They were very solicitous of Severn, and insisted they would sit with Keats while Severn went to catch some fresh air. He was relieved to get out of the small rooms which seemed to be closing in on him daily.

Dr. Clark tried various diets on Keats in an attempt to find something that would give him more strength. In January, he ordered that the poet be allowed only a single anchovy with a morsel of bread each day. Severn thought such a strict diet inhuman and, when the doctor was not present, would bring soup and a few vegetables to Keats, which his friend nibbled half-heartedly.

Severn never told Keats what the doctor had said, but somehow the poet knew.

"My death," Keats said one January day as Severn sat with him, "may stretch on for months, but I have already prepared for that. Joseph, please fetch me the laudanum you purchased in Gravesend."

Appalled, Severn stared at Keats.

When Severn did nothing, Keats glared at him. "It is my right," the poet said rather peevishly. "I have paid for it, you know. And besides, as my death is certain, I only wish to save you from the long miseries of attending it and beholding it."

Severn said nothing. His mind was awhirl. He knew he couldn't obey Keats, even though he didn't want to see his friend suffer anymore. Within a moment, though, Keats had lost his good nature and was raging at him.

The argument continued all day, until Severn finally confided in Dr. Clark. The doctor took the bottle away with him, and that was the end of the argument, much to Severn's relief.

The next morning when Severn entered his room, Keats merely stared at him while the young artist ducked his head guiltily.

"Could you bring me paper and pen?" Keats asked, his voice so faint Severn had to step closer to hear him. "And ink, too."

"Are you going to work?" Severn asked, a hopeful tone in his voice.

Keats shook his head. "I've ... letters to write, Joseph."

Severn brought him the articles he requested and sat by the bed. He watched as Keats struggled to push his hand across the page.

"If you like, Johnny," he said gently, "you could dictate the letters to me." "No!" Keats smiled to try to lessen the sting of that, because he could see the tears in his friend's eyes. "You can help me on some, but not these, Joseph. They are too personal in nature."

Somewhat mollified, Severn nodded. Before he left the room, he saw Keats pen a wobbly salutation. "My dear Shelley-"

Later in the day Severn posted the letter to Percy Shelley, and in the next week Keats wrote several more to the poet which Severn posted for him. After that, Keats could no longer hold the pen in his hand. The following evening Athina and August came by, and when they left an hour later, Keats was sleeping fretfully, his face unnaturally white.

Severn was grateful for their calls because they allowed him to leave the rooms for a while, and yet it seemed that Keats was always much worse after a visit from them. Perhaps it was mere coincidence. The artist thought. While he was attracted to the women. too, he was slightly repelled by them, and he could not reconcile the two feelings.

He thought that when Keats was not around the women, he feared them, but when they arrived, he seemed only too happy to see them.

Several times, Severn tried politely to turn the women away at the door, claiming Keats was fast asleep, but each time Keats, hearing their low voices, would ask for them, and Severn would stand aside and let them come into his room.

There was nothing else he could do.

CHAPTER 19

Can death be sleep, when life is but a dream.

—On Death

S omehow, the two women had quietly entered his bedroom, even though it was very late at night and so very dark he could scarcely see, and he hadn't heard them knock at the front door and rouse poor Severn, but he didn't mind. Not at all.

Genuinely pleased to see them, Keats smiled at the sisters, and they returned the expression, and he could feel the warmth spreading throughout his body. The warmth always accompanied her ... them. He smiled drowsily, knowing that this must be a dream, a very pleasant one. He had so many of those recently, and at times it was hard distinguishing what was real from what was not, but even that didn't matter any longer.

A strong white light glowed and spread throughout the room. Joseph had long ago blown out any candles and gone off to his own bed. Perhaps it was the moonlight. Yes, see, it streamed through the open curtains, and there in the whiteness stood the two women.

So beautiful, the light, the women.

They stood by the bed now, so close, that if he could have lifted his hand he would have touched one or both of them.

Athina reached over him and brushed his fevered forehead with her cool lips. He shivered, his body at once icy and burning, and a moan escaped his lips. Under the heavy bedcovers he twisted, writhing as the feelings darted through him.

And slowly August began unbuttoning the bodice of her dark gown, letting it slide off her moonlit arms. Then she unfastened her skirt, and it slipped with a sibilant rustle onto the floor. She stood only in her shift, and with a quick gesture that startled him, she pulled that off and stood nude in the light.

He gasped. He had never seen a woman so exquisitely made; not even her sister was as flawless. She was like a statue, he thought, as cold to the touch as one hewn from marble, as perfectly formed with each curve and line just right, and yet ... he licked his lips in anticipation. The inner heat burned fiercely, and he could feel the gathering lust.

August's pale breasts jutted out, firm and full, and her waist was impossibly narrow, her hips curved and womanly, and then a dark triangle between them. She stepped forward, and he watched in fascination as her breasts moved ever so slightly.

She bent over him, a cool breast brushing his face. Reflexively he opened his mouth, then felt the hardened nipple being pushed into his mouth. He was unresisting. It tasted like dusk and moonlight, ice and fire, and he licked it with his tongue, then caressed the nubbin gently with his lips. She moaned and pressed herself closer.

A flash of movement caught his attention and out of the corner of his eye, he watched as Athina, too, began undressing. She removed each article of clothing so slowly, so painstakingly, that he wanted to shout for her to hurry. Unlike her sister, she did not toss her clothing upon the floor, but rather folded each piece and set it carefully on the chair.

He throbbed in response, and a sob caught in his throat. Her body was not as lush as her sister's, but it was equally beautiful, and her breasts were perfect globes in which he wanted to lose himself. The triangle at the junction of her white thighs gleamed honey gold in the moonlight, and already on his tongue he could taste that exquisite honey.

She joined her sister by his bed, then wordlessly slipped under the covers with him. August did likewise, and even though the bed was not great in size, it was wide enough to accommodate them comfortably.

Athina murmured something, then kissed him, while her sister lightly touched his face.

Their kisses were ice-cold, burning-hot, and he craved more.

August rose above him, then swept her lips across his chest, while she caressed his face, his arms. Maddeningly slow her hand inched down his thin body until she reached his manhood. It throbbed with a pain and pleasure he had never thought he would know, and she raked a fingernail across its tender top.

He shrieked, but the sound was swallowed by Athina who kissed his lips, pressing her tongue into his mouth. She sucked at him hungrily, as if she could draw his very breath from his lungs, and for a moment, he panicked, and fought against her, but August held his arms down, and in a moment his struggles ceased.

They continued their attention to him, and his desire overcame any fear.

He arched his back, as the two women petted him, kissed him, and he reached out blindly, not caring which woman his hands found. He fondled icy nipples and squeezed full breasts, sought those dark wells of womanhood, and when his fingers slipped in easily and were caught with tightened muscles, he shuddered with pleasure. Those muscles pulled at him. as if they were sucking on him, drawing him to them, and he reached over, bestowing a tender kiss upon the dewy hair.

His breathing grew ragged, becoming panting as August's lips followed her hand, and she began licking his hardened shaft. Voluptuous pleasure rippled through him as August's mouth moved up and down him, and blindly he reached out, taking Athina's face in his hands.

He kissed her, hard, his mouth forcing hers open, his tongue thrusting against hers, even as his groin responded, and he rammed against August. She chuckled, a low sound, then simply opened her mouth wider and took him in, and he cried aloud. He had never experienced anything like this, never before, and never, he knew, again.

He was gasping for air now, and wondered how they could breathe so evenly. A ripple darted through him, and he moaned aloud.

Athina smiled lazily at him, then pulled away momentarily. She rubbed herself, her beautiful breasts and her musky sex, across his face, then his chest and stomach; all the while her sister continued her delicate and tantalizing ministrations.

In his veins a white-hot heat boiled, and he thought he would explode, and he tried keeping it from happening too soon. But the desire was stronger than he, and he had time only to clutch at one of Athina's breasts, when the heat rushed along, too fast for him to stop, and burst out of him. He heard August's low murmur, and that too sent a thrill through him.

Beneath her mouth and hands and sex, he bucked, and pumped, his legs entwined in hers, aware and yet not aware of the hands and teeth tearing at his chest and groin, until he was completely drained and exhausted. Then he fell back onto the bed, limp. He was drenched with sweat, his dark hair plastered across his forehead, and even the hairs on his chest were damp. He was so winded he was nearly choking for lack of air.

Yet, even though he was obviously spent, the sisters did not let him rest; rather, they murmured wordlessly and ran their cunning hands across his arms and legs, touching his flaccid penis.

Gradually, though, and against all his expectations, his body began awakening once more, and he stirred, moving legs and arms vaguely, and then because he could do no more, rolled over onto his side. Lips unwarmed by his earlier kisses trailed across his hip, tickling him, onto the lean curve of his buttocks.

Hands like winter reached across him, raked nails on his skin, then kissed the wounded places where dots of blood welled up. The tongues, so gelid and sharp, lapped at him, and he felt the sisters' mouths move downward, caressing and licking his fevered skin, and around, away from his back until they reach his stomach.

Icy prickles darted through his skin, and to his astonishment his manhood expanded. Someone laughed-Athina, he thought, although he could not be sure-and seized him, and he throbbed against her hand. She squeezed hard, and he cried out in pain, and in pleasure, too, and then she was licking him, rimming the top of his penis with her long tongue, lapping at the shaft, down until she nuzzled against his testicles, where she nipped the soft skin.

The fire boiled up again within his veins, and he wanted to stop it, wanted to roll over onto one of the women so that he could give her … them … love, so that they could receive some pleasure, too. If only he could move, if only his body would respond to his commands, and then he could kiss her and caress her properly, as he wanted to, and then he would slide ever so gently inside her, and thrust, deeper and deeper, bringing them both to great heights of joy.

But he couldn't, and now he was being held down, his back firm against the wet and clinging sheets, and he felt the odd prickings along his inner thigh, on his penis, on his stomach, and he cried out, as pleasure and agony mingled and exploded once more, and as blackness spread across him.

The following morning, Thursday, Severn walked into Keats's room and nearly fainted at the horrible sight before him.

Blood was everywhere. The sheets were stained, as was the carpeting alongside the bed, and even several long and twisted streaks smudged the formerly pristine walls behind the bed.

And there lay Keats, half in bed, half out, not conscious. He was deathly white now, his bruised eyes closed, his chest barely rising and falling. He had red marks on his stomach and groin, but Severn did not study them.

Severn sent a message across to Dr. Clark to come at once, then began the painful task of cleaning up his friend. He wept as he did so, completely unaware of the flow of warm tears. In all that time Keats never opened his eyes or even stirred.

The doctor arrived just as Severn was removing the soiled sheets, and Dr. Clark frowned at the bloodstained material. He bent over Keats, now attired in a fresh nightshirt, and listened for a few minutes, then stood up and shook his head. Tears burned in Severn's eyes again as he looked away.

"The end could come any moment, Mr. Severn." Clark frowned. Once again, solemnly, he shook his head and there was a sorrowful expression on his face. "I will send a nurse this afternoon. I'm afraid there isn't anything else I can do."

After Severn showed the doctor out, he sat down beside his friend and thought about what was to come. He pressed his face into his hands. After a long moment, Keats's eyes slowly opened, then focused.

"Joseph." Blood, spit up from his lungs, flecked his swollen lips, and Severn leaned forward, wiping it off with a handkerchief. He could not bear to look at the spreading red stain.

"I'm here, Johnny."

"Joseph, did you ever see anyone die?'

"No." And he thought of the young boy Keats had been when he had sat with his mother and watched her die little by little.

"Well, then I pity you."

Severn said nothing; there were no words left in him, certainly none that would comfort his friend. He only wished that there was something he could say, if not for Keats, then for him. But there was nothing; nothing but an overwhelming numbness.

Keats had much that he wanted to say yet to his friend, but he couldn't find the strength to speak. Unformed words tumbled in his mind. He was dying, he knew that, and he knew why. It wasn't consumption, as the doctor thought; rather, he was dying because of the love of the Kristonosos sisters. He would have smiled-or wept-had he been able. He never thought that love could be so deadly.

And too, he knew now that his young brother Tom had not died of consumption. No, Athina had taken care of the boy; and Athina— somehow, and still he did not understand the method—had killed Tom.

Just as she and her sister were killing him.

He closed his eyes. Soon it would be over, all the worry, the pain, all gone.

Later in the day the English nurse came to the apartment, and Joseph left his friend's room to sleep. Yet each time he started to drop off, he would jerk awake. How could he sleep, knowing that Keats might soon slip away forever?

The hours passed like days, and finally Severn rose, and he sat beside the nurse. Keats's color was worse than it had been earlier in the day; his eyelids were pale, almost transparent, and there was a slight blueness about the lips that Severn hadn't noticed before.

The next day, Friday, February 23, Keats called out weakly to Severn, who went at once to the bedside.

It was around four in the afternoon, and although Keats had slept a few hours the night before, he felt worse than ever. His eyes were gritty, his mouth dry, and his hands trembled whenever he reached for something. And tears came all too easily.

"Severn—I—lift me up-I am dying-I shall die easy—don't be frightened—be firm, and thank God it has come!"

Gently Severn did as he was asked and lifted him up, and Keats's breathing eased momentarily, and then the phlegm gurgled deeply within the poet's throat, and his breathing became strained. Severn held him for hours and talked soothingly of his art and of the music he loved almost as well, and all the while the sounds from Keats were so dreadful that Severn wept.

Around eleven that night, Severn saw that his friend had fallen asleep, and so he laid him carefully back onto the bed. But Keats did not stir. Severn knew then that he was not sleeping. Keats had died.

He gazed down at the wasted body of his friend, as tears slipped from his eyes. He hunched over in his grief. The long months of struggle and agony for his friend were at last over. At least, Keats had not lingered any longer. At least, he was at rest now.

In the unnatural quiet of the room, he thought he heard a faint sound. Confused, thinking that he had been alone with Keats, he blinked and looked up. The light was dim, and so he saw nothing at first.

But then, he saw that only a few feet away from the bed stood the Kristonosos sisters. They had come to see how Keats fared, and now he must tell them the sad news and comfort them. But even as he thought that, he hesitated, and, with a sudden chill, realized they were smiling.

_1824_

A heavy, smothering darkness had slipped into the sitting room while
Byron talked of the short life and agonizing death of John Keats, and
for a few minutes after his voice ceased, neither man moved. The
room was perfectly quiet; normally, while they talked, they could
hear the voices and shouts of the men in the rooms below Byron's.
Now: only silence.

Byron rose slowly and lit a nearby lamp. The yellow light washed
across his pale and drawn features, captured the intent look in his dark
eyes. As if every movement brought him pain, he swung around stiffly
and gazed at Winston.

"Well, Mr. Early? What do you think of that terribly sad tale?"

"I have always enjoyed Mr. Keats's poetry, and I am sorry he died
at such a young age. But 'twas simply a coincidence," Winston asserted
as he shifted noisily in his chair.

He had sat very still during Byron's long recitation, and now that it
was over he wanted to move around, to get up and pace about the
room, but with some effort he restrained himself. He feared his actions
would look as if Byron's story had somehow adversely affected him,
and of course, no such thing had happened. He licked his lips, a
nervous gesture.

Byron continued gazing at him.

Again, Winston's tongue flicked across his lips. Why were they so
dry?

"You can't know all of this, can't know if it's truly what happened
to Mr. Keats—after all, as I might remind you, you weren't there, my
lord. And besides, the sisters did nothing wrong, as far as we know. I
am assuming that you must have talked to Severn sometime after
Keats's death."

Byron nodded.

"Severn admitted, after all, that he did not care for them, so what
he might say about the sisters is nothing more than petty slander. There

could be no connection, none whatsoever. None," he repeated, as if he needed reassurance.

"But there is," Byron said, his voice weary. "The women drained him of his life—and of his creativity. You'll see." He rubbed his hand over his face, grey with fatigue.

"No one witnessed that night with Keats when the sisters supposedly came to him and—" Winston's voice stopped, as he looked away, embarrassed at the memory of Byron's words.

"But they came to him."

Winston pressed his lips together. "Then prove it, my lord."

Byron held up several folded pieces of paper. "But I do have these."

"And they are what?" Winston asked, more sharply than he intended.

"Letters. From John Keats to Percy Shelley, those precious few letters Keats managed to write, which Severn posted for him."

"Your proof is in there? Then let me see them!" Winston reached out with one hand.

"In due time, Mr. Winston, in due time. And the moment is not right yet."

"When will the right moment come?"

Byron did not seem to hear the young man's words, but instead spoke, his eyes focused on nothing. "Keats was buried in Rome in the Cimitero di Protestanti, only a few feet away from the grave of William—But no. I fear that I'm getting ahead of myself."

Lord Byron poured them fresh drinks, wiped his face with a handkerchief, then coughed into it, and began his second story.

PART III
SHELLEY—ITALY: 1818

Death has set his mark and seal
On all we are and all we feel,
On all we know and all we fear.
> —*Death*

In the dark eyes a power....

> —*To Constantia, Singing*

CHAPTER 20

Willie Shelley liked their new home. He didn't know if Clara did. After all, she was just a baby. And besides, she didn't talk much. Certainly not to him. She just sat and gurgled.

The children were at the far end of the garden, near the arbor. where the bushes were the most dense, the vines most overgrown. and Milly, their nurse, had told them to wait just a moment. and she would be back.

But he had been waiting a long time, and he was tired and hungry, and he wanted to go inside because the little flying bugs bothered him.

But he had to wait.

He had a bright red ball that he and Milly had been playing with, and now, bored, he tossed it to his sister, sitting on a soft blanket a few feet away from him. It smacked her right in the middle of her chest, and she started to cry, her small pale face screwed up with the effort.

Willie glanced over his shoulder, then hurried to get the ball before Milly came out to see why Clara was crying. But Clara always cried. She wasn't even a year old yet, a whole year younger than he, but she still cried all day and night. He sat down with the ball and rolled it around his legs which stuck out in front of him.

It was getting a little dark, and the bushes were bigger than he was and strange-looking now that there wasn't much sunlight, and Willie was a little scared. He bit his lip and stared down at the ant crawling on his leg. He brushed it away.

Clara was still crying, when he heard the bushes rustling. He watched a leaf on the end of a branch tremble.

A bird.

A cat.

It was so dark.

He blinked, trying to see what was in the bushes, then glanced back at the house. He could barely see it now. He knew he should run and get Milly, but she and his mother had told him never to leave Clara by herself. And Clara was still crying, and he couldn't pull her to her feet and take her inside.

The rustling continued, growing louder now and closer, too, and Willie felt a warmth spreading between his legs. He had wet himself.

Suddenly a woman stepped out of the bushes into the clearing, and he exhaled, not realizing he'd been holding his breath.

She wore a pale dress that seemed to glimmer, and he thought she was very pretty, although he couldn't see much of her face in the darkness. But her eyes were very deep, and dark. She bent over Clara, whose face was as red as his ball.

"Here, now what is this, little one?"

Clara continued crying, although she looked up at the newcomer.

The woman picked Clara up in her arms, holding her carefully, and spoke quietly to the baby. The woman's head was bent low over his sister's face, and all Willie could see was the long hair hiding the baby like a curtain. Then finally Clara stopped crying.

She held the baby for a little while longer, rocking her and singing softly, then she stooped and put his sister back on the blanket. Clara was asleep, one hand at her mouth. Her red face was much paler now.

Willie looked from his sister to the beautiful woman, who smiled at him, then left just as suddenly as she'd arrived.

Puzzled, Willie sat there, turning the red ball over and over in his hands. A few minutes later Milly came out to fetch them.

Mary Shelley was slightly concerned the next day when Clara slept so late. Usually the little girl was up before anyone else, cheerfully ready to start her day. But today Milly reported at breakfast that the baby still slept and had spent a peaceful night.

After she was finished with her brief meal, Mary went into the nursery to check on her daughter. She thought Clara looked pale, and wondered if the baby was ill. She put her hand on the small forehead, but it felt no warmer than usual.

Well, sleep wasn't harmful, she reasoned, and so she instructed Milly to let the baby sleep as long as she wanted. Besides, Clara was a fretful baby, and as long as she was asleep, Mary could work. Willie was quietly playing with his toys. He waved to his mother, and she blew him a kiss.

A faint smile tugging at her lips, she returned to her unpacking. Mary Shelley and her husband, Percy Bysshe, and the two small children, had moved just a few days ago, on June 11, to the Bagni di Lucca.

The Baths were a fashionable spa, and the town had several comfortable inns. a casino where dances and dinners were given, and numerous summer villas on the steep wooded slopes. This old Etruscan town had been ruled as a principality until 1814 by one of Napoleon's sisters, and was highly recommended by Eustace's *Classical Tours Through Italy*, a work which Shelley trusted deeply.

The town was set among some of the loveliest hills the Shelleys had ever seen, and on the mountains grew deep groves of oak and chestnut, with vines cultivated at the base of the mountains.

The house her husband had found for them, called the Casa Bertini, was built on a rather modest scale with three floors, an elegantly tiled roof, and freshly painted shutters. It perched near the top of the unpaved, dusty road that wound up through the village and into the hills. The Casa Bertini looked upon the road from a small terrace garden, while the back was beautifully overgrown. At the end of the garden Shelley had found a rough arbor made of laurel bushes, and here he would work.

Momentarily, Mary frowned as she glanced around the cluttered sitting room. Crates still made walking through the room circuitously, and everything which had been unpacked needed to be washed or dusted. So little done in the hours she had been working. She was tired of constantly moving from one town to another, but it was necessary, she knew—they were always one or two steps ahead of the bill collectors.

She stooped to select some of Shelley's books to put on the few shelves they had, then paused to wipe the dust from her face.

Her face was very pale, with a well-shaped nose and a mouth neither too thin nor too full. Her shoulder-length light-brown hair was arranged demurely on either side of her head, and she was not at all surprised to find a cobweb adorning one curl.

Her forehead was wide and white, and she possessed earnest hazel eyes that the poet William Wordsworth, a frequent visitor in her father's household, had said no man would forget when she grew a little older. At the time she had been amused by his praise, but had never forgotten it. She was quite slender and tall, although not as tall as her husband, and her delicate hands were one of her chief attractions, although she didn't consider them that extraordinary.

Now, she realized ruefully, they were spotted with dust and ink stains, and sported several recently formed calluses from all the packing and unpacking she had done in the past few months.

Some thought her just pretty: others called her beautiful. Either way, Mary Shelley didn't much care. She was not overly concerned with clothing, either, and while she displayed good taste when she so desired, she did not put herself out in trying to wear the latest designs, which was just as well as the Shelleys were continually short of funds.

She arranged the books carefully, knowing they would be the first thing Shelley would notice upon his arrival home. He was off, strolling through the countryside-working. he claimed. She had work of her own, her writing to do, but first she must settle the chores.

This year had seen the publication of her first novel. *Frankenstein*, conceived while visiting Lord Byron at his villa in Switzerland. and she had become an instant celebrity with her gothic tale. And she wanted to start on another novel she'd thought about while en route to the Baths.

She was due money from her publisher, but she couldn't expect that to arrive anytime soon; she knew enough never to expect the check to arrive on time, too. Also, it bewildered her that the public always assumed that the "acclaimed" writers were rich. Certainly she and Shelley weren't, nor were any of the other poets or writers of their acquaintance. Her father was heavily in debt, and so much of their money was funneled to him; too, Shelley was generous-too much sometimes, she thought-in giving money to friends.

And then there was the matter of her father-in-law. Sir Timothy was not at all pleased with the marriage and the fact that they had left England, and the money that was supposed to come freely to Bysshe was only occasionally doled out.

Just another way in which the father sought control of the son, she thought wearily.

Oh, well, perhaps she would work this evening, when the children were once more in bed. Perhaps Clara would be good, and go to sleep right away.

Morning passed into afternoon, and late afternoon passed very slowly into evening. She was carefully wiping the dust from a volume's leather spine when Shelley arrived with a cheerful hello and planted a kiss on her grimy forehead. He wrinkled his nose fastidiously, then chuckled as she stuck her tongue out at him briefly.

She studied her husband, something of which she never tired, and wondered that he had been attracted to her. He was slender, and tall, although with his round-shouldered stance-a legacy from his youth when he'd towered above classmates-he didn't appear quite as tall as he actually was. His dark hair was long, abundant and curling, and windblown as always. As usual, he'd pushed it back from his face.

His reddish eyebrows rounded gently over his brilliant blue eyes, which were dreamy at rest, yet flashed with a wild sapphire light when he was excited. His nose was long and narrow. his mouth well-formed with ruddy lips. He possessed a singularly high voice. Some called it strange, but acquaintances thought nothing unusual about it, and Mary found it exceedingly pleasant. He was so handsome, she thought.

As always, he was dressed casually, his collar open, his neckpiece long gone. And he had grass stains on his shirt and pants.

He smiled. "How are you progressing, my love? Finding everything?"

She wiped a hand across her cheek and left a smudge. "I think so, although I won't know for a few days. There's so much left."

"I know." He sighed. "Where are the children? Willie didn't greet me at the door."

"Milly's giving them their dinner; they'll see you afterward." She turned back to the boxes. "Did you get any work done?"

"Some, although I'm not really happy with it." There was silence for a few minutes. then: "Mary."

"Yes, my dear." She waited. She knew that tone of voice. He had done something, something he wanted her approval of.

He smiled. "I'm afraid I've taken the liberty of inviting two guests for dinner tomorrow. I knew you wouldn't mind, my dear."

"What?" She stared at him, not sure she had heard properly. "Dinner guests when the house is barely settled, Bysshe?"

"Well, yes." His expression faltered slightly.

"Oh, Bysshe."

"I'm sorry," he said quickly, his words rushing together. "I met them while I was out strolling, and we had such an enchanting discussion that I longed to have you meet them, Mary. Truly you'll like them."

"Are they women?" she asked.

Shelley nodded sheepishly. "They're sisters, and half-English, I think. And quite extraordinary looking. too."

Two more women, Mary thought a little sadly. To add to Shelley's harem, or at least that's what his enemies. and unfortunately they were many, called it. She was accustomed to such behavior, although she didn't always like it. He had grown up with five younger sisters, many of his good friends were women as well. She was slightly jealous of other women; and she had good reason to be of some. She knew that Shelley had not been faithful to her, although they had never spoken of his indiscretions.

Secretly, in one deep never-admitted-to part of her, she feared that someday another woman would take her husband away from her. And she had reason to fear that, too. Had she not herself taken him away from his first wife?

Mary had been very young, only sixteen, and in love, desperately so. She could not imagine living without him. Shelley had reciprocated, and there was nothing to do but run away together, even though he was married with two children.

The impetuous couple became a scandal in England, had temporarily estranged her father, had lost many friends. but despite all of the adverse reaction, she had never regretted what they had done.

She was the daughter of Mary Wollstonecraft, the women's rights advocate, and while her mother had not lived long after her birth, Mary's father had raised her with her mother's liberal beliefs, of which the sanctity of marriage was not one. Her mother had borne one child out of wedlock, and had only married Mary's father when she became pregnant again.

Shelley swore over and over that he loved Mary more than any other woman he'd ever known, but that didn't mean that such a thing couldn't happen a second time, and each time a new woman entered her home, that old fear stirred in her breast. She wished she could have him all to herself, even though she knew that was selfish. Besides, he was a famous man, and no matter how she felt, she must share him with the world.

The world, though, did not have to include two extraordinarily beautiful sisters.

"Mary?"

She thought he looked a lot like Willie then, and how could she resist him?

"Oh, very well," she said at last.

His face brightened, and he kissed her again. "Thank you, my love. I know you won't have cause to regret this. Believe me, the sisters are most extraordinary."

"I've no doubt," she murmured.

CHAPTER 21

For she was beautiful-her beauty made
The bright world dim, and everything beside
Seem like the fleeting image of a shade.

— The Witch of Atlas

"Here they are at last," Shelley exclaimed—rather unnecessarily, Mary thought somewhat crossly—as he leaped to his feet, "the Misses Kristonososes. Ladies, please enter."

Shelley and his small family had gathered in the small parlor, hurriedly cleaned and arranged that afternoon, the crates packed out of sight, to receive dinner guests.

He shook the hand offered to him. "I'm glad you could come this evening."

"We wouldn't miss this occasion for anything," Athina Kristonosos said sweetly.

He smiled at her, then turned. "This is my wife, Mary."

"How do you do," Mary murmured, surveying the strangers from under her eyelashes. She had expected attractive women, but not two

126

breathtakingly beautiful ones, whose forms were so … well, the only word was voluptuous. No wonder he had invited them home to dinner after a single conversation. She noticed that Shelley's gaze kept straying from one face to another and from one bosom to the other's. Certainly a large amount of flesh showed, she thought waspishly, as she studied her guests' gowns.

The blonde wore a white lace dress over a satin slip, the skirt bottom being trimmed with ornate lace entwined with tiny pearls and full-blown roses. The bodice was pale rose-colored satin, very tight and low-cut. White lace slashed the short rose satin sleeves. Her golden hair was arranged with a few light ringlets at her temples, but otherwise cascaded down her back. Elbow-length white kid gloves and a necklace and earrings of pink pearls completed her ensemble. She carried a small ivory fan, with which she toyed.

Her sister wore a black crape dress over a sarsenet slip of the same color, with a bodice cut square and tight to the shape, her bosom being even more noteworthy than her sister's, Mary thought. Roses and scallops embroidered in gold thread decorated the hem, while a rouleau of crape intermixed with jet beads trimmed the bosom and back. The long sleeves were banded with jet beads. Her black hair was parted in the center, then braided and brought around the crown of the head. She wore chamois leather gloves and shoes, and her earrings and necklace were antique blood red rubies.

Beautiful women beautifully attired. Mary glanced down at her own attire. She'd never cared overmuch for clothes, but suddenly she regretted it. Her gown, although of a once-fine brown tabby, was several years old, and even when new was never as fashionable as these two dresses. Her kid slippers were old, and she knew there was a faint stain on one. There was also a tiny rip on the right side of her gown. She sighed.

"Good evening," the dark-haired one said, clasping Mary's hand.

How cold it was! Mary thought, seeking to pull her hand away quickly, yet without appearing rude. The other's skin was as cool as marble, even through the material of her glove.

"How do you do, Mrs. Shelley," said the blonde woman somewhat shyly.

Her hand was just as cool, and Mary wondered why. Was there something physically wrong with them? Perhaps they were always cool to the touch; she knew some women were like that. But the chill of their skins was almost unnatural. Her husband, of course, would not have noticed such a detail; obviously, he was besotted with their lovely eyes and smiles. And their rather lush bosoms, too.

"And whoever is this handsome young man?" Athina asked softly as she noticed Mary's son and knelt before the little boy.

"This is my dear son, William," Shelley said proudly. "Now, Willie, can you say a proper hello to the pretty lady?"

"'Lo." Willie, his shoulder-length hair fair and silky, his eyes the brilliant blue of his father's, glanced shyly at his mother, and Athina reached out to stroke his plump cheek. His eyes widened slightly, and curiously, the woman put a finger to her lips.

Immediately Mary took a step forward, then stopped as her son smiled. There was nothing wrong, she assured herself, yet she was puzzled by the gesture.

Clara Everina, for once not crying, was duly shown, then Milly Shields dropped a slight curtsy. After the introductions were finished Milly firmly ushered her youthful charges from the room to the nursery where their dinner waited.

"They're lovely children," Athina murmured. "So beautiful ... so vibrant."

"Yes, the most exquisite faces I've ever seen on children," her sister said. "Dear William has your extraordinary eyes, Mr. Shelley, which makes him a very lucky boy."

He grinned. "Thank you, but I think he quite looks like Mary. Don't you agree?"

"Oh, yes."

"And Mr. Shelley said you had a third child? A daughter named Allegra?" August queried, gazing steadfastly at Mary.

The woman's unblinking stare unnerved Mary slightly. "No, Allegra is my stepsister's daughter. Currently she's visiting her father."

The two sisters looked at one another, but said nothing.

Among the circles in which the Shelleys traveled it was widely known that Allegra's father was Lord Byron, and that he was not disposed toward marrying the girl's mother. The little girl was beautiful, and possessed the same cleft in her chin as did her father. But while everyone knew, no one spoke of it.

"Would you care for something to drink, ladies?" Shelley asked in his role as genial host.

The women politely accepted the amber sherry he poured for them. August sipped at hers delicately, Mary noted, while Athina drank more quickly. Shelley refilled her glass.

Mary sat quietly, staring at her sherry, then glanced at her husband. She was uneasy with her guests, and wished that the evening was done.

"How is it that you and your sister came to meet my husband?" she asked quietly.

August answered. Mary noticed that she did most of the talking. "We were out strolling, and he approached us, asking us for directions. It seems he had become turned around in his wanderings."

Shelley laughed. "'Twas remarkably silly, but fortunate over all, don't you think, my love?"

"Oh, yes." She knew her husband would never hear the irony in her voice.

"I must tell you, Miss Kristonosos, that after some thought I have renamed you and your sister," Shelley said as he filled his glass again.

August raised one eyebrow. "Oh?"

"Yes, I thought you needed names more appropriate, and so you have become-at least to me-the Morning and the Evening Stars."

Athina glanced down at her hands, while August said with a faint smile, "Really, you flatter us greatly, Mr. Shelley."

"Not at all."

"My husband has always been interested in the heavens," Mary said, then wished she'd remained silent. The older sister looked at her, and Mary could feel the chill of the gaze. Once more she stared down into the depths of her glass.

With Mary remaining silent, Shelley and their guests chatted. The sisters had recently been in Switzerland, it seemed, as had the Shelleys, and so conversation turned to the remarkable sights in the Alps.

Milly announced that dinner was ready, and they went into the dining room.

Shelley, who sat at one end of the table, arranged for the sisters to sit on either side of him, while Mary sat at the other end.

As the maid served the dishes, Mary noticed that the sisters ate little of the barley soup and fresh salad, and when the meat was brought in, August politely declined, as did her sister.

"I'm sorry," she said with a half-rueful smile, "I forgot to mention that my sister and I eat only vegetables and fruit."

"How remarkable!" Shelley said. "You see, ladies, I, too, embrace vegetarianism as well." He flashed a pleased smile at them.

"We don't meet many people of our inclination."

"No, one doesn't, but I think it has much to recommend it. Of course, it's not very popular right now, but someday, I think it will be."

Mary had tried vegetarianism for a while, living on broths and vegetables and fruits in season, but she had felt listless and had fallen ill frequently, so she had resumed eating meat, despite Shelley's disapproval.

The discussion turned to poetry, as it often did, and Shelley asked August her taste in poems.

August set her glass down, still nearly full yet, and smiled. "'... *far I have loved/Thee ever, and thee only: I have watched/Thy shadow, and the darkness of*
thy steps,/And my heart ever gazes on the depth/Of thy deep mysteries. I have made my bed/In charnels and on coffins, where black death/Keeps record of the trophies won from thee ...'"

"*Alastor!*" he exclaimed happily. This poem had been composed in 1815 while they were still living in England. He beamed at Mary, then at the visitors. "You know my work!"

Mary was amused; after the years of acclaim, Bysshe still could not believe that his name might be recognized by others, and that there were actually those who read his poetry.

"Yes, I know your poetry, Mr. Shelley. I was in London some time ago and was fortunate enough to obtain a copy of that marvelous volume. In truth, I travel with it always. Would it be too much to ask of you to inscribe it for me sometime?"

"I would be delighted, dear lady." He smiled at her, then at his wife.

"'*I met a traveler from an antique land ...*'" Athina began softly.

"You, too, Morning Star?"

"My sister and I have always enjoyed poetry, Mr. Shelley, and have always found poets, writers, artists, and others of a creative bend to be the most stimulating of companions," August replied. "There seems a special energy about those who create. Do you not find that so, Mrs. Shelley?"

"Yes, I agree. Some of my earliest memories are of my father talking with writers, poets, and philosophers." Charles Lamb had visited her father, as well as Southey and Samuel Coleridge. "Those evenings they came to visit were so exciting."

"And in turn those creative men infused you with an energy of your own, is that not so?"

"Yes, I think so." She had not really looked at it that way before, but now she realized that August was correct. She had often gone to her room after those visits, and, too excited to sleep. had started writing.

"I am sorry that I have not read your novel yet, although I have heard much good of it. Perhaps you will inscribe a copy for me?"

"Certainly, Miss Kristonosos." Mary was a little flattered that the woman knew of her novel, and yet she could not help but wonder if the woman had said that simply to mollify her. Sometimes it was terrible having such a suspicious nature. And sometimes it proved to be quite useful.

"What are you currently working on, Mr. Shelley, if I may ask?"

"A poem entitled *Rosalind and Helen*. Actually, I began it some time ago."

"And tossed it aside," Mary said, "until I found it once more and thrust it at him. I do wish to see it finished before long."

"And now I obediently work on that, although there are others broiling in my mind. With our travels, it hasn't always been possible to work, and in fact I haven't yet settled down here."

And whose fault was that? Mary wondered. She had managed to work, despite having the house and children to look after. Ah, well. ...

Once they were finished with the meal, Mary suggested they go into the parlor. They drank coffee, then after Shelley brought them each a glass of sherry, Mary complimented the sisters on their excellent English.

"We deserve no credit. Our mother was English," August replied, "and our father Greek, so that both languages are equally natural to us. Also, our parents encouraged us to learn as many languages as possible. I speak ten or so, and Athina can converse in nearly fifteen."

"That is a truly incredible feat." Shelley exclaimed as he gazed at them. "You must find it extraordinarily helpful in your travels."

Fifteen! Mary thought, dismayed. She spoke only French and a smattering of Italian.

"Yes, we do. However, I am afraid that, as well as my sister speaks so many languages, her Italian needs improvement." Athina looked down demurely. "That is one of the reasons we're here-to help her."

"And do you plan staying long here?" Mary hoped not. As irrational as her feeling was, she wanted these enchanting women gone; she wanted them out of her house, out of the Baths. She didn't want them lingering any longer than necessary.

"No, Mrs. Shelley, we won't linger very long."

It was almost as if the woman had read her thoughts, Mary told herself, and felt a touch of cold settle along her spine.

"There's so much in Italy that we desire to see and explore. We will be leaving in a few weeks."

Shelley looked disappointed, but Mary experienced a vast relief.

"What a shame," she murmured cheerfully.

"We're only staying here a short time ourselves," her husband declared to Mary's surprise. "But I'm not sure where we would go from here, perhaps Rome. You see, Mary can't bear solitude, nor I society — surely this is a case of the quick coupled with the dead."

The Kristonosos sisters glanced at one another for a moment, then began laughing softly.

Their low laughter brought a strange tingling sensation to Mary. It was almost … she couldn't quite put a name to the feeling … and she wondered if she hadn't been a little too quick judging them: the sisters were rather nice and interesting, weren't they. The laughter stopped, and she shook herself, wondering at her thoughts a moment before.

They chatted for some time, then finally August glanced at the clock on the mantelpiece. Both hands were nearly straight up.

"Well, we must be going home now. It is getting quite late, and I don't want to overstay our welcome -at least not the first visit,"

"I'm sure this won't be the only one," Shelley responded graciously.

Mary said nothing.

August rose gracefully and smiled charmingly at the Shelleys.

"Thank you for inviting us to dine with you. We had a delightful time this evening, and I know we shall be seeing you again, perhaps while we're out walking some evening. At least, I hope so."

How odd, Mary thought, that the sisters had not responded with an invitation to their house.

Athina murmured her thanks, barely audibly. and then Shelley was insisting on walking them home. Mary said nothing, because she knew it would be of no use.

Afterward, Mary left the parlor. The evening had been enjoyable in a way; and in another, she'd been more bothered than she could ever remember. She glanced into the dining room; Milly had cleaned it properly. Wasn't it odd that August and Athina had scarcely eaten anything? Vegetarians usually ate large portions.

More than passing odd, she told herself. And returned to the parlor to wait for her husband.

CHAPTER 22

The moon made the lips pale, beloved—
The wind made thy bosom chill—

—Lines

After a week, they were settled into the new house, and Mary decided to forget her writing for a week of rest. She joined Shelley to walk for many enjoyable hours through the thick chestnut woods, where they followed the course of the river, or of paths cut into the mountain.

Before breakfast or after dinner, they rode, renting the horses in the village. In the evenings they watched the glorious fireflies, and the planet Jupiter rising over the mountains to the south, and the pale summer lightning spread across the sky. Two evenings that second week they attended the lively dances held at the casino.

During their third week at Casa Bertini. though, Shelley began exploring on his own, taking only a lunch and a book to read later. On his first expedition, he found a spot surrounded by precipitous rocks, where the fall of water plunged into a deep basin adequate for bathing. Atop the rocks stood tall alders, and above them, the great chestnut trees standing in strong relief against the blue sky. He promptly pulled off his clothing, sat down with his volume of Herodotus, read fo0r am hour, then leaped into the waters.

He did not tell Mary of this incredible spot, preferring to keep it private, and day after day, he returned to it. He read volume after volume there, but his own notebooks remained empty. From then on he spent less time with his wife.

One late afternoon, as he read, he yawned over his book. Virgil wasn't holding his attention today, so he carefully set the book aside. He lay down on his back and stared up at the sky, so blue and not a cloud in sight, then after a moment closed his eyes. He would rest for a few minutes longer perhaps, then bathe, before he dressed and went home.

Mary wasn't expecting him for hours more so he needn't rush. He smiled. She was a wonderful woman, and he was lucky to have found her, and yet ... he didn't want to rush home quite yet. The children would be noisy and Milly would be scolding them, and Mary would be thinking of her own work. No, better to stay here where it was so peaceful and rest a little. He yawned again, and quietly sleep stole over him.

When he awoke later with a start, he saw that the sun had already begun setting, and that only a silvery light surrounded him. Too late to bathe now, he thought; the water would already be cooling. He reached out for his clothing, when a hand touched his arm. Startled, he looked up at his intruder.

It was August Kristonosos. She smiled, her dark eyes gazing down into his brilliant blue ones. For a moment, neither moved, and then, his breath held, he drew her down to his side.

Each twilight, Shelley met August beside the pool of water, and each night they made love. Their lovemaking was glorious, and wonderful, the wildest and most passionate he had ever experienced. Even better than with Mary, who had proved to be his most ardent lover so far.

Mary.

Sometimes he would think of her when he was with August, and guilt would flood him, and he would force her image from his mind. This was not the time for his wife, only for his charming lover.

But still he couldn't forget about his wife. Of course, he had said nothing to her of this new development, nor would he. Certainly he'd said nothing of his other affairs, and all had turned out well. Mary had a sharp tongue sometimes, and he didn't want to be at the receiving end of it. Still, he was convinced that she suspected nothing.

The golden days passed quickly, although each hour he was away from August, Shelley burned with desire. He wanted to spend each moment of the day and night with her, to brush her soft face with his fingertips, to kiss her breasts, to stroke the silken inner thigh, to bury his face in that musky garden.

He begged to see her during the day, but each time she laughed, claiming it was impossible. Even though he wept, she would not change her mind. She was so cruel to him, this mistress, and yet he did not think he could live without her.

Sometimes the days, and the nights, passed slowly, as though he moved with difficulty through a dream world, and when Mary talked to him, he couldn't hear her words. After a few minutes, she would simply stare at him, then rise and leave the room. He ate little, and did not notice how pale and listless he was becoming. He saw his son and daughter only rarely, and when he did, he thought how shrill and strident were their little voices.

One evening, nearly a month after their first tryst, Shelley and August were once more in their secret bower. They made love again and again, and Shelley, exhausted in trying to please his lover, fell back against the grass. He had difficulty breathing tonight and forced himself to calmly inhale deeply. And to concentrate on what his dear August was saying. Something about how she would be alone in Italy now, because her sister must return to England very soon.

"You won't leave, will you?" he asked anxiously, taking her hand. He could not bear thinking of that; he forced the thought from his mind, and focused on her dark eyes, her beautiful face.

"No, I am quite sure that Athina can handle our affairs quite adequately by herself."

She smiled, a wry expression, and the besotted Shelley never noticed the dark cloud that slid across the pocked face of the moon.

CHAPTER 23

She is still, she is cold

—Ginevra

L ate in August, Shelley, with some reluctance, visited Byron in Venice.

The journey, over two hundred miles, took a full week and somewhat fatigued Shelley, but finally, late on Saturday night, the twenty-second, he came to his Venetian lodgings in a black gondola while rain lashed at the windows and lightning flashed across the water.

The following afternoon he went to the Palazzo Mocenigo, where Byron lived with his current mistress. He had waited until he judged that Byron would be finished with his toilette for he was notoriously slow. Too, he did not wish to interrupt Byron and his mistress.

Byron's valet, the very quiet Fletcher, let Shelley into Byron's study, and Byron was genuinely pleased to see him,

Vigorously Byron pumped his hand, "I'm glad you came, Shelley,"

"Mary was concerned about Allegra." He waited a moment, then said, "Is she here?"

"No," Byron said with a thin smile, "I've sent her on to a convent, where the nuns can better take care of her. Wine?"

"No, thank you, Byron." Actually, the little girl was the very reason he had come so far. Mary was concerned that her stepsister's daughter was living in the same house with Byron's mistress-a low, coarse woman, rumor had it. Well, at least he could reassure her upon that matter now. He would question Byron about the convent later. As for the mistress, he didn't know yet.

"Is Mary with you?"

"No, she and the children stayed behind. Clara wasn't feeling well, and Mary didn't want to risk traveling with her."

"Very wise of her," Byron murmured as he moved across to a comfortable chair and sat. "I have a suggestion, Shelley. I've rented a country villa at Este for a few months. Why don't you bring your family to stay? The villa is large, and you and the children will have plenty of room."

"Thank you, I think we might." His tone was not very enthusiastic. If he went to Este, he would not be able to see the delightful sisters.

Byron leaned forward suddenly.

"Tell me, Shelley, are you well'?"

"Of course, I am. Why do you ask?"

Byron stared at the deep, dark circles under his friend's glorious blue eyes, circles that had not been there when last they'd met. Too, Shelley looked drawn and pale, although Byron knew his friend took long walks at the height of the day. And something lay veiled behind those blue eyes, something like fear.

Fear of what, though? He asked himself. Byron decided the best course was playing ignorant.

"It's nothing. My mistake."

Shelley smiled.

Uneasily, Byron said, "Come, let's not stay in any longer. Shall we go for a ride?"

"Of course."

A gondola took them across the lagoon to the Lido, a long, sandy island where little grew but thistle and seawrack. His groom had

Byron's horses waiting for his regular afternoon ride, and Byron could tell that Shelley enjoyed the gallop along the sea immensely.

For hours they talked of many things, of Mary and their many moves, of Byron's recent completion of the fourth canto of *Childe Harold*. They talked of Allegra and the convent, and Shelley felt reassured about the child.

On their way back across the lagoon in the gondola, Byron pointed out a small island on which sat a windowless and dreary building. It was topped by an open tower in which a bell now clanged.

"Are those faint cries of help I hear?" Shelley asked a moment later.

"Perhaps so," Byron replied. "That is the local madhouse. Come now, let's return."

Shelley glanced back at the stark black tower against the crimson sky and shuddered.

Their conversation continued when they reached the palazzo. Byron's mistress joined them for dinner, and Shelley was surprised to discover she was an Italian noblewoman, quite intelligent and charming. Later she excused herself and went to bed, while the two men talked nonstop until five in the morning.

Shelley returned to his inn. He had decided going to Este would be good, and he sat down and wrote to his wife to go at once to Byron's villa. He sent the letter express, knowing that it would be a full ten days before he saw her and the children. He also directed a letter to August, asking her to meet him in Este.

Shelley again visited the next day with Byron, and the day after Shelley left for Byron's villa, I Capuccini. Byron elected to remain in Venice for the time being. The villa was built on the ruins of an old Capuchin monastery, and was cheerful and full of light, and spacious, just as Byron promised.

Este was nearly at the foot of the Euganean hills, and before them stretched the wide green plains of Lombardy. A pergola, a wooden trellis covered with vines, led to a summerhouse where Shelley decided he would set up his study. At the end of the garden was a large dilapidated Gothic castle, which had once been home of the Medici family, and was now the habitation of owls and bats.

Shelley began working on a new poem, *Prometheus Unbound*. He had been thinking for some time on the nature of good and evil. For some reason he thought of August at that moment, and he wondered when she would arrive with her sister. Soon the lines flowed smoothly from his pen. *By such dread words from Earth to Heaven/My still realm was never riven;/ When its wound was closed, there stood/Darkness o'er the day like blood.*

Mary arrived on Saturday, September 5, just six days after her twenty-first birthday, and three days after Clara's first. She had celebrated — as it were, she thought wryly — by packing Shelley's books at the Casa Bertini. She was worried about Clara, who was still ill. The trip had taken longer than usual because she was forced to stop often due to the child.

"Now," Mary told the baby once they arrived, "we can rest." As she leaned over the cot in the pleasant nursery Milly had arranged, she stroked the little girl's forehead. It was unnaturally warm. The baby appeared weakened, as though she could not move her arms or legs, nor even her head. Her eyes were dull, too; another sign of fever, Mary reasoned.

She called for water and cloths, then undressed her daughter and began sponging her with the cool water. Perhaps that would help the child from burning up in this illness.

As she moved the wet cloth across Clara, Mary noticed a rash on the child's chest. What could have caused it? As Mary touched the rash with her fingertips, Clara opened her eyes wide and moaned.

Quickly Mary withdrew her hand. When she was finished bathing the baby, she wrapped her up carefully and held her close.

"You'll be all right, my love," she whispered and, rocking Clara, sang softly to her until the little girl fell asleep.

The next day Clara was much better, for her eyes were clearer and she talked a little, but Mary determined to bring Clara to a physician in Venice. She didn't want to take any chances.

But she and Willie were forced to stop at a small inn along the way and take rooms because Clara had worsened even in these few hours. The baby breathed harshly, as if she couldn't get enough air into her tiny lungs, and her face was red from the fever which had returned.

Mary sent a note to her husband, and some hours later he met her at the inn. Shelley stroked the baby's pinched face and looked up at Mary to see his concern mirrored in her eyes. He hadn't given much thought to his children for weeks now-his thoughts had been occupied with August, and he felt badly. Now, he would do what he could to make it up to them.

They placed Clara on a small bed arranged especially for her in their room. Mary looked exhausted. Shelley told her to go and rest; he would stay with the child until she was ready.

Relieved, Mary nodded, then left to rest in the parlor, but though she tried to sleep, she was unable.

She feared for Clara's life. Clara for whom she'd wanted so much. She had lost her first child, a daughter who lived only a few days, and she still had not gotten over it completely; and she did not want to lose another one. She closed her eyes, but she kept seeing poor little Clara's face.

Sensing the upset of his parents, Willie began crying, and Mary pulled him onto the settee with her and stroked and rocked him until finally he fell asleep, a fist curled by his mouth.

In the next room Shelley raised his head from his chest abruptly and realized with shame that he had fallen fast asleep. Darkness had fallen some time ago. No doubt, he thought with a faint smile, Mary had slept, too, which was good; she had needed it.

He rose and lit a candle and came back to Clara's bed. On the pillow alongside her too-white face was a tiny droplet of blood.

Clara was dead.

CHAPTER 24

The breath of nightlike death did flow
Beneath the sinking moon.

—Lines

The Shelleys could scarcely believe that the life had gone out of the tiny girl, but in little more than a day the girl was laid to rest.

Secretly Mary blamed Shelley, for she thought that if it had not been for the hard journey to Este, Clara would not have died. Surely the trip had contributed to her daughter's death.

Shelley blamed himself, too, but for a different reason. Clara had died because of his marital indiscretion. He felt that, though he knew it didn't make much sense. August had had nothing to do with the little girl's death, but his daughter had died nonetheless as some sort of punishment to him. He knew he should give August up at once, and he vowed that he would. Now, if only he could keep that vow. When she arrived in Este, he would tell her she must leave.

Mary and Shelley did not speak of little Clara, and each sought relief from their grief in their own manner. Mary lavished more attention upon Willie, while Shelley grew more withdrawn. He feared hurting his family again. Each misunderstood the other's actions, and thus a rift began developing between the couple.

And when August came upon him strolling one night on the estate, he knew he would never give her up.

Shelley had to get out of the house, and so on the twenty-fifth of September, without any notice whatsoever, he called upon Lord Byron.

Byron studied his friend, whom he had not seen since Clara's funeral. Something more than grief had left its mark on Shelley. The dark circles Byron had noticed previously had grown more pronounced, as had Shelley's pallor. Too, he trembled uncontrollably. Was this some terrible disease which had captured Shelley in its web? Or ... or what? He wondered. What could be worse than grief for a loved one?

"How is Mary?"

Shelley shrugged indifferently.

Byron was surprised. Was there a rift between the two? They had always been close, far closer than Byron had ever been to his own wife whom he'd left in England.

Shelley gestured sharply, then tried smiling, although it was a feeble expression.

"Well, enough dreariness, my friend. I didn't come for that, you know. I need diversion. Let us talk of something else."

Byron was relieved to change the subject from death, never a favorite subject of his. "Yes. Actually, I began a new work at the start of the month and am pleased with its progress. Would you like to look at it?"

Shelley took the manuscript from Byron and began reading *Don Juan's* First Canto. "*I want a hero: an uncommon want.*" His eyes raced down the page, then to the next one. When he was finished, he leaned back and stared at his host.

"Brilliant. Absolutely brilliant."

Byron grinned. "Of course."

Shelley chuckled. Byron was glad to see his friend relax.

"And what of you, Shelley? Have you managed to work at all?"

"A little. Something I call *Julian and Maddalo*. Originally I intended to send it to Hunt for the *Examiner,* but now I'm not so sure of it. I think I'd best finish it first, because I determine its direction."

"I would like to see it when you're done, if you wouldn't mind."

"Of course not. And I'm honored with your request. Once I'm done, you may sit in judgment."

They talked for some time of their other work, and of the poems of fellow poets. Finally, sometime later, a lull occurred in the conversation. Then Shelley leaned forward and lowered his voice, even though they were the only ones present.

"I have met the most incredible woman, Byron," he said, his eyes fixed, unblinking, on the other man.

"I have no doubt that you would fall in love with her instantly, as I did."

Byron's lips curved into a sardonic smile. "Would I now?" He stood and fetched them both glasses of wine. He suspected he would need it.

"Yes." Shelley nodded fervently and took a long sip.

Byron had never seen his friend this ardent and yet so wooden. If Shelley possessed a passion for her, why wasn't that passion showing in his voice? It was in his eyes, or was that something else?

Byron smiled tolerantly. "Well, then tell me more about this exquisite."

"She is so wonderful … they both are, Byron. I call her sister, Athina, the Morning Star, and she—the one I love with all my heart-is the Evening Star. They are quite the most beautiful women I've ever seen … absolutely breathtaking. The older one, who is my lover, is named August, and has hair the shade of midnight. Her eyes are like ebony." His eyes had taken on a dreamy look, as if he wasn't quite aware of his surroundings, and his voice was a whisper.

"Her lips like roses." There was irony in Byron's voice.

With effort Shelley fixed his gaze on his friend.

"No, not at all, Byron. More than that … like blood."

"Not a very romantic simile."

"But it is," he insisted, "and once you've met her, you'll understand. She … her lips … are ice and fire, blood and snow." Shelley licked his lips.

Byron, oddly repulsed, glanced away from his friend. What could it be? Certainly infidelity did not disturb him...

"Very well," he said indulgently. "When shall I meet your paragon of virtue and beauty, and all that is good and wonderful?"

"When she's ready for you."

CHAPTER 25

The rose has fled from his wan lips, and there
That kiss is dead

—Fragment of the Elegy on the Death of Adonis

A wind swept across the ocean, while above the lightning jabbed at the water, and his only light was a white star. The storm raged, nearly overturning his small boat, but he held on, eyes closed at times, until the charmed bark reached shore.

On the white sand, bare except for matted thistles and weeds, a skull and seven dry bones, sat a woman as beautiful as morning, and her dark hair had fallen loose, a single green sea-flower in those dusky tresses. She rose gracefully, loosening her star-bright robe and shadowy hair, and sang.

He did not know the language, but it was marvelously fair, and touched him in his heart. He stepped out of the boat, and she took his hand, her coolness against his warmth. Wordlessly she led him away from the shore, through the mist of this sunless land and the golden rain, and they walked inland past vast pines and cypresses. They

147

reached a great ivory stair, and at its top passed through a wide portal whose moonstone roof was carved with lifelike sculptures.

Beyond was a vast hall with a roof of diamond lit by the glorious lightning, and a diamond spire, and a floor of amethyst. The man and woman passed ten thousand columns of veined emerald, and a fountain filled with blood, and a garden of lilies and roses and violets.

He stopped to smell the perfume, but she plucked at his hand and he followed.

And when they at last reached a throne of sapphire, he saw a second woman sitting there, as if she had been waiting for them. Her hair was as fair as the other's was dark. The two women kissed one another, then him, their lips as cold as ice, and then, smiling at him with her bright eyes, the fair one beckoned for him to come sit at her feet. A single white flower decorated her hair, its odor as sweet as death, and he longed to touch its pure petals.

He rested his cheek on her soft knee, felt her caress him with her long silken tresses, and as the two women sang softly, he closed his eyes and entered the golden gates of sleep.

When he awoke, he found himself in a gondola, and it was rocking from the choppy water. Rain fell soaking him to the skin, while overhead thunder boomed ominously. In the distance he saw an island, and on it was a tower, stark against the black sky. The gondola stopped at the shore, and he stepped out of it, only to see the boat drift away. He heard only the azure silence.

He turned and faced the blood red tower, and wondered where he was and how he came to be here. But, even as he began walking toward it, he heard piteous cries and fierce yells and the clap of tortured hands. He didn't want to go there, but he had no choice.

He climbed the stairs into an old courtyard, weeds growing in the crevices of stained stones, and as he passed the grey walls, blood-dabbled hands reached out from crevices and plucked at his clothes. He looked away from the maddened faces.

Steps led upward, and he counted them, then lost count. He seemed to climb for hours, and then at last he reached the tower's pinnacle, and there in the cloud-shadows of midnight he saw her.

This Lady wore a gown woven of starlight and smoke, and was wrapped in a gauzy veil. Her ebony hair fell in waves below her waist. And even though her back was to him, he knew she was as beautiful as her sister. When she turned at last and raised her white hand in greeting. he recognized her, and she smiled.

And in her eyes, and in her face, and in her touch was Death.

Shelley was shaken by this dream, which came in December. He and Mary were spending the winter in Naples, where they took rooms at No. 250 Riviera di Chiaia, which looked out through tall windows onto the Royal Gardens, and beyond to the blue water of the bay, and the mountainous island of Capri.

Shelley. at the east window, gloomily watched the plume of smoke above Vesuvius turn to a dull red glow, and he was reminded of the fountain of blood in his dream, and he knew he must make some effort to keep his spirits high. They were to visit Pompeii that day.

In the ancient ruins of Pompeii, he and Mary walked through the silent streets, gazing at the splendid mosaics, and the Greek bas-reliefs in the temples. Under the intimidating portico of the Temple of Jupiter, they paused for lunch, where in silence they ate oranges and figs and bread and apples, and listened to the distant thunder of Vesuvius.

They returned by the eastern gate as the sun was just setting and the shadows lengthened across the road, and walked through the carved marble tombs standing along the consular road.

Once or twice Mary thought they were being followed, but she dismissed that as absurd. Yet from time to time she would pause to glance behind her, and once she thought she saw a dark form dart behind one of the tombs.

She had reason to think dark thoughts, because the estrangement between her and her husband had grown no better. They chatted, and sometimes at night he came to her bed, but that was more and more infrequently, and she wondered if he was having yet another affair. Too, his health was suffering, and she was worried about that. Several times she had tried to raise the subject to him, but he had simply looked at her with those blue eyes, grown so cold now, and she had said nothing.

Because they thought his health would be better there, they moved to Rome in early March, to lodgings at the Palazzo Verospi, No. 300 Corso.

The Corso was the most fashionable area in the city, being a very long narrow street full of hotels, banks, palazzos, churches, and villas. Their house was only a three-minute walk from the Pantheon.

Shelley found himself hard at work on *Prometheus Unbound*. He had finished Act I at Este. He was very tired now, no matter how much he slept and so he reasoned that he might as well get little sleep and set to work, as get too much sleep and no work. He had enjoyed his mistress's company in Pompeii, and soon he knew she would be here in Rome.

The daylight hours he devoted to poetry and to Rome, most of the night hours to August, and he saw little of his family.

Shelley was fascinated with the Forum, the Coliseum, and the Baths of Caracalla, and he took frequent walks there. Sometimes he went on solitary moonlight strolls. The elms were just budding, and the warm spring winds brought unknown, yet all sweet, scents to him.

In mid-April, Shelley's guilt asserted itself, and he began reading *Paradise Lost* out loud in an effort to spend some time with Mary and Willie—Mary listened for hours as he read. Willie sat on the floor, leaning back against his father's leg.

By now Willie was just slightly over three years old and was a strong and lively-and often headstrong-child. He worshiped his father and mother. More and more, Mary thought, he began looking like his father. What a handsome lad he would be when he grew up.

In May they moved to the last house before the Trinita; immediately below it were the three landings of the Spanish Steps and the Piazza di Spagna. A pleasant house with large airy rooms, it had lots of sunshine during the day and a pretty little garden.

A few nights after the move, as Mary was reading Boccaccio's *Decameron*, she paused to look around the room with a puzzled expression. She'd asked Milly to send the boy in to say good night. Where was he?

Mary got up and found Milly, who said he'd gone in earlier to talk with his mother. Where could her little boy have gone?

Worried, she searched through every room in the apartment, looking behind draperies and under beds and in large boxes where he sometimes liked to hide as a game, and she had reached the first floor again when she thought she heard her son's childish voice coming from the garden. She stepped through the open door and in the darkness caught a glimpse of Willie in his nightshirt as he darted through the trees.

He must be playing some new game, she thought at first with amusement. Then she caught a glimpse of something else, too—a figure in a dark gown, and her smile quickly faded.

"Willie?" Mary's voice was sharp. "William? Are you out there?"

After a few seconds, his reply came, although reluctantly. "Yes, Mama."

"Come here at once." Her tone was sharper than she'd intended, but she couldn't help it. Through her fear, she could feel her heart thumping.

She heard him say something in an urgent tone, then he was running toward her. In the light streaming from the house she saw his nightshirt was not clean, and he had a smudge of something dark, dirt perhaps, on one round cheek. He stopped in front of her, his pudgy hands clasped behind his back, and looked straight ahead.

"What were you doing out here?"

"Nothing." His gaze was locked now on his dirt-streaked toes.

She looked around, but the garden was empty and silent now. Had she just imagined that she had seen a woman with her son? Was there just the merest hint of a perfume lingering in the air? A strange musky scent, she thought, then shrugged.

"Was there someone out there with you, William?" Solemnly he shook his head. "Are you lying?" Once more he shook his head. She sighed, knowing he wasn't telling the truth, and knowing that nothing, short of a strapping, would make him admit it. "Come along now, it's long past your bedtime. You worried me, William, by wandering out there, which was very wrong. Milly thought you had come in to see me."

He nodded. "I'm sorry, Mama."

"I know you are, dear."

She took his hand, and he was dutifully tucked into bed. She swept the dark hair off his forehead and brushed the fair skin with her lips.

Mary sat down and picked up her book, but she couldn't concentrate on the words. She sighed and told herself that she shouldn't worry so. Perhaps it was nothing, and she was only tired. She wished that Shelley were here tonight so that she could talk with him, and perhaps he would take her in his arms. But he was never here in the evenings anymore. He needed to rest, too, she thought: these days he was far too pale and quiet.

Enough of this, she told herself sternly. He was with his mistress; she knew that-without proof-by now, and she suspected, irrationally she knew, that the woman was August Kristonosos. And that disturbed her more than any of Shelley's other infidelities.

CHAPTER 26

Rest, rest, and shriek not, thou gentle child!

—To William Shelley

Willie was far too excited to sleep. He wiggled under the covers, then clapped his hands over his mouth so he wouldn't laugh aloud.

The beautiful lady in the garden earlier had said she would come and say good night after he had gone to bed, so he mustn't fall asleep because he didn't want to miss her. He mustn't do that, or he wouldn't be a good boy. His eyelids fluttered downward, then he sucked in his breath as he heard the sound of her skirts.

"Asleep already?" she asked with a warm chuckle.

She sat on the bed, alongside William.

He nodded his head drowsily, then shook it. "No, I wasn't." This lady was so pretty. She made him feel very important.

The woman laughed again, a low sound that made his body tingle, and she stroked his cheek with her cool hand. He sighed happily as he snuggled under the covers. Then she bent over and hungrily pressed her cold lips against his own warm ones.

Her kisses were even better than Mama's.

Early the next morning Milly, still in her nightclothes, rushed into her mistress's room.

"Mrs. Shelley, come quickly. Something is wrong with William!"

Mary leaped from the bed and ran into the nursery. The boy was feverish. Yet, thank God, he was still alive.

He scarcely moved as she examined him. Warm to the touch; he needed a sponge bath. She unbuttoned his nightshirt, and started to pull it off over his head, then stopped, staring in horror. There was a faint rash upon his small chest. It looked just like the one Clara had had before her death.

Immediately she sent for the doctor, then paced as she waited for him. At last he came, but gave her no diagnosis. He suggested that he bleed her son, saying perhaps then the rash would disappear. The boy must rest.

Infuriated, Mary had him escorted out.

Over the day Willie improved and could even sit up and take some nourishment, and when Mary told her husband that William was sick, he suggested that they leave for Naples, which might be better for William.

Bitterly, she kept silent; she could not forget that the move to Este had caused Clara's death. No, this time, she said, they would stay put. She would not subject the child to the strain of travel.

Later in the week Milly came to Mary. She had been gossiping with other servants in the English colony, she said, and had learned that in the past month several other children of English families had died, apparently of a similar fever and rash. This news did nothing to ease Mary's worried mind.

Shelley stayed home more, now that his son was not well, and for that Mary was grateful. But Willie's condition did not continue to improve.

He suffered no pain, which was good, but his illness made him exceedingly lethargic, and he slept a great deal now. And dreamed, too. Sometimes he would call out in his sleep, or often awoke, trembling and crying.

In a strange way his behavior reminded her of her husband's, of those odd dreams which still woke him nearly every night.

Were the two connected? And if so, how? Did Shelley have the same illness as William, an illness that progressed more slowly in an adult?

She had no answer.

On June 2, Willie took a sudden turn for the worse. His fever rose steadily, and after that a moment never passed when he wasn't burning alive from it. His cheeks, once rosy with youth and health, now were reddened with the fire of death.

Each day the little boy woke weaker and weaker. Once, in the morning on the sixth, he opened his eyes, and murmured "pretty lady."

Shelley thought his son meant Mary, but she was sure he didn't. She thought of that night she had seen him in the garden with someone, a shadowy lady. She mentioned the incident to her husband. His face paled, then he said he saw no reason to link that with Willie's illness.

However, Mary wasn't convinced.

As the day wore on, Willie worsened. Finally, he slept unnaturally, all the while seeming to become smaller and whiter.

On June 7, at noon, under the gaze of his exhausted parents, and with his father holding his hand, William Shelley died.

For two days Mary was bereft of hope or even reason. She wept as she had never done before, and wished that she, too, would die. Sometimes she fell asleep, but it brought her no rest, for slumber was punctuated by terrible dreams. Dreams of the Kristonosos sisters, and William, hand-in-hand with them, and they were both smiling and staring hungrily down at him.

Mary would call to her son, and he would turn his head and look at her as if he did not recognize her, but then he would walk away with the sisters. Each time she woke from the dream screaming.

On the third day, Mary found strength to leave her bedroom. Willie had to be buried; she had to be there. She rose from her bed and washed her face and hands in cool water, dressed in a fresh gown, brushed her hair, and left her room.

That afternoon, a sunny warm day, the Shelleys laid their son to rest in the Cimitero di Protestanti. Mary watched as the tiny coffin was lowered into the ground, then she turned away.

That night Shelley came to her, and they held one another tightly without words.

Not long after that, Mary discovered she was three months pregnant, and begged to leave Rome, the city of Willie's death. They went to Leghorn for the summer, and moved to Florence in October.

CHAPTER 27

My head is heavy, my limbs are weary,
And it is not life that makes me move.

—Fragment: Death in Life

In Florence the Shelleys found lodgings in Madame du Plantis's house. They attended the ballet and the opera, but within days Mary found that she could not continue these activities without great difficulty because she was now advanced in her pregnancy. Soon she stayed home on the sofa or in bed, reading.

The single constant, she thought one evening when Shelley was out, in all the moving around that they had done was that he still saw August Kristonosos. Mary didn't know how they planned it, or how the woman could keep up with them, but somehow the trysts were still accomplished. Every time they moved, Mary saw the woman while she was out walking or shopping, or even simply glancing out the window; it was all deliberate upon August's part, she knew; clearly August wanted Mary to know she had arrived, and sometimes the woman would smile sweetly at her.

She thought she had long been past the period of truly being upset about her husband's infidelities, but she knew now she wasn't. Probably because she realized that Shelley wasn't going to give his lover up. What particularly worried her was that the affair had gone on for so long, and that Shelley's steady physical deterioration had begun about the same time.

During October Shelley was working hard. The lines were coming smoothly. It was the only way in which he could keep from thinking about poor little William. And there was August as well. He smiled drowsily. That kept him occupied as well.

On Friday, November 13, Mary, with Shelley at her side, gave birth to her fourth child after an easy labor. The baby was small but healthy, and his parents named him Percy Florence, christening him after his father and his birthplace.

Slowly, Mary abandoned her grief as she tended the new baby. He was a delight. She vowed that this child would stay healthy. She wouldn't lose this one.

The weather in December and January turned bitterly cold; often there were severe frosts. Mary stayed at home with young Percy and often remained in bed, working on her journal, while Shelley continued on his nightly expeditions, no matter how bad the weather. He had adopted a huge serge winter cloak, with a grey fur collar which framed his pale face.

In January Mary began a new book, which she called *Castruccio,* and which would illustrate the manners of the Middle Ages in Italy.

She was working hard on it early one afternoon when she heard Shelley and Milly talking in another room. Something about their conversation caught her attention; perhaps it was the low tones they used. She set aside her writing board and pen and paper, and walked carefully to the door to listen.

"—Gibson's young nephew, who was visiting her during the winter," Milly was saying. "Her maid claims she doesn't know how her mistress will break it to his parents. They're quite elderly, you know."

"How did he die? He was the healthiest of lads, as I recall, and strong, too."

"A fever and a rash is what Mrs. Gibson's maid said, sir. And then he wasted to death, but the doctors don't know what the disease was."

Mary could hear the sharp intake of her husband's breath, and she wondered if his thoughts paralleled hers. Little Clara and Willie ... She forced herself to concentrate on what Milly was saying.

"—others, too."

"Others?" Shelley's tone was sharp. "What do you mean, Milly?"

"I mean that young Richard isn't the only one to die, sir. Mrs. Gibson's maid says at least five other young men, and three children, have had that fever and rash. And this is all within the week, sir, and she's not one to exaggerate."

"Good God! Please, don't say a word of this to Mary. You know how she will worry."

"I won't, sir. You have my word on that."

Mary retreated from the door, then sat abruptly on the bed. Deaths like those of her daughter and son, and all within the past week. Her husband's nightmares had grown worse in the past week, too.

What was the connection?

There had been deaths in Milan and Naples and Rome, and even in Venice, when they had stayed at Este. Death had followed in their footsteps. So also had August Kristonosos, and to Mary this could mean only one thing: The woman had arrived in Florence.

It was time, Mary decided, to move once again. They would go to Pisa, and if August Kristonosos followed them, she knew she must do something.

With each passing month Percy Florence grew stronger, and yet a cold fear had lodged within Mary's heart. She grew more possessive of him, and was unwilling to let anyone else take care of him.

"I just want to hold him, Mary," Shelley said, his tone reasonable.

She clutched the baby more tightly, and he began fretting. "No."

"Just a moment" her husband coaxed. "I'll stand right here."

"Very well." Reluctantly she handed the baby to his father, and watched as Shelley held Percy Florence close. She had noticed in her preoccupation with her son that Shelley's looks had deteriorated. His eyes were not as bright; there seemed to be a slight film across them, and he had lost more weight, weight which he could not afford to be without. She stepped closer and put her arms around him and leaned her head on his shoulder.

Shelley gazed down at her in surprise.

Mid-year Shelley learned of John Keats's health and financial difficulties.

"Write to him at once, Shelley," she said, "and tell him that he may come and stay with us for as long as he needs to regain his health."

Surprised, Shelley raised an eyebrow. "Are you sure of this, my dear? I know that you do not care overmuch for guests."

"If Mr. Keats has no one else to turn to, we must do something. We cannot let him suffer."

"Very well. I am delighted." He, too, wished to help Keats, for he liked the man and his poetry, as well. And it was well known that Keats had little money.

Shelley did write the letter, inviting Keats to stay, and he received a reply sometime later. Keats graciously declined the offer.

During the summer he received several other letters from Keats, and as he read them, his eyebrows drew together in a frown. Was Keats mad? Was he losing his mind from some brain fever? What he wrote was preposterous, simply impossible. But as outraged as Shelley was, he did not burn the letters. Rather, he folded them up and tucked them into his desk. Why he wanted to keep them he didn't know; he just had to.

Summer had fled Pisa, with autumn arriving hard at its heels, and Shelley was gloomy as he shrugged into his coat. The wind blew hard outside, while falling leaves whispered at the windows.

It had been a long day. He and Mary had argued. Again. They did that frequently now, where before they never had harsh words. They argued about his work and hers and about money, and about giving money to her father, who needed it.

Finally he had shut himself away in his study, but had been unable to concentrate enough to get any work done. He left the apartment for an extended walk. When night came, he turned toward the area where August lived, not far from them.

As always, August plied him with good wine when he arrived, and stroked his face and murmured soothing words as she listened to him complain about Mary. Then she took him to bed.

"You must tell your wife, my dear," August breathed afterward against Shelley's ear, "that you cannot hide from me. Not any place in Italy, nor any other country in Europe. Not even England."

He nodded, as if not really comprehending her words, then said, almost petulantly, "I've tried talking her out of moving, but she insists, and at first there was Clara, and William, to consider. Now there is Percy to think of, of course."

"Of course," she repeated solemnly. "And how is little Percy Florence?"

Every time he visited, she inquired after his son. He remembered how she had looked at Clara and William. Nonsense, he told himself.

"Very well. He's a strong one. He'll have his birthday in two weeks."

"Sometime you must bring him here so that I may see him. I would love to play with him. How beautiful he must be, too, if he looks like you."

He smiled and kissed her cold lips. "I don't think that would be possible. Mary hardly lets him out of her sight."

She smiled, but said nothing.

Shelley leaned back, resting his head against her soft breast as she stroked his temple, and he could feel his weariness leaving him. He closed his eyes and luxuriated in the comfort.

"I have good news, my dear," August said. "My sister will soon be returning to Italy."

"Excellent! I'm looking forward to seeing her again. I thought she would be back long before this."

"I did, too, but the matter she has been attending took far longer than she anticipated. But soon it will be over. She writes that she looks forward to seeing you once more as well."

"Good," he murmured.

"She likes you as much as I do, and dear Athina will do this to you," August said, shifting so that she could kiss his eyelids, "while I do this." Her mouth dropped to his, and she forced her tongue against his, and

161

over the next hour she demonstrated the affection the two sisters would show him.

And when he lay back, weary and drained of any energy, he did not notice the odd red rash that burned like a brand across his stomach and loins, nor did he see the strange smile on his lover's face.

The date was October 31, 1820. It was the day that Keats and Severn reached Italy.

CHAPTER 28

The lady found her lover dead and cold.

—The Sunset

Percy Florence Shelley celebrated his first birthday, and Mary felt part of the burden she had carried for the past year lifted from her. Somehow, deep inside her, she knew he was safe. Her little boy, her only child, would live.

During the winter, though, Shelley's health worsened steadily, and was particularly bad over Christmas. Shelley, rallying in March, insisted that more exercise was just the thing he needed to improve, and so in April he hurried to Livorno, where he purchased a boat, planning to sail it back to Pisa.

Mary was alarmed, because Shelley had never learned to swim, but he reassured her before he left that he would be all right. What he did not tell her upon his return was that while he and another friend had been sailing, the boat had capsized; and Shelley would have drowned, had not his friend pulled him to safety.

When he returned home, he found a letter from Leigh Hunt waiting for him. As he walked into the parlor, he opened it, then paused to read the missive. His face drained of color.

Mary looked up from her reading; she was doing research for her new novel. "What's wrong, my love?" Fear clutched at her.

He sighed and sat down, his face grey with weariness. He rubbed his face, and she thought how tired he looked, and how ill. "Hunt writes that John Keats died in Rome two months ago."

"What? But I thought he had been getting better after moving there."

"He did for a while, then his condition grew worse. The doctor thinks it was consumption, the same as his brother Tom."

"Poor Mr. Keats," Mary said, and there were tears in her eyes.

"Yes." Just after the first of the year they'd received the first of a series of letters from him, saying that he and his friend Joseph Severn had settled in the city, and Shelley had felt a chill upon reading the address, which had been only a short distance from where Willie had died. The Shelleys had planned visiting them, but Shelley had been too ill at the time, and then they had gone on to Leghorn and not Rome. Now, it was too late.

Saturday, August 4, was Shelley's twenty-ninth birthday. Two days later, at ten in the evening, he arrived in Ravenna, where Byron now lived in the Palazzo Guiccioli, a grand house with a marble staircase. He told Byron he just wanted to visit.

Much to his amusement, Shelley encountered at the palace eight enormous dogs, three monkeys, five cats, an eagle, parrot, and a falcon, and ten horses in the stable-and of course a mistress, a beautiful Italian countess, and much more to Shelley's liking than the street-walkers and bakers' wives Byron had previously seduced.

Byron welcomed his friend heartily, and Shelley thought he looked well, although his hairline had receded much since they'd last met.

Byron, on the other hand, was appalled at the great change in his friend. Shelley had lost more weight, which he could ill afford, and sometimes he scarcely seemed to be of this world. If he had been a religious man, Byron would have crossed himself. If ever he saw death walking, this was it.

That night the two men stayed up all night, talking and reading and discussing Byron's poems. Toward morning he showed him the new cantos of *Don Juan*, which Shelley admired. Obviously, Byron thought, Shelley was healthier than he looked.

Finally, they retired, Shelley to a magnificent chamber that was almost intimidating in its vastness. Byron loaned him a personal servant as a valet for the duration of his stay.

Both men rose casually at midday or later, ate breakfast at two, worked or talked or lounged until six. At eight they dined lightly but well, and spent the night talking of poetry, politics, Byron's women, diseases, and emotional life until six the following morning, whereupon the pattern repeated itself.

On the third day there, a tired Shelley wrote a letter to Mary, and the following day he made a pilgrimage to the tomb of Dante, where he spent most of the pleasant day by himself.

He decided it was time Byron knew the second reason for his visit. Recently Byron had moved his daughter again, because he had decided that she was not really his daughter, after all, and that a simpler Italian convent education would be more than sufficient.

"Mary has asked me to visit Allegra, Byron. I hope you won't mind." Shelley waited for the other to answer.

"Of course not. Why should I mind?"

Shelley just smiled slightly. Byron was indeed unpredictable.

The next day Shelley went out to the convent in the middle of the marshes of the Romagna, some forty miles outside Ravenna, where he found the five-year-old Allegra taller, but also more delicate and paler than when he had last seen her. She was also more serious, and her talk was full of Paradise and angels. He wasn't sure that a convent education was best for her.

The girl was dressed in white muslin, with an apron, and black silk trousers and sturdy shoes. Her black hair fell in curls over her shoulders, and her eyes were just as deep a blue as he recalled.

Gazing at the cleft in her chin, Shelley thought there could be no doubt as to her paternity, and he thought Byron was a fool in denying such an obvious matter.

Although she was shy at first, Allegra soon grew friendly. She begged for him to play with her, and at last he gave in. They played hide and seek, although he had trouble keeping up with her and was often winded and had to rest a few minutes. Once, an impish grin on her face, she rang the bell summoning the nuns from their cells, and then sometime later she showed him her own little room and bed. He thought of the beautiful palace Byron lived in, and thought it a shame that Allegra couldn't be there.

Momentarily he felt sadness, for his own Clara would have been nearly the same age now. Tears began filling his eyes, and so he forced that grey mood away, and stooping slightly said that he had brought a hug and kiss from her father, which he delivered fondly. Then he gave her a gold chain and some sweets.

They talked for some time after that, and when the sun was setting, he said he must leave. She looked sad for a moment, then said she was glad he could come.

"Do you know when I might come home?" Allegra asked softly.

"No, my dear, I don't, but I will talk with your father about it. That I do promise."

She nodded, then he walked away. He turned once and waved, then left the grounds of the convent.

Allegra waved cheerfully, although tears had filled her eyes.

Behind her, a shadow waited.

Shelley returned to Pisa and reported to Mary how he had found the little girl, and for some reason Mary found Allegra's description unsettling. Why would the little girl, obviously so healthy, be pale? Perhaps, Allegra was simply sad because she missed her father and mother; after all, Byron had forbid Allegra's mother to see her. That must be it, Mary decided, and yet her uneasiness would not subside.

On his brief visit Shelley had persuaded Byron to come live in Pisa, and on November 1, the flamboyant poet arrived with five carriages, six menservants, nine horses, dogs, monkeys, peacocks, and ibises. Some of his animals, he regretfully reported to the Shelleys, had had to be left behind in Ravenna, but he assured them he would soon collect more.

Byron found the palace they'd rented for him delightful, particularly liking the dark and damp cellars, which he called dungeons, and on some nights he would sleep down there.

Byron, who now lived just across the street. From the Shelleys, came to visit often. And again he was disturbed at the change for the worse in his friend. Yet whenever he asked Shelley if he was ill, the man shook his head. How could he deny it? Byron glanced at Mary, whose face reflected his own concern.

"Well, Shelley," Byron said quietly, "you may claim that you feel splendid, but I am more honest and admit that I do not. I've been experiencing these uneasy dreams that wake me in the middle of the night and leave me trembling without explanation. I can't always remember what they're about, though, and that I find damned curious. Odd sort of thing, don't you think?"

"Yes," Shelley replied with a curious lack of interest, "but then dreams are like that."

Byron continued musing aloud, as if he hadn't heard him. "Generally, there's something about women in them, I believe. Yes, that's it. There's always a woman in my dreams, and sometimes two." He winked broadly at Shelley, then chuckled. "But that isn't surprising, is it, old fellow?"

Shelley said nothing, while Mary smiled politely. Strange that Lord Byron, too, was disturbed by odd dreams. Dreams, too, that resembled Shelley's in content. Shelley had told her little of his, but she had no doubt of their nature. One look at his aroused body told her.

She appreciated Byron's concern; perhaps he would be able to help her husband. She had tried persuading Shelley to return to the doctors, but he refused outright, and no matter how much she argued, he never changed his mind on the matter.

Since the beginnings of his illness Shelley had been enchanted with August. No, rather he was besieged emotionally and intellectually and physically by the woman and her sister, and curiously, as she recalled now, so had other men they'd met. No man had a bad word about the half-Greek sisters.

No one but her.

She shook herself. Allegra. The child was about the age her dear Clara would have been. Suddenly Mary grew cold. All too clearly she recalled how her husband had described the child. Pale. Like her own Clara before she died. Like Willie. She remembered, too, how Athina and August had gazed at the two children that evening when they had come to dinner so long ago. Almost hungrily, she realized.

And now Clara and William were dead.

Could Allegra be next?

The next morning Mary woke up her husband some hours earlier than he was accustomed to rising.

"What's wrong?" he asked as he struggled to sit up. He failed, and propped himself up on his elbows.

"I think you ought to visit Allegra again. I'm worried about her, Percy."

He smiled sleepily. "Don't be, my dear. She was all right when I saw her."

"But what if she's ill?"

"Then the nuns will take care of her, or they will send for a doctor."

"Percy."

"Enough, Mary, please. Byron and I were up late last night, and I need to sleep some more."

Unsatisfied, she rose and dressed and checked on Percy Florence. As she held him, she wept for the little lost girl.

Later in the day Shelley confided that only a few days ago, he had had a strange dream; in fact, he'd had two dreams.

"In the first my own image arose and turned around and asked, 'Are you satisfied?' What do you make of that, my dear?"

"I don't know," she replied slowly. "What of the second dream?"

"There, I was walking along a beach and it was a stormy night. Suddenly I saw Allegra appear, arising from the angry sea and clapping her hands in greeting of her old playmate. I ran toward her, but when I reached the water, I saw only bones."

Mary was shaken by his words, and held him tightly. She raised her face to him, and he kissed her tenderly, just as he had in the first days of their courtship. For no reason that she could determine, tears blurred her eyes and she swallowed hard.

Mary said nothing, but her dread would not pass. She moved through her daily work almost mechanically, and at night went to bed fearing what the next day would bring. She kept Percy at her side constantly.

In April word reached the Shelleys from the convent at Bagna-Cavallo. Allegra had died.

In a way it came as a shock to none of them, although Mary wept openly. Even Shelley had tears in his eyes, while only Byron seemed unmoved.

The nuns reported that Allegra's death had been caused by a sudden wasting disease. She had not suffered at all, but had simply slept her life away.

And the day of her death was when Shelley had dreamed of her.

CHAPTER 29

Horror covers all the sky,
clouds of darkness blot the moon,
Prepare! for mortal thou must die,
Prepare to yield thy soul up soon—

—Victor and Cazire

Lord Byron was greatly saddened by Allegra's sudden death, although he did not outwardly show it, and when he visited the Shelleys one day in late April he asked how such a thing could have happened. The little girl had seemed like a healthy child. Mary said she thought she might know. Shelley was not yet with them, and she glanced once over her shoulder, as if checking to make sure that she and Byron were alone.

"How?" he demanded.

"I do not know the method, sir, but I think that the Kristonosos sisters are responsible for your daughter's death. Just as they are for the deaths of Clara and Willie." He could only stare, as if she'd suddenly gone mad. Was she actually accusing those two lovely sisters of this horrible deed? He had not met them yet-but Shelley had talked about them incessantly, and Byron was sure they couldn't be blamed.

Mary took a deep breath, and clasped her hands together to keep from trembling. She was very pale, but her eyes gleamed.

"There is something ... evil ... about those women, sir, something that eats away at the life of those around them. Look at my husband, Lord Byron. Have you ever seen him so pale or lifeless? He was never this ill until he made their acquaintance. I think they must both be ... succubae, or something equally wicked."

She leaned forward, regarding him intently. "Believe me, sir, the deaths of our poor children-and many others as well, I sincerely believe-are caused by those women. Remove them, and you will have no more unnatural deaths." There, it was said at last; her accusation finally out in the open. She waited for his reaction, which was not long in coming, either.

"Madam, you are mad." His tone was outraged. "I am appalled by your conjecture. Its fanciful origin lies wholly in your mind. You are overwrought yet at the loss of two children, which is quite understandable, but as for the causes of their deaths and Allegra's, we must look elsewhere. The Kristonosos sisters are by reputation very kind and considerate ladies. Why, look here, Mrs. Shelley, I have a thoughtful condolence note from Miss Athina, even though we've not met. Would a monster respond in such a way?"

Mary stared at him. Grief for her lost children had not swayed her reason. She knew she was as sane as Lord Byron.

"Look here, Mrs. Shelley, have you spoken to your husband of this matter? What has he said?" His tone was impatient now.

She looked away. "Once I attempted to tell him, but he laughed at me. He wouldn't listen fully to my story, and since then I've said nothing."

"I see. Well, Mrs. Shelley, if your husband sees nothing to alarm us, then we must remain calm. Is that not so? After all, he is a man of remarkable judgment."

He's no judge of the sisters, she told herself. No man could judge them impartially. But she knew with all her heart that a monster could also wear the face and body of a human. Neither Shelley nor Byron listened to her, but she knew that the sisters would kill again. She prayed only that her husband and his friend-and her baby son-be spared.

In mid-April an addition was made to the Byron-Shelley circle in Pisa. Edward John Trelawny, poet and adventurer, arrived in the city.

Twenty-nine years old, he was a giant of a man, six feet tall, with broad shoulders and a tapering physique. He had a curling mass of dark hair, swarthy skin, and pale grey eyes, and white teeth that glittered through a heavy black beard. Mary thought there could be no more a physical opposite of her husband than this man.

A Cornish man, Trelawny had entered the Royal Navy at thirteen, where he had served with distinction in the war with Napoleon. He had lived in India, and among his many daring exploits was the capture of a privateer which he later commanded. He and Shelley met now through the auspices of another friend, and from the start they took to one another.

For hours Shelley and Trelawny talked about boats and sailing, and then they began designing their own craft with Trelawny saying that he knew an expert boat builder. Immediately Byron decided then that he wanted one as well, only he desired his larger than the others. Daily the three men together, or with some of their English acquaintances, went sailing on the Arno.

Mary was not particularly happy with these nautical excursions and after a week had gone by she motioned Trelawny aside into the garden. She hadn't had much time to talk to him by herself; either Shelley or Byron was with the man day in and day out.

"What may I do for you, Mrs. Shelley?" he asked gallantly.

"I must confess, Mr. Trelawny, that I have some fears about these outings."

"Fears, madam?" His grey eyes studied her calmly, and she knew he was thinking that she did not seem like a woman who feared much.

"Yes." Here she lowered her voice. "You see, Mr. Trelawny, my husband cannot swim at all."

"He can't!" Trelawny stroked his beard thoughtfully. "He never said a word to me."

"Of course he wouldn't admit that, which is why I have informed you. And that is why I fear those long hours sailing."

"Well, don't worry any longer, Mrs. Shelley. I will teach your husband to swim, and that will be that."

"Thank you."

He took leave of her shortly after that, and left the Shelley house. Night was falling, and he wanted to reach his rented quarters before it was completely dark. He had work to do tonight.

The air was cool and felt good against his skin, and a faint breeze ruffled his dark hair.

Trelawny passed several citizens out after dark, and they nodded toward him. He smiled and kept walking. He didn't live too far from the Shelleys, but he preferred taking the long route home. That way he saw more of the city.

He heard the echo of a shoe against a cobble from behind him, and he glanced over his shoulder. All he saw were shadows. He stepped into the light coming from a window and paused, but heard nothing.

He shrugged and continued on his way. Perhaps it was a would-be thief out for what he could plunder. Well, Trelawny thought, grinning fiercely, he would show that man a thing or two.

Again he heard a footstep, so soft as almost not to be heard, and he frowned. There was something different about this, but what, he didn't know. His skin prickled, but not from the breeze. He felt the beginnings of something almost unknown to him: fear.

There was something more than a simple thief following him. Something. Someone. And whenever he looked, he could see nothing but the dark and darker shadows. and his fear grew.

Quickly he licked his lips and lengthened his stride. He would be home soon, and safe there, he thought. Or so he hoped.

When he was only a short block from his home, he paused. Edward Trelawny ran from no one, he told himself. He pulled a cigar out of his pocket and gathered together a few matches.

"I'm waiting," he said calmly to whoever or whatever was out there in the darkness. He sniffed the cigar, savoring its deep aroma. He lit a match, and in that flickering moment saw a white face not more than a few feet away from him.

The person—man or woman. he couldn't tell in such a short time—seemed to hiss at him and draw away, and he was struck by the depth of its dark eyes. Long after his match had burned out, and he had dropped it to the ground, he could still see those eyes.

Trelawny couldn't tell if the creature was still there, and so he lit another match and applied it to his cigar, and even though he didn't see who was following him, he began walking to his house, being extremely careful to keep the match lit.

What a sight he must present, he thought ruefully. Trelawny the adventurer holding a burning match in front of him as' if it were a blazing torch. He grinned at the image, and yet that wasn't all too far from the truth, he knew. The creature had seemed to pull back from the flame. Interesting.

He heard no more footsteps and dropped the match, then quickly went up the steps into his quarters. There he went at once to the parlor and, even though the night wasn't that cold, built a blazing fire in the fireplace. He sat down by the flames and stared into them, unable to forget those compelling dark eyes.

CHAPTER 30

Ask the cold pale Hour,
Rich in reversion of impending death,

—Hellas

Toward the end April, at Mary's insistence, the Shelleys moved to the seashore, to the Casa Magni at San Terenzo, a half mile north of and just around a promontory from Lerici, on the Gulf of Spezia.

The white house had an arched stone portico and a veranda supported on seven arches that faced the bay only a few feet away from the door. It looked quite charming from the outside, but Mary knew from the past few years that that didn't mean the inside was fine.

And this time she was right. The ground floor was clearly uninhabitable, for waves washed across its flagstone floor when the sea was rough, and so it was used for storing boat gear. On the floor above, a large unpainted main room with peeling plaster was reached by a dingy staircase at the back, and off this chamber were three smaller rooms, which at least had tall windows to let light in. The ones to the left and right were the Shelleys', and faced the terrace and the sea. The servants and children slept in the back of the house.

This was the first time they had slept in separate bedrooms since they were married, and she missed the reassuring touch of her husband at night. But she told herself it was only for a short time. Soon she would have him to herself again.

Mary was none too happy with her new home, and she wondered at Shelley's ill choice. The walls were cracked, plaster fell from every ceiling, and all too few floorboards were unbroken, and she worried that Percy Florence would fall through one. The kitchen building was small, and its wood stove smoked uncontrollably.

Further, she was again pregnant, and had she known that before the move, she wouldn't have suggested it. But now that they were here, they would stay, she decided. They had no choice.

She had only one consolation-the house was remote, making it that much more difficult for August Kristonosos to follow them. And that was nearly worth living in this frightful hovel.

Shelley liked the wild solitude of the Casa Magni, and the immense forest of ilex and pine rising on rocky slopes behind the house. The only means of communication was by boat or along the narrow beach, two hundred yards or so to the hamlet of San Terenzo, with a little church and a ruined castle, and very little more.

Mary started at once to establish her newest household, while Shelley contented himself with working in the day and taking long nightly strolls along the beach. Since they had moved, his health had improved substantially. Sometimes Mary followed him, managing to keep out of sight, because she feared he was meeting someone. But she never saw him stop to talk with anyone, and after ten days her fears were put to rest.

They had been there only a few weeks when Shelley's specially built boat arrived, much to his delight. He had wanted to call it *Ariel*, after the sprite in *The Tempest*, but Byron had interfered, and the name *Don Juan* had been painted in black letters on the white sail. Both he and Mary were irritated with Byron's presumption, but there was always time to change it, he decided.

Mary begged him not to go sailing by himself, and for once he gave in to her.

Sometimes she would go to the door of his study and watch him as he worked, his head bent over his paper as he concentrated, completely unaware of her presence, and she would feel a tightness growing in her chest. Tears would sting her eyes, and she would dash at them with her hand. She loved him, and she knew she was losing him to the other woman.

If only she could convince him, and yet whenever Mary broached the subject, Shelley coldly said he wished to hear nothing ill about August. And so Mary was forced to keep her fears to herself. He would see she was upset and tell her not to worry.

In June Shelley completed *The Triumph of Life*. As he waited for the ink to dry, he reread the poem. It was one of his best, he thought without prejudice. But he wanted Mary to read it; she was always his best critic. She told him when it was good, and when it needed improvement. So he went in search of his wife. He presented the poem to her.

"What do you think, my dear?"

As Mary read the lines, she grew terribly cold inside, and her hands trembled so that she could scarcely read. "*So came a chariot on the silent storm ... and a Shape/So sate within. ... /Beneath a dusky hood and double cape/Crouching within the shadow of a tomb.*"

It was good, more than that, really, but she knew, without a doubt, this would be his last poem. Mary began crying, and Shelley took her into his arms, holding her closely, and that made her tears flow all the harder. It was, she knew, now only a matter of time before she lost him for good.

She was riding along the narrow beach at night, and the sand seemed to gleam with a silvery light. The wind was blowing, and her hair streamed loosely, flying about in the breeze.

Up ahead she saw a dark figure, and she pulled the horse to a quick stop. It pawed the sand, and flared its nostrils. Then it whinnied, as if from fear. She knew it did not want to go past the figure; she, too, didn't want to because she feared it. But she had to. Shelley was there, somewhere past that dark form, and he needed her, and she knew she had to go to him.

She kicked her heels into the horse's flank, and it reared, its forelegs pawing the air, and from beyond she heard a dark laugh.

Beneath her the horse trembled, then sidestepped in its nervousness. She patted its sweating shoulder and talked reassuringly to it. Slowly the beast became still, and still speaking calmly, she urged it forward.

Stiffly it trotted toward the figure, and as Mary approached it, she saw the form grow larger and darker until it seemed like a giant bird of prey. It rose from the ground and swooped down upon her, and raked its diamond-tipped talons across her stomach. She cried out as agony speared through her, and the bird of prey laughed, and the voice was that of August Kristonosos.

Mary sat up suddenly and screamed. Pain shot through her belly and she screamed once more.

Shelley lit a candle and rushed into the room. "What's wrong, Mary?"

She shook her head, unable to speak, and only clutched her stomach in answer.

"The baby?"

She nodded, tears of pain rolling down her cheeks. She looked up at him and tried to talk, but still couldn't. He stroked her cheek, then called the maid and sent her to go fetch a doctor in the village.

Jolt after jolt of pain tore through her, and now she felt the blood between her legs.

She cried out as she realized she was losing her baby. Shelley left the room momentarily and returned with blankets and more sheets, and with a large bowl of ice. He tried to staunch the flow of blood, but there was too much. He had only to put a sheet against her when it was thoroughly soaked, and then he would have to replace it.

He put fresh blankets around her, then began packing ice around her lower body. If he didn't do something, she would bleed to death.

The pain seemed to be easing somewhat for she was no longer screaming or whimpering, but still Mary clutched his hand. He stroked her forehead, heedless of the blood on his hand.

Finally, the blood flow slowed, and Shelley breathed a sigh of relief. Minutes later, Mary seemed to fall asleep, and he bent down to kiss her softly. He waited until the doctor, out on another call, came some seven hours later, then went to wash up.

"That was quick thinking, young man," the doctor said approvingly as he inspected Shelley's work.

"Thank you." He rolled down his sleeves. "She lost the baby, though."

"Yes, but she's young yet and so are you. There'll be plenty more of them."

Shelley nodded, but said nothing, and watched silently as the doctor instructed the maid in how to clean Mary up and what to do for her in the next several days. Mrs. Shelley, he said, would not be able to get up for at least four days, and perhaps longer.

Mary did not wake even when they turned her, and finally, Shelley returned to his study.

In the morning, when she woke somewhat rested, Mary told Shelley of the strange dream at the onset of her miscarriage.

"It was her," she said.

"What?"

"It was August Kristonosos in my dream; she was the bird of prey. She caused the miscarriage."

"Mary, hush now," he said soothingly. "You're tired, and have undergone an ordeal. You must rest for the next few days."

"I know what I saw," she maintained staunchly. "She caused it."

"Hush," he repeated and brushed his lips across her forehead.

He rose and left the bedroom and walked out onto the veranda. He stared at the sea, so grey today like his mood, and knew that his wife was right.

Late in the month Leigh Hunt and his large family arrived from England. Shelley had long wanted to bring his friend to Italy but had always been unable to afford it, until finally Byron said he would sponsor the trip, as well as allowing the Hunts to occupy the ground floor of the Palazza Lanfranchi in Pisa. In May Byron had moved to the villa Dupuys in the village of Monternero above Leghorn, and thus he wouldn't need Lanfranchi for a while.

Mary slowly improved and was back at her own work within ten days. Shelley watched after her each day and insisted she rest whenever she felt the slightest bit fatigued. She was pleased with his attention, and in those days felt closer to him than she had in many months. She regretted it when her convalescence came to an end, because he seemed to draw away then.

Even though he had not seen her for some time, Shelley still longed for August and her sweet and maddening kisses. And constantly he dreamed of her, too. Each night she came to him in his dreams, which was why he believed Mary and her dream.

Some mornings he found it almost too much for him to rise, but he forced himself to get out of bed. He had too much to do, too many things left before—But enough of that dreary thought, he told himself.

Now that everyone was settled and Hunt was on his way to visit Byron in his new residence, Shelley decided he wished to sail to Leghorn. He still did not know how to swim, for although Trelawny had tried numerous times, he'd despaired of him learning.

On July 1, Shelley and a man from the village sailed the boat out of the bay and down the coast to Leghorn. They covered the distance in seven hours, and docked at half past nine in the evening. The next morning they went ashore to Byron's immense villa, where Shelley and Hunt had an emotional reunion.

"Good God, Shelley, you look terrible!" Hunt blurted out. Byron had warned him that their friend looked ill, but he hadn't expected to see what looked like at first glance a walking cadaver. He glanced quickly at Byron, who shook his head.

"Tactful as always, Leigh," Shelley said with a slight twist of his lips. "Mary has been ill-she miscarried-and I've been caring for her."

"I see." Hunt knew there must be more to it than that, but he would prudently refrain from saying any more, at least until he could take Byron aside.

Trelawny arrived the next day. In the evening, after the terrible heat of the day had abated, the group of four Englishmen sat in Byron's garden among the fragrant roses and jasmine and heliotrope and talked about poetry and politics and watched the fishing boats and flickering lights on the bay.

"Aren't you bored in such a remote place?" Hunt asked Shelley as he sipped his wine.

"No, not at all," Shelley said. "You really must come back with me sometime. I know Mary would like to see you. You could bring the children, too. That would give Percy Florence someone to play with." Idly he brushed away a small flying insect. "I have my work, of course, and there is the *Don Juan*."

Trelawny leaned forward. "You don't take her out by yourself, do you?"

Shelley smiled and stared down at his long fingers laced together in his lap. "Of course not."

Trelawny glanced at Byron; both men knew that Shelley was lying.

"Well tomorrow we can recommence swimming lessons, if you so desire," Trelawny said. "You would have two of the best teachers." —

"If you insist."

"Shelley, you have to learn to swim at least enough to keep yourself afloat, if you are to continue boating," Byron said. "It's too dangerous otherwise. You know that—"

"Yes, yes, yes. I appreciate your concern. But there really is no reason to worry."

Hunt drank more of his chilled wine, and wondered why he didn't believe his friend.

The next day Shelley accompanied the Hunts to Pisa and saw them established there. On Sunday Hunt loaned Shelley his copy of Keats's last book of poems, for Shelley was curious to see them. He thought of the odd letters Keats had sent to him, then brushed that thought away.

Shelley returned to Leghorn to sail home, and found that Byron, as quixotic as ever, had decided to move back to Pisa. Secretly, Shelley suspected it was because Byron feared that Hunt's numerous children, a rather undisciplined troop, would somehow damage his palace.

Monday, July 8, Shelley, another Englishman named Williams, and a sailor boy planned to depart from Leghorn at two in the afternoon. Trelawny had planned to accompany them on Byron's new schooner, the *Bolivar*, but because he had no clearance papers, he was forced to wait. It was under his prodding that Shelley had reluctantly arranged a crew.

The heat that day was particularly oppressive, but Shelley looked cool and nautical with a double breasted jacket of linen, a cambric shirt, white nankeen sailors' trousers, and black leather boots, and he was in particularly good spirits. It had been good to see Hunt again.

Although they saw low clouds gathering on the horizon to the west, they still set sail after two. Shelley was impatient to return home, and he knew Mary would worry if he stayed away much longer. They were still ten miles from San Terenzo.

Shelley loved sailing, but he still hadn't learned much about it. He tended to tangle himself in the rigging and often read Sophocles while trying to steer. Several times he had almost fallen overboard.

Trelawny drew Williams aside. "Believe me, sir, you will do no good with Shelley as a crewman until you heave his books and papers overboard, shear the wisps of hair that hang over his eyes, and plunge his arms up to the elbows in a tar bucket!"

Williams only smiled, and within a few minutes he returned to the boat.

As the *Don Juan* sailed out of the harbor, Trelawny watched his friend's progress through an eyeglass. He also kept an eye on the storm that seemed to be rising in the gulf. He would have liked it if his friend had delayed sailing, but Shelley was ever his own master.

An hour out of Leghorn, the light faded from the sky, the wind increased, and clouds gathered.

"We're in for weather!" the boy shouted, glancing at the ominous clouds.

Shelley looked up from his Keats and nodded. He felt no fear at the prospect of a storm, at least not yet, and he instructed the young sailor to tie down their gear. He continued reading. There was something familiar about one of the poems. He frowned slightly, tapping a slender finger against the binding. He tried to catch the elusive memory, but couldn't.

High waves crashed against the sides of the boat, and Shelley lurched across the deck, grabbing onto the handrail before he was flung overboard into the water. The cover still bent back on the book, he thrust it into his jacket pocket.

"Go below now, Shelley, for God's sake!" Williams shouted.

"What about you?" he shouted against the wind. Spray drenched his face.

"I'll be down in a minute or so."

Shelley nodded and made his way down the narrow hatch to the little cabin and paused as he heard a low laugh from the shadows. Or had that been simply cargo shifting or the squeaking of the boat's timbers?

"Who's there?" he asked sharply.

"Come, come, my love, you must know by now," said a woman's voice.

Shelley stared, unable to believe what he was seeing, as August Kristonosos slid out of the shadows. She wore a dark flowing gown that was nearly transparent and which showed that she wore nothing underneath. And yet he could only stare at her beautiful face.

Her lips had never been redder nor her eyes darker, and as he watched, she licked her lips, a sensuous gesture that brought a rush of warmth to him. Nor had he ever seen her as bewitching. He wanted her now, on the floor of the cabin, as if they were animals.

Then he blinked.

"August, my dear! What are you doing here?" Had she somehow stowed aboard? But that was impossible, he told himself. The cabin was too small, and they had checked it before they left Leghorn. "I don't understand how you came to be here."

"No?" She was closer now.

A second voice joined hers. "You still do not understand, Shelley?"

He whirled around, and in the faint light could see Athina, who was approaching him from the far end of the cabin. His smile wavered. What was this? Was Williams somehow behind this hoax? But surely his friend knew nothing of the women. His desire was nearly overcome by his surprise and curiosity.

Athina slipped her arms around his neck and pressed herself against him. Her breasts burned into him, and involuntarily he groaned. He ran a hand down her smooth hip, then touched that damp area between her legs. She was ready for him, and he wanted her very much, more than he'd ever wanted her.

"Mary understood us," August said, as she kissed him, her tongue forcing his mouth open. "She always has, while you were always the innocent. Poor dear. But then men always are."

"What?" Mary had understood them? Whatever were they talking about? He knew that Mary had never liked August, but she had only been jealous. Hadn't she? Or was it something more?

The sisters did not reply, but rather with their incredible strength, they pulled him down to the floor and held him there as they kissed him.

Outside the wind howled.

CHAPTER 31

Death is here ...

—Death

At midnight on Monday a horrendous thunderstorm roused Mary from her slumber, and with each clap she shuddered, although she didn't know why.

She went into the baby's room and brought Percy Florence back to her bed, and there she held him all night long, as though seeking comfort from him. He smiled and touched her cheek with his pudgy hand, then fell fast asleep. She knew Shelley would never set out in weather like this, and for that she was slightly reassured.

Tuesday, the ninth, it rained all day and the sea was calm. When a very wet Trelawny reached Casa Magni, he was surprised to learn that Shelley hadn't arrived yet. As he shed his outer clothing, he talked of trivial things, never mentioning that Shelley had sailed already. He pretended that nothing was amiss, because he didn't wish to further upset Mary.

The following day, though, Trelawny rose early and rode directly to Pisa to see if Byron had had word of Shelley and his friend.

Byron wasn't pleased at being roused before noon, but when Trelawny explained why he was there, the poet's irritation evaporated.

"Message from Shelley?" Byron said, as he sank into a chair. "Isn't he home?"

"No." The one word was curt.

"Then—" Byron leaned forward, unable to complete his sentence.

"I don't know, and Mary hasn't heard from him, either. This might be one of his pranks, or …" He left the thought uncompleted. "But I'm afraid it's far more serious, Lord Byron. I will order an extensive search begun at once."

"Good. Let me know as soon as you hear of anything, Trelawny."

"Of course."

Although nervous about her husband's delay, Mary remained in fairly good spirits and organized a picnic for herself and the baby. She refused to allow her mind to dwell on what might have happened; they were delayed, that was all, she said, they were delayed.

Friday, July 12, strong winds blew all day long, and still Shelley had not returned. At noon Mary received a letter from Leigh Hunt, addressed to her husband. She opened it immediately. and as she read the short note, she sank into a chair.

Pray write to tell us how you got home, for they say
that you had had weather after you sailed Monday—

The letter dropped from her fingers.

It could not be over, not like this. She refused to accept it. Shelley wasn't dead. Unable to rest until she knew, Mary hired a carriage the next day and went to Pisa, to see Byron and ask him if he had heard any word of her husband.

It was past midnight when she arrived at the Casa Lanfranchi.

The Hunts were all asleep, but Byron, who was already in bed, rose when Fletcher told him the identity of his visitor.

"Good evening, Mary."

"My lord." She was twisting a lace-edged handkerchief in her hands, and when she realized what she was doing, she let her hands fall to her side. "I'm sorry to disturb you so late, but I had to know if you have any news of my husband. He's overdue at Casa Magni, and I'm very worried."

The expression on his face became grim. "I'm sorry, Mrs. Shelley, but I haven't heard anything. Your husband and Williams did indeed sail on Monday. Trelawny was here a few days ago, and said he would organize a search. I haven't heard from him again."

The color drained from her face.

"Would you care for a meal? You must be exhausted as well; I'll have a servant prepare a bed. It is a long drive back, and it is late."

"Thank you, no, my lord. I must leave. There might be some word, you see."

Byron nodded sympathetically, and escorted her to the door. And although it was now long after midnight, she set out for Leghorn.

As she rode in the carriage, Mary, who had not slept in over twenty-four hours, thought she heard a woman's low laugh behind her.

Fearfully she glanced over her shoulder, but saw no one; nothing was behind her except the black of the night.

Trelawny, still making inquiries in Leghorn, met up with her the next day and said that so far no one knew what had happened to the *Don Juan* and its occupants. He had wanted to give her hope, but he couldn't. He believed now that his friend was dead.

Trelawny offered to accompany her, and the couple went on to the tiny town of Via Reggio, where, they had learned, a little boat and a water cask had been found some five miles down shore.

When Mary saw the craft, she sighed with relief.

"It's not the *Don Juan*, Mr. Trelawny."

"Aye, better and better, madam."

He didn't want to build false hopes, and yet perhaps the *Don Juan* hadn't sunk. Perhaps it had somehow escaped. And yet if so, why hadn't Shelley contacted his wife? Still the boat could have been blown to Corsica, or Elba, or even farther.

He stroked his beard. "Why don't you return home to wait for news? You'd be far more comfortable there than riding around from town to town. I'll stay here for some word."

Mary allowed herself to be persuaded, and as she crossed the river toward home, she felt the water splash about the wheels, and a feeling of suffocation came over her. As she gazed down at the river, she saw two great lights burning, and a voice that was not hers cried aloud, "That is his grave."

Still, even though she wept, she could not give up and admit that he was truly dead.

Early the following day Trelawny set off on horseback to scour the shore; by now the coast guard had entered the search, too, and Trelawny was offering a reward for any information.

Mary waited until Thursday, July 18, neither eating nor sleeping, but simply sitting. For hours on end she held Percy Florence in her arms and rocked him. Sometimes she would sing a lullaby to him, but mostly she sat silent. Waiting.

Trelawny could not bear seeing her suffer, and so he left for Leghorn once more to see if there was news. He was weary from his many travels this past week and from the little sleep he got each night, but he couldn't rest; not until he knew.

Mary stayed home and watched Percy Florence play, and yet every time she looked at the child, she saw Shelley's face, and tears filled her eyes.

Trelawny returned at 7 P.M. No one was in the big room; only one lamp burned there.

Mary came out of her room. Trelawny's face was grim, and Mary stood a short distance away, her hands clasped together, her breath held.

"Is there no hope?"

He shook his head. "Shelley has been found."

"And?" Her voice was barely over a whisper. Her heart hammered, and she hoped beyond hope that he still lived. Perhaps he had only been injured. Perhaps. Tears stung her eyes.

"He was found washed ashore between Massa and Via Reggio just today."

It had been ten days since the storm.

Mary staggered, and Trelawny rushed to her side and eased her into a chair.

Trelawny, Byron, and Hunt appeared to claim Shelley's body.

As Trelawney stared down at the grisly remains that had once been his good friend, he blanched. He was thankful Mary wasn't here. The face and hands and those parts of the body not protected by clothes had been eaten away by the fish. But he could recognize the slight figure by the jacket, and the volume of Sophocles in one pocket, the volume of Keats in the other. He thought she need not know the details; he did not think he could forget the sight himself.

He glanced at Hunt, whose face was pale. Hunt kept gulping, as if he were about to be sick. Byron's eyes were closed, and his lips were moving. Surely not a prayer, thought Trelawny ironically.

Because of the fear of plague, the Italian authorities would not allow the body to be shipped back to England, and so Shelley's remains were promptly buried on the beach in quicklime.

The body could not be transferred elsewhere, and so Trelawny suggested that the remains be burned on the shore, as the ancient Greeks had once done. The others agreed; Trelawny interviewed officials, signed papers, and paid fees until permission was granted for the ceremony.

On August 16, just twelve days after what would have been Shelley's thirtieth birthday, Lord Byron, Edward Trelawny, and Leigh Hunt gathered on the beach at Via Reggio to burn the body of their friend. Mary could not bring herself to accompany them to the ceremony and remained secluded at home.

At noon the three men, with Italian authorities watching, built a great bonfire. In the Greek fashion, Trelawny sprinkled incense, oil, wine, and honey over the remains of his friend. Children from the countryside gathered to watch the spectacle, but curiously none of them spoke as they watched.

Byron, who could not bear to be close to the pyre and who was overwhelmed with sorrow but wanted no one to see his emotion, swam out to sea and watched from that distant vantage point, while a weeping Hunt remained alone in Byron's carriage. A grim Trelawny murmured a few words, then placed Sophocles in the pyre as well. He kept the Keats volume.

He lit the bonfire.

No one spoke as the flames roared.

Trelawny watched as a solitary sea bird circled overhead. It was almost as if the spirit of their friend still lingered, he thought sadly.

By four in the afternoon the fire had finally died to red and grey embers, and Byron had long ago returned to shore.

The three friends waited until the embers cooled and then gathered the ashes into a small velvet covered walnut case.

"I'll take it," Byron said as he picked up the box. Trelawny had made a move toward it, but stopped when he saw the expression on the other's face. Byron would return to Pisa, where Mary Shelley was now staying, and then he would hand over the box to her.

According to Shelley's desires made known while he was still alive, he had wanted his ashes interred in William's grave. Byron gave Mary the walnut box, which was then placed in a coffin, and then buried in Rome at the Cimitero di Protestanti.

Mary watched as the grave slowly filled with dirt, and as she turned, Trelawny's arm supporting her, she saw the newly raised grave marker of John Keats. Her son and husband, and Keats. All of them dead, she thought bleakly, then closed her eyes.

Trelawny and Leigh Hunt escorted her back to Pisa. She planned staying there for a while, and then—what? She didn't know where to go. As she looked at Shelley's books, she began weeping again.

Atop the desk was the volume of Keats's poems which Trelawny had given her a few days earlier. She set it aside. Inside the desk she found a box containing Shelley's correspondence.

She untied the ribbon on the first stack, and sitting down began to read. This letter was from John Keats and was dated the year before he died. She frowned as she scanned the letter, then quickly read another.

She picked up the book. It was called *Lamia*. She began reading. Her frown deepened.

Could it be possible? However incredible, had he known Athina Kristonosos? Mary remembered that the woman had returned to England. To conduct family business, her sister had said, but was that truly the reason?

Each time that Keats mentioned Athina in his letters it was with the same euphoric tone she had heard her husband use when mentioning the Kristonosos sisters. Keats said that the woman had tended his brother, and then, after Tom died, she had tended him. The latter letters, though, were darker, and he hinted that Athina seemed to drain him somehow. He was growing more ill by the day, but each time he saw her, she glowed with more beauty.

She read Keats's last letter slowly, then read it again. She thrust it aside and wrote a short note to Byron, asking him to come see her.

He came that very afternoon, and found, as he had expected, Mary wan, her face pinched, her eyes reddened. He bent over her hand.

"Thank you, Lord Byron. I have summoned you for a reason." He raised one eyebrow inquisitively. She went over to a small writing desk, and from the center drawer drew out a packet of letters.

He waited, curious.

"As you might imagine, my lord, I have had much to do recently, and while I was sorting through our papers, I found these. They are, as you can see, letters from John Keats to my husband. In one of the first of them Mr. Keats mentions that a beautiful blonde woman, half-Greek, came to the house repeatedly to visit his younger brother Tom. Tom grew sicker, the woman continued visiting, and then Tom died. After that, she and Keats continued seeing one another, and I have no doubt that they were intimate. That seems to be the pattern." This last was spoken with some irony.

"Mr. Keats reports that the doctor did not know the cause of his brother's death-although consumption was suspected-but that he wasted away slowly, and that he ran a high fever, and his stomach and loins were covered with a rash." She paused. "And then much, much later Keats, a very young man, died of consumption, the doctor said. But he also had a rash."

She looked Byron in the eye. "The woman who visited the Keats brothers was Athina Kristonosos."

His lips curved into a half smile. She was hammering away again at this old theme, was she? Amazing how jealous women could be sometimes. No doubt she was half out of her mind with grief over her husband. That could unhinge even the strongest of minds.

"That proves nothing, Mrs. Shelley. The woman might simply have been visiting in England at the time: nothing else can be inferred by it."

"Read the letters, Lord Byron."

She handed them to him: and he began reading. The first mention of Athina was almost casual, but by the last letter Shelley had received, Keats wrote almost reverently about the woman. The same way Shelley had spoken about her and her sister. And yet there was fear, too. Keats believed he was dying, somehow, at Athina's hand, and yet. incredibly, he wanted to do nothing about it.

These written words were far more convincing than what Mary had said: even he could see what lay beyond the words. "No." An inaudible, reluctant half moan escaped from him:, she couldn't be right.

"My husband met those two women at the Baths, and how casual a meeting it appeared at the time. They came to our house later, and how they stared at the children-Clara and Willie. August and Athina Kristonosos gazed at the children, Lord Byron, as if they were tidbits to eat. And now our children are dead, all except poor little Percy Florence, who somehow has escaped their devilish notice thus far.

"Allegra, too, proved of interest to them; they often asked my husband about her and *where she was slaying*. Our children aren't the only ones to die at these women's hands, my lord. Mr. Keats and his brother did, too. And then there is Shelley."

"Madam, he drowned."

"Perhaps." Here she leaned forward and lowered her voice a little. "What if he was already dead by the time the boat capsized?"

Speechless, he stared at her.

"There have been numerous other deaths, too; suspicious deaths of writers and poets and artists in each place we lived-and *each time the Kristonosos sisters were present.* Those who died abruptly were creative and young. As for the children like ours, is there anything more filled with life and energy than a child, who has his life ahead of him? I remember clearly that August Kristonosos discussed creativity with my husband. She was particularly emphatic in saying that writers and artists and poets emanated a great energy.

"As you recall, the longer Shelley knew the women, the more lethargic he became. Sometimes, he found it hard to rise from his bed."

Byron recalled that all too well but Shelley had adamantly denied being ill.

"I think she and her sister were draining him of his energy, of his life."

She shook her head.

"No doctor had a good reason for any of these deaths. Look at my own children's example-look at poor Allegra. All of them wasted-drained of their life; all of them healthy before the sisters made their acquaintance." She leaned forward, and her eyes gleamed, but not in the way of a madwoman, he thought. and that made him more uneasy. "There is another thing. Do you remember the volume of poetry found in Shelley's pocket?"

"Yes. Keats's, I believe."

She nodded. "Its title was Lamia. I think that Mr. Keats suspected what the sisters were, but couldn't prove it." Byron looked puzzled. "Lamia is another word for succubus, you see, those deadly spirits that come to men at night and suck their lives from them." Suddenly her voice had dropped to a whisper and he had to lean forward to hear her words-"And now, Lord Byron, I fear you will be the next to die."

1824

Winston did not speak. He could not. After a few moments, though, he realized he had to get up and move about and think, so he rose shakily and paced about the small whitewashed room. The lamp cast long, deep shadows in the corners, and as he passed them, involuntarily he glanced away. Byron's gothic tale had filled him with superstition. he told himself: he must be reasonable.

Finally, the young man returned to his chair, dropped into it, and put his head in his hands.

Burning thoughts that couldn't be real roiled through his confused mind, and he wanted to cry out that what the other man had said were lies, fairy tales, nothing more than that. Byron was a spinner of tales, as had been Shelley and Keats.

And yet ... yet he couldn't believe that. When he raised his head at last. he understood why Byron wore the look of a haunted man.

"It's impossible," he whispered, his voice hoarse.

"Impossible, my lord. How can you know all that you have told me here tonight? How can you prove this? There's no proof at all."

"But there is," Byron said. He stood and crossed the room and returned with a bundle of letters. He dropped them in Winston's lap.

"Keats's letters to Shelley," Winston said.

He did not move; it was almost as if he feared to touch them; as if he would become part of this madness somehow.

"Go ahead. Read them."

Reluctantly Winston untied the ribbon and unfolded the first paper. He scanned the lines quickly, went on to the next, and the next. When he was done, he swept them from his lap.

"Keats also wrote me." Byron handed him several more letters.

They contained much the same as the letters to Shelley. Line after line of praise for Athina, and yet fear was there, too. A fear that was known, and could not be denied. Too, Keats mentioned the strange dreams he had, erotic dreams. The type of dreams that Shelley had had, and Byron, and now Winston.

"But—"

"Remember what Shelley told me. I asked, 'When shall I meet your paragon of virtue and beauty, and all that is good and wonderful?' And his reply was: '*When she's ready for you.*'"

"Let me tell you the third tale," Byron said and began his own story.

PART IV
BYRON—ITALY: 1822

She walks in beauty, like the night
Of cloudless climes and starry skies;

—She Walks in Beauty

I had a dream, which was not all a dream.

—Darkness

CHAPTER 32

"And now, my lord, I fear you will be the next to die."

Byron forced himself to smile at Mary Shelley's preposterous words. Well, after all, he told himself cynically, what could one expect from the woman whose mind had conceived the gothic tale of *Frankenstein*? She was distraught, mad; Shelley had been mad; they were all mad. God knows, he certainly felt mad at times.

"Madam," he replied in his most soothing tones, "I understand that you are grieving over your sudden loss, that your thoughts are not as steady as they should be, but perhaps once you have rested a little and time has passed and you've thought matters over again-"

"My thoughts, my lord, are as steady as yours or any other man's." Mary Shelley regarded him coolly, and not at all with the look of a madwoman. Momentarily his resolve wavered. "I know that you don't believe me ... that you don't want to because of what it implies, but you must, if you are to save yourself. Is your life not worth at least that, sir?"

Byron raised an eyebrow.

"You've read the letters, now please read the poem." She handed *Lamia* to him.

A little reluctantly he accepted the book. Its cover had been bent back, as if recently read and then thrust quickly into a pocket, and it showed signs of extreme water damage.

"Is this the copy that was found with your husband?" he asked gently.

"Yes. Mr. Trelawny was kind enough to save it from the bonfire for me."

"Well, then I cannot take it," he said grandly as he handed it back to her.

But she simply pushed his hand, and the book in it, away. "You must take it, my lord; after all, it is you that the sisters will look to now that Mr. Keats and my husband are dead, and this one poem may be your only defense."

He was more shaken by her words than he wanted to admit, perhaps because Mary was so calm. He could see the grief there, but he knew that it ha not overruled her reason.

"One thing more, my lord."

What could this be now? "Yes?"

"Do you have dreams?"

"Of course."

"No, I mean dreams that wake you in the night and leave you frightened, dreams whose contents you cannot remember, dreams that are more nightmares and which bewitch, yet terrify you."

How the devil did she know? Had Fletcher been blathering again? Damn that man; he would have a talk with him when he got home.

"Yes," he admitted, almost hesitantly.

"So did my husband—they woke him nearly every night after he met the Kristonosos sisters. And Mr. Keats had them as well."

He rose. "Madam, death is never a favorite topic of mine. Forgive me, but I must take my leave." He bowed over her hand and returned to the Palazzo Lanfranchi.

As for the book of Keats's poetry, he went directly to his study and set it on a shelf.

There was time enough to think about Mary Shelley's strange words. And while he did not dwell on them, he did not forget her words.

"What do you plan, Trelawny?" Byron had invited both Trelawny and Hunt to dine with him, and now, after a fine meal, they sat on the terrace overlooking the Lugarno. Salmon tinges painted the sky, and the water looked almost pink with the sun's reflection. The heat of the day had dissipated, and a cool breeze had sprung up to ruffle Byron's hair.

"An excellent question, my lord." The Cornish man thoughtfully stroked his beard. "I have offered for Mary's hand." He smiled at the astonished looks of the others. "Weren't prepared for that, were you? I have admired her for some time. But alas, the lady has turned me down. She says she thinks Mary Shelley such a pretty name that she does not wish to give it up and intends to have it upon her headstone."

He sipped his wine, then took a puff from his after-dinner cigar. That had been one reason Mary turned him down. The other was her great love for Shelley, and he respected her for that. He would always be her friend, no matter what.

Trelawny stretched, then stared at the lit end of his cigar. "Well now, I think I'll go back to England. What about you, Hunt?" Leigh Hunt sighed. He had longed for years to come to Italy, all the while prevented by grave financial difficulties, until finally, when Lord Byron had sent him the passage, he and his family had been able to come. And only a few days later, his closest friend was killed. It was a dreadful beginning for his Italian trip.

"Once more—I see you grinning, Trelawny—Lord Byron and I are starting a new journal. One of his most recent poems will be in the first issue. Do you have anything to contribute, Trelawny?"

"I might in a few weeks. I have not been writing much poetry as of late."

"Of course." Hunt watched a small craft drifting by the terrace, then glanced away. The sight brought back too many painful memories of Shelley. He must change the subject. "You know, I met the most extraordinary women last evening."

"Oh?" Trelawny arched a dark brow. "Who might these young ladies be? Does your wife know that you are flirting with the ladies of Italy?"

Hunt laughed and shook his head. "I assure you that this was the most respectable of meetings."

"Indeed," Trelawny said mockingly.

"Yes, what of these ladies?" Byron asked. He sipped his wine and stared at the water. His bulldog, Moretto, lay at his feet. "You know that I am always interested in new acquaintances."

Both Trelawny and Hunt chuckled.

"Well, as I said they are quite the most beautiful women I've ever seen, and even more remarkable is that they are sisters," Hunt was saying now. "Almost like day and night."

Byron started.

"And they are half Greek. Truly they are the most charming creatures, and they say they would love meeting you, Edward, for they've always enjoyed your poetry. I said they must be sadly mistaken because the Edward Trelawny I know is a most feeble poet." Hunt's amused look evaporated as he glanced across at his host. "Byron, what's the matter?"

"Nothing, nothing at all." Byron rose to his feet, and started toward the door to the palazzo, then paused as he remembered his two guests. "I'm sorry, I'm not feeling well. I must rest now."

Hunt and Trelawny watched with bewildered expressions as their friend went inside. After a moment, they looked at one another. Trelawny thoughtfully stroked his beard, took another puff on his cigar, and watched the smoke unfurl above his head.

"Now, what do you think is the matter with him?" Hunt asked.

"I don't know, Leigh, but it looked like he'd seen a ghost."

When he reached his study, Byron told himself he was only imagining things. Hunt had never mentioned the names of the two women; the pair might be some other half-Greek sisters, and not the ones who had known Keats and Shelley. He refused to consider the chances of that.

He sat at his desk, pulled out paper and ink, and began writing. In his work he could forget. But the lines made little sense. Frustrated, he crumbled the paper and tossed it away.

Over the next few days Byron worked hard, and each night he and Leigh Hunt stayed up till nearly dawn as they discussed plans for their new magazine. One afternoon, as Byron gazed at the numerous frolicking Hunt children, he remembered what Mary had said. How soon before they fell ill?

Utter nonsense, he told himself briskly. The little Hunts were as healthy as horses, and just as quiet, too, he thought, uneasily watching them run up and down the grand staircase.

One night, in late August, he realized he'd had little time to read, and he decided to rectify that. He went into his study to choose a volume, and the first book his hand rested upon was the one Mary Shelley had given him. He shrugged. Why not? It might prove amusing. If nothing else, it might put him to sleep.

He retired to his bedroom and his grand bed, empty except for himself tonight, and crawled in, then picked up the slender book and opened it. *Upon a time, before the faery broods,/Drove Nymph and Satyr from the prosperous woods.* Yawning, he let the volume fall to the covers.

What tripe. He reached over to extinguish the candle and closed his eyes.

He did not have to wait long before falling asleep.

CHAPTER 33

He stood—how long he knew not, but it seem'd
An age—expectant, powerless, with his eyes
Strain'd on the spot where first the figure gleam'd,
Then by degrees recall'd his energies,
And would have pass'd the whole off as a dream,
But could not wake;

—*Don Juan*

Nightfall and he walked along a tree-lined avenue. It might be Italy, but he didn't recognize the place, what he could see through the veil of darkness. Certainly he had never visited here before.

Ahead were the ruins of an old house, dark and bulky against the night, and for some reason he found it compelling. Something soft brushed against his face, and he whirled, but whatever it was, was gone now, although he thought he heard faint laughter, like a woman's, floating back to him.

Byron continued walking. He didn't know where he was going, or where he had come from; he simply knew he must go to the ruined house.

It was silent, too, along this avenue; too quiet, he thought. He heard none of the usual sounds of the night from the birds or small animals, nor did even the slightest of breezes rustle the leaves dangling over his head. Once a silken strand of a spiderweb swept across his face, and irritated, he pushed it away.

Underfoot fallen leaves from the previous autumn crunched as he strode down the wide road. He was closer now, only yards away, and he thought he saw someone, a lone figure, waiting just outside the ruins.

But a few minutes later when he reached the front of the house, no one was there. Imagination, he told himself, nothing more.

Yet an air of expectancy lingered about the ruins. What was he … were they … waiting for? The glass in the house's many black windows glittered with starlight. He pushed his way inside, past vines gone wild and fallen masonry, and found the roof and part of the upper floor had caved in long ago.

He could not go farther into the house without bending double, and then resorting to crawling. But, surely as there was nothing here to see, he did not have to go any farther, and he could leave now.

He blinked, thinking he had just seen a glimmer of light ahead. He couldn't leave just yet. And he remembered the figure he thought he had seen outside.

He pushed through the fallen boards and broken glass, past crumbling plaster and rotting material, and in the center of the house, where the house was open to the sky, a garden grew.

Strange saplings, their trunks twisted into grotesque caricatures of human faces, as if the result of too little light, and squat grey-green shrubs abounded, while sinuous vines snaked about broken marble pillars, and arched overhead forming a tenuous trellis. Diseased-looking white blossoms profusely covered the vines, spreading a too-sweet perfume through the isolated garden. Mottled mushrooms flourished like a carpet underfoot. A single scarlet blossom bloomed.

An ebony-colored chair, a relic from some long ago room, stood to one side. He brushed the damp leaves from its decaying needlepoint seat and sat. He knew he must wait. The light here was curious, he thought; almost like moonlight, and yet more powerful. He wondered if the sun ever reached the garden. The area was open, but that didn't mean the sun shone here. and somehow he didn't think any of the plants here owed their lives to the warmth of the sun's rays.

Gradually his eyelids lowered in the coolness of the garden, and his head drooped forward to rest on his chest as he began to doze, and he was startled when cool hands slipped around his neck.

"Were you waiting for me?" she asked, her breath frosty against his ear.

Startled, he twisted around and saw his visitor was a young woman. A beautiful one, too, he added, with long luminous black hair. She was smiling at him, her lips glistening, as if she had just licked them a moment before. Her perfume was strong. sensual, a welcome counterpoint to that of the sickly flowers. and a familiar agitation stirred within him.

"Yes," he said, removing her arms and rising, "I was waiting for you."

Beyond reason, he knew who this was. August Kristonosos.

Instantly he reached out, and without hesitation August slid into the circle of his arms. She pushed closer, and he felt her body meld against his. She was pliant and cool, and everywhere she touched him, he was inflamed. He could wait no longer.

Deftly he unbuttoned her dress, a filmy black gown that slid off her shoulders and fluttered to the ground. As she stood naked in the moonlight, he gazed ravenously at her perfect form, at the full breasts with their dark nipples, the narrow waist, the smooth hips and thighs with the tangle of black hair there.

He had never seen a woman like her; never had one like her.

He ran his hands down her body, as if searching for some flaw, but he found none, and then he jerked her roughly against him and kissed her full mouth, his lips hard against her icy ones. His mouth crept down to the hollow in her neck, and he licked the skin there, so cool against his tongue.

As he kissed her, she was deftly ridding him of his clothes. He paused to take off his boots, and then they were both naked. She was so beautiful that he ached.

She was grace and sensuality and primeval Woman. And he wanted her, wanted her more than anything. Even more than life.

A breeze swept through the ruins bringing a faint whisper of moisture, and overhead they heard an ominous rumble. It might rain upon them in this open area, but he didn't care.

Her fingers pushed through his curly hair, tugging occasionally at a lock so hard that tears filled his eyes, but he ignored the pain because the pleasure was even greater. Her hands swept across his body, brushing against his chest, his hips, his thighs, his already stirring manhood.

August pressed her damp groin against his, and he felt the throbbing between her legs. Already he was hot and aching, and she was driving him mad by rubbing herself against him, against his hard penis, pressing until it was nearly flat against him. He ground his teeth in pain, and she slowly backed away with a satisfied smile, then beckoned.

Daintily she stepped away, then laid down in the garden, her bed soft grey moss. She propped herself up on her elbows, then spread her legs wide.

"Come to me." It was an invitation he could not resist. Within seconds he lay alongside her and stroked her body, her skin velvet-soft beneath his fingers. His hands skimmed across her arms, her breasts, her hips, then he cupped one breast in his hand, bringing his lips down to the nipple. He kissed, then began teasing it with his tongue, while she moaned and spread her legs wider, and the scent of musk mingled with that of sweet flowers.

He slipped one hand across her flat stomach to the dark triangle. She was cold there, as always, and he knew he would warm her; he would build a fire within her, just like the fire that was consuming him now.

He was ready for her, and he rolled over onto her, but just as quickly she pushed him onto his back in the moss. Surprised, he gazed at her.

"Not yet," she murmured, and her teeth sank into his shoulder, drawing blood. Pleasure instantly replaced pain when suddenly she slid her skilled fingers down his penis to the sensitive head. Alternately she rubbed and massaged him, then once dragged a sharp fingernail across him, and his eyes opened wide. She kissed his lips hard, bruising them and drawing blood, which she carefully licked away, and he groaned with dark pleasure.

As she straddled him, she gazed down at him, and he thought how magnificent and white her teeth were, how red her lips, almost like newly shed blood. She reached down to the bite on his shoulder, still oozing slightly, and lapped at it with her tongue. He squirmed.

She crouched over him, kissing and stroking—sometimes nipping—him, and almost always drawing a little blood. She thrust her tongue into his mouth, and then slipped out to trail down his chin to his neck, then his chest. She inched farther and farther down his body until her moist mouth hovered over his throbbing penis. She licked and sucked it, caressing its tender tip with her tongue, and he panted as the unbearable heat surged through his loins. Her tongue traced along the sensitive skin underneath, then down the length of the shaft.

He closed his eyes; his hands were already balled into fists at his side. He could hardly stand it any longer. Surely she knew he was ready to explode. Surely she could see that.

Now she kissed tenderly the skin inside his thigh. Her soft hair trailed maddeningly across his leg, tickling him, and her breasts brushed against him, and he grabbed at them, but she was already out of reach.

His insides twisted with want; he had never desired a woman as much as he did now. Never. He thrust his hips up, seeking her, any part of her. Laughing softly, she slid the entire length of his shaft into her mouth. He groaned aloud. He was being sucked down into a never-ending dizzying vortex.

Blinking lights and alien sounds and colors whirled around him, as she drew her mouth up and down the hard shaft, and then he thought she would swallow him whole, and her teeth nibbled and gnawed, and the pleasure and the pain were indistinguishable, and he thrust harder, deeper, and he pumped, screaming as he did so, and then just as the explosion came, she withdrew.

He blinked, hardly believing what she had done, but she just laughed and straddled him, her dampness against his. She rubbed against him, so that his penis was flat against his stomach, and slid back and forth.

He felt her moistness as it lubricated him, and she would ride forward to the tip, then back toward the base, all the while smiling down at him.

The fire soared through him again, burning through each inch of his body, and then he possessed no restraint. He was spurting wildly, pumping uncontrollably, his hips jerking up and down, and a sticky wetness sprayed on his chest and face. Just as quickly, her inner thighs clamped down hard on him, and he felt himself sliding into her. She rose up, then plummeted down, slamming against him so that it took his breath away.

Above him she twisted and bucked like a wild animal, withdrawing, then impaling herself on him, until he thought she could take no more, but each time she did. He went deeper and deeper, and his hands roamed across her face, her breasts, her arms. She leaned forward slightly and brought her gyrating hips down, milking every last ounce of passion from him.

Her body sucked the very vitality from his, riding him until one great explosion followed another, until he thought he was so limp he would never be able to make love again. But he was wrong. Each time she fondled and caressed, and coaxed forth his passion, each time a little less than before, though. Sweat poured from him, dampening the lust-fired skin.

And finally, when he could respond no more, when he had nothing left to give her, he lay there panting on the grey moss, and she withdrew, flicking his limp member with a careless finger, then curled alongside him. She kissed his ear, then ran her tongue along his jaw line. Murmuring, she nuzzled against him.

He was exhausted as never before. No woman had ever done this to him. Never. He was so tired physically and mentally that he could scarcely see or hear, and yet she was talking to him in her low soothing voice, but he couldn't make out the words.

He reached out to her, and she held his hands and kissed the fingers one by one. He shivered and murmured her name.

She laughed and kissed him gently on the mouth, and he could not believe that the fierce animal a short time ago was her.

Then he felt her slipping away from him, taking her cool body from his fevered one, and he was lying alone in the bed of crushed moss.

Slowly, dizzy from that slight movement, he sat up, and as he gazed around at the ruined rooms and the garden, he knew finally that this was no dream.

CHAPTER 34

The present is hell, and the coming tomorrow
But brings, with new torture, the curse of to-day

—To Caroline

In September Mary Shelley left for Genoa and a short time thereafter Byron followed. It took some time for his servants to pack his numerous possessions, because he never threw anything away, but finally his caravan arrived on the night of September 30.

He and the Hunts traveled up the hill to the suburb of Albaro, and there they parted company. The Hunts and Mary Shelley would share a villa, Casa Negroto, while a mile up the hill Byron would live at the Casa Saluzzo, a white many-windowed villa overlooking the harbor of Genoa. Its spacious back rooms peered into a walled overgrown garden, which in some ways reminded Byron of that odd garden.

The stone building was tall and square with a four-sided French roof, and a high-ceilinged drawing room.

At last the noisy Hunt children were out of his house, gone with their babbling and sticky fingers and shrill laughter, he thought with relief as he settled down for a glass of wine one night shortly after he moved in. He had enjoyed his conversations with Hunt, but the rest of the family had strained his nerves. Now, Mary Shelley must cope with them. Mary … he hadn't seen her since he had come to Genoa, and he knew he must pay a call upon her soon. But if he went, she would look at him with those serious hazel eyes of hers, and he would know immediately what she was thinking.

She would be wondering what he was doing about the Kristonosos sisters. But what was there to do? He hadn't seen either woman; they had not yet approached him. True, there had been that dream involving August, but since then his nights had been wonderfully dream free. He frowned slightly. At least, he *thought* he didn't dream.

There was no threat, he told himself, repeating it ever so often.

That curious night had grown blurred. At the time, he thought it real, but as the days had passed, he had decided it must have been a dream, after all. Surely, he'd dreamed because of what Mary had suggested.

What he could not explain, though, was his lack of vitality. This past month he could scarcely work; he had felt as though he had been drained somehow. And that he would not even think about. Yet the effort of picking up a pen was too much. For the most part he slept, and ate a little, then went back to bed, all of which caused his Italian mistress to complain.

He set his glass down and went outside. An avenue of tall cypresses led him to a pavilion, and there, on a wooden bench, he sat and stared around at the twilight garden. The air was cool, welcome after the heat of the room he'd been in. A slight breeze ruffled the slender stalks of bright flowers. The grass around the pavilion shimmered, as if it were waves upon the ocean.

He closed his eyes against the memories of Shelley that flooded back. How he had hated seeing that vital man half-eaten by fish, then reduced to nothing more than a jar of ashes.

He shuddered, then opened his eyes at a sound from outside the pavilion. It had grown dark now, and as his eyes adjusted, he glanced about, listening. He didn't hear anything again. No doubt it was some cat out prowling around. Nothing more.

And yet, a doubt lingered, and with no hesitation, he rose and quickly returned to the house filled with bright lights.

In the following weeks Lord Byron visited Mary Shelley occasionally, often bringing with him work for her to copy so that she might earn some money, and sometimes she would come up the hill to pay a brief call upon him. Their conversations were always very general, and she never mentioned the Kristonosos sisters, even though Byron expected it. He asked after Percy Florence, and she remarked that the boy was growing each day, and that it was a pity that Shelley couldn't see his son. To that Byron had nothing to add.

Several times Hunt came to Casa Saluzzo, without benefit of his large family, and he and Byron spent many hours talking. Their new magazine had had one issue so far, and had been far from a universal success. Even so, they weren't discouraged.

"It's because we no longer have Shelley," Hunt said morosely one early October evening as they sat in the garden. "It would have done better with a poem by him in it."

"You had one of mine," Byron replied somewhat waspishly.

"Of course, of course, Byron," Hunt said quickly, "I didn't mean to insult you, but you really do know that it would have been more successful with one of his." He sighed. "Poor Shelley."

What Byron knew Hunt really meant was: Poor Hunt. The man hadn't yet come to terms with Shelley's sudden death. God knew, Byron thought, the man's family was of absolutely no help to him.

Both men lapsed into silence that lasted for a few minutes, then Byron stirred. He reviewed that strange conversation with Man. and he wanted to see what Hunt thought.

"Do you know what a succubus is, Hunt?" Certainly he knew what an incubus was-a male demon—and he was sure that a succubus was simply a female one, but he wanted to hear what the editor said.

"Yes, it's a demon that takes the form of a woman and then has … well … visits a man at night and takes his vital fluids from him. You know." Hunt's cheeks were red.

Thoughtfully Byron tapped his fingers on his knee. "What about a lamia?"

"Do you mean like the one in Keats's poem?" Byron nodded. "Well I think Lamia was the daughter of Poseidon and a mistress of Zeus. Hera was jealous of her—as with all Zeus's women—and had Lamia's children destroyed, and changed her into a creature like a snake, but also a woman. Lamia then lured victims to her and devoured them. I believe that in Rome she later became identified with a bloodsucking witch."

"There's a snake in Keats's poem. *'She was a Gordian shape of dazzling hue,'* and *'Her head was serpent, but ah, bitter-sweet!'"* In the past week he had read through the entire poem several times. It disturbed him.

"Yes, I do think Keats must have read the legend sometime. Burton's *Anatomy of Melancholy* popularized it, as I recall."

"But is that all that a lamia is, Hunt? Once Mary Shelley said something about it being another name for a succubus."

Thoughtfully Hunt stroked his chin, then sipped his wine. "Let me see if I can remember. Lamias—or lamiae, more correctly—could take on the forms of many things. Some authorities said mermaids were lamiae, which, of course, is utter nonsense; still others said that the lamiae hissed liked serpents and fed on the flesh of the dead. Bloody awful stuff, if you ask me, and not something to tell a child." Hunt shuddered and drained the last of his wine from his glass.

"Yes." He remembered how August had stared at him in his dream, that compelling look in her eyes, the one that forbade him to look away. Like a serpent's gaze, he thought uneasily.

"Wait, I've just remembered something else."

"Yes, Hunt?" Byron said, his tone carefully amused. He didn't want the other man to know how serious he was on this subject.

"Another interpretation of the legend was that after Hera robbed Lamia of her children, she vowed vengeance. From that moment on she began enticing children and murdering them; she also had the power to seduce men and suck their blood." Hunt poured himself more wine. "Is that sufficient?"

"More than enough," and Byron's voice was strangely muffled.

Long after Hunt left that night, Byron paced about the lower level of his villa, with old Moretto faithfully following at his heels. He could not sleep, would not sleep.

Mary Shelley contended that her very young children, and Allegra, his bastard daughter, as well as grown men—yet all of them fairly young—were killed by August and Athina Kristonosos.

Leigh Hunt claimed that in the legend Lamia enticed children to her and murdered them. And she seduced young men and sucked their blood.

But legends were only that. and nothing factual, or if they had been based upon a fact, the details grew muddled with the years and the retellings.

What if it was not blood of babes and men that the lamiae sucked?

Both Hunt and Mary had said a succubus sucked out the vital fluids of men. What if that was more than blood, more than seminal fluids?

What if it was the vitality of youth that was taken from their bodies? Nonsense!

But he did not convince himself. He took down the Keats volume, but thrust it away again. It was only a creation of Keats's mind; nothing more. And yet ... a poem about a woman who was indeed a serpent. And what of Shelley's poems? Byron recalled lines from the poems Shelley had allowed him to read.

Alas! I have nor hope nor health,
Nor peace within nor calm around ...
Yet now despair itself is mild ...
I could lie down like a tired child
And weep away the life of care
Which I have borne and yet must bear
Till death like sleep might steal on me ...
My head is wild with weeping for a grief
Which is the shadow of a gentle mind ...
Hearest though the festival din
Of Death, and Destruction, and Sin ...
My head is heavy, my limbs are weary,
And it is not life that makes me move ...
The death knell is ringing ...

Shelley's later poems were tilled with the images of death and darkness. As for his last poems, Byron didn't know. Only Mary had copies of those, and according to Shelley's father's wish, she could not publish them for some time.

No, no, no, he told himself, and once more paced through the nearly empty rooms.

Further, Mary had said the children and men died of a wasting disease. He had seen that in Shelley, but Keats was supposed to have died of consumption, like his brother Tom. But what if it was something which masqueraded as that disease, and which the doctors misdiagnosed? There had been others Mary mentioned. All writers or poets or artists—and poor innocent children.

All creative. All young.

Byron paused before a mirror and stared at the silvery reflection of his pale face. Most certainly he wasn't wasting away; perhaps he was a little wan, but then he hadn't been out in the sun much.

Nor was he running a fever, as Mary claimed the others had before their deaths. He had dreams, odd ones at that, but then any number of men did. As for a rash upon his stomach or loins ... she'd mentioned that as well-another symptom. Byron laughed aloud. How ludicrous!

Still laughing, he pulled up the tail of his shirt. He would prove Mary wrong, no matter what. See, there was nothing—

He stopped and stared, unbelievingly, at the faint dappling of red that spread down his chest and disappeared below the waistline of his trousers. Faintly, as though from very far away, he heard the mocking laughter of a woman.

CHAPTER 35

Thou incubus! Thou nightmare!

—The Deformed Transformed

In January 1823 Lord Byron celebrated his thirty-fifth birthday in Genoa. Even though he was not old in years, he felt aged, and tired, and ill, despite what he said to Mary when she asked how he was.

Since October his strength had been sapped. Each day was a struggle against an overwhelming weariness; each movement was taken as if he had lead weights tied to his limbs. Some days it was simply easier to sit at his table with his head in his hands and his eyes closed, and do nothing but think.

In December, on the very last day of the year, he had finally met the sisters. Even to that moment, he had thought he might be saved from the same fate as Keats and Shelley, but one day as he was out, two women approached him. When he saw their beauty and the sly smiles upon their lovely faces, he knew who they were; and he knew he had been wrong. Dreadfully wrong.

They had called him by name, even though they had not yet been introduced, and his hand had been cold as he shook those dainty ones

215

offered to him. He smiled, but knew the expression was sickly, for he knew those exotic eyes, flirting with him, regarded him only as prey.

His nightmares increased. His unrest increased, but still he could not completely believe the obvious. He had to be sick, he thought; the sisters couldn't cause this exhaustion in him. After all, he had met them only the one time. After that he had avoided them. But, one part of him countered, it wasn't necessary for him to see them; they could visit him nightly, as they wished.

On his birthday he pulled up his nightshirt and looked once more at his stomach. The rash looked much angrier than the first time. He brushed his fingers across the redness, then flinched a little at the unexpected tenderness. Numbly he looked away.

The next day Byron saw Mary. She mentioned the Kristonosos sisters and asked what he was doing about them. He simply smiled and said there was little that could be done. She gazed at him, her face so serious, and then shook her head.

A week later a young friend of his, a promising writer, was found dead in his home. He had died, authorities said, of a wasting disease. But was that really the cause of death? Byron wondered.

Shortly afterward two other acquaintances in the English colony at Genoa died. A wasting disease. All three had been in their twenties, and all had been writers, or poets, or artists. All were creative, and young, and now they were dead.

And those were only the deaths he had heard about, what about those men—and children—who weren't English and who died? How many "wasting" deaths went unnoticed? How many could be traced to the sisters? Perhaps dozens, he thought, or even more.

Why, then, was he still alive?

Perhaps, because he was such a great poet, he reasoned with no undue pride, he had more to give ... more creativity ... and the sisters knew it, and so milked him for however long it took.

He shuddered, then made himself rise from bed and get dressed. He was damned if he would continue lying here, feeling sorry for himself.

Late on a mild January night, as Byron and Leigh Hunt strolled along the beach. talking about their respective work, Byron thought he saw August and Athina Kristonosos some distance ahead of them. He stopped, strangely reluctant to go on.

Hunt glanced at his friend's face. "What's the matter, Byron?" Hunt looked up and down the beach to see what could be the cause of his friend's agitation, but all he saw were two women deep in conversation.

"Nothing's the matter." A full moon was out tonight, and when the women had finally turned, he'd seen he was mistaken. Yet in that instant fear and excitement had gripped him, and even now his heart still beat rapidly. For one wild moment he had wanted them to be the sisters, and he was disappointed.

Was he mad? No, just bewitched, or rather, enamored of August and her equally beautiful sister. Yes, they were enchantresses, but of a far different sort than Mary claimed.

"Have you ever loved another woman other than your wife?" Byron asked.

"What?"

"Have you ever loved another?"

"Well ..."

"Come now, Hunt, I won't tell her. Your secret is safe with me."

"It's not a secret," Hunt said, his tone peevish. "But yes, I did love another woman besides Mrs. Hunt. It was long before we married, though, and I have forgotten her name in the years since."

"What a shame," Byron mused. "Have you ever loved two women at once?"

"No, I haven't. I leave such things up to you, my lord."

Byron smiled bitterly.

Early in February Leigh Hunt told Byron that he and his family were thinking of leaving Genoa soon.

"Leave? Why is that?"

Hunt brushed back a lock of hair that had fallen into his eyes. "I don't think the air agrees with my children. The two oldest boys and girl seem ill."

"Ill?" His voice was sharp. and Hunt looked at him strangely. "How?"

"Well, they're suffering from some sort of lassitude. My poor wife has the devil of a time trying to rouse them in the morning; they just fall back to sleep! And they're very quiet now, my lord. I think you would scarcely recognize them."

Hunt was painfully aware of Byron's more than moderate dislike of his children's unrestrained behavior. Byron had been particularly disapproving when his children had broken several windows at the Palazza Lanfranchi, and there had been the matter of the scribblings across a wall, not to mention the incident with the goat on the stairs. But it had all come clean in the end, hadn't it?

"My eldest boy has a most peculiar rash across his stomach. Most peculiar. The doctors don't know what to make of it."

Byron felt a little faint. as though he were standing in a closed room and he was about to suffocate, yet he and Hunt were talking outside in the garden at his villa. It was happening just as Mary had said.

He spoke, his tone urgent. "Yes, then you must leave, Hunt, for the children's sake. Go where the air proves more beneficial. Perhaps Mrs. Shelley could suggest a more congenial location."

"Yes, she's far more familiar with the Italian climate than either my wife or I."

"Do it soon, Leigh," Byron said, "wherever you decide to move, for God's sake, make sure it's far away from Genoa."

CHAPTER 36

Along my bones the creeping flesh did quake

—A Spirit Pass'd Before Me

In April, Edward Balquiere, a young Irishman and a member of the London Greek Committee, paid a call upon Lord Byron to discuss the Greeks' war of freedom.

For some time Byron had been thinking of going to Greece; in fact, long before his death, Shelley had urged him to do so. Yet somehow the trip had always been postponed. But the plight of the Greeks never left his thoughts.

The more Byron listened to Blaquiere, the more intent he became. He had money saved; he could provide the Greeks with a large amount of cash, gunpowder, and medical supplies, all of which they desperately needed. And as Blaquiere suggested, Byron could be of great use to the Greek provisional government.

But he was tired, tired of moving. However, there was that wonderful ideal of freedom for which the long-oppressed Greeks fought. How could he turn his back on that cause? He couldn't. And if he went to Greece, perhaps the sisters wouldn't follow. They seemed settled in Genoa; in Greece he would be free of them.

And perhaps the life here was a little too comfortable, a little too stifling. And it appealed to his craving for sensation.

"I'll go," he announced.

Immediately the two began planning for Byron's expedition. Byron invited Trelawny along because he knew the Cornishman loved a good fight. Trelawny was traveling, but Byron dispatched a letter to him at once. Then he would need five horses as well as other supplies. He smiled. Old Fletcher wouldn't be happy. He thought Greece all rocks and robbers. There was so much to do and so little time for it, because he'd said he would leave for Greece sometime in the summer.

He forced himself to act against the lassitude that sometimes seemed to overwhelm him; he was determined not to give in to it-or to the sisters, if indeed that was what was causing his affliction. Perhaps, he thought with some amusement, it was simply ennui.

May went by in a flurry of business.

The Hunts decided to move to Florence, and in June Byron paid the Hunts' passage there. The children seemed a little better; Byron hoped they would recover completely. He took Mary some work to copy and told her of his plans. She said she thought him wise.

He met with Blaquiere on July 11 at the representative's inn, telling the Irishman he planned to leave in a week.

Afterward, Byron set off for home on foot along the quiet beach. The day had been warm, but the night had turned windy, with the promise of a rainstorm not too distant. Off on the horizon lightning glimmered. At times, through the clouds, a full moon spread a silver light around him.

He whistled a cheerful tune, but as he went further from the town, the more the music sounded too loud and grating, and he stopped. Now all he heard was gravel crunching underfoot, and, to his right, the water lapping gently at the sand.

And that sound turned his thoughts to other matters. Had it already been a year since Shelley had drowned? It didn't seem possible, but this was July 11, and Shelley had died on the eighth. He brushed his hand across his face, wishing he could remove the weariness and age that had come over him this past year, and that somehow Shelley could be returned to the living.

But Shelley was dead, and he feared that only one cure existed for his malady.

Ahead and on his left bushes and arched trees formed a natural bower where he often stopped on particularly hot days, lingering in the cool shade for a while before continuing on his way up the hill farther along. The bower was also a natural trysting spot for the locals, and Byron had immediately adopted it, spending much time there wooing several shy young women when he was not plagued by the strange lassitude.

As he went past it, smiling at his memories, he naturally glanced into the bower. At that moment the clouds slid away from the face of the moon, and he could see nearly as well as in the daytime.

And he wished he hadn't.

On the ground lay a man, his pants and shirt torn off his body. Byron stopped, thinking the man had suffered some sort of seizure. He took one step forward, then stopped again. He was not alone. Stooping above the fallen man was a woman. And as she lifted her head, he saw the glint of her eyes in her white face, the fall of the blonde hair, and he knew at once who it was.

The victim turned his face, cried out weakly in Italian, and raised one hand in supplication. The woman made a hissing noise, not unlike that made by a serpent, and the man shrieked, a terrible hollow sound that cut its way to Byron's soul; the hand dropped to the ground.

Byron stared at that limp hand, and knew the man was dead. He raised his eyes and saw the woman straighten, smoothing her hair. Then smiling, her lips glistening in the moonlight, she advanced toward him slowly.

He did not wait. Fear riding him, he turned and ran as fast as his lame foot would take him. He ran to the only place where he knew he could find shelter—Mary Shelley's villa.

After a few minutes Mary answered the thunderous pounding at the front door, the delay doubtless because she had been abed already. She was surprised to see Lord Byron, much disheveled and out of breath, stagger into the dark room.

"My lord, what is the matter?" she asked. She set her candle down and helped him to a chair.

He gasped, and she realized that he had been running some distance. She could imagine that only if he were somehow desperate, and yet why?

He tried answering, but could not. While he caught his breath, she fetched a bottle of brandy and two glasses. From his face she thought he would need it. Finally, the redness faded, and his breath came much more easily, although he could not rid himself of the trembling that racked his body.

"Mrs. Shelley, I fear that I have done you a great wrong," he said as he took out a handkerchief and wiped his face.

"And how is that, sir?" She handed him a glass of brandy, which he accepted gratefully and almost drained in one swallow.

"I wronged you by not believing your story about the Kristonosos sisters." Mary's gaze never wavered from his face. "I was a fool. I admit that freely now, madam. You see, I saw her tonight ... that woman ... Athina Kristonosos ... and if I had not witnessed it, I would never have believed it! She killed a man-this dainty petite blonde-even as I watched, and then she started walking toward me. And I knew she would do the same to me." He shuddered.

Mary brought her chair closer to his. "My God, who was it?" He shook his head. "I didn't recognize him, but I presume he was Italian. She had been bending ... over him." He looked away and the brandy she had once more poured into his glass nearly sloshed out. "It was ghastly beyond belief."

To her credit, Mary did not sit back and announce that she had told him so. Instead, she took his hand in hers and tried to still the trembling. "I am sorry that you were forced to accept my story under these circumstances. How terrible it must be for you." He nodded, a quick convulsive motion. "What will you do now, my lord? Your trip is not for a week, but surely it is too dangerous for you to stay here now."

"Yes! She recognized me, God help me, and now they will come for me! I know that with all my heart." He drank another glass of brandy.

"May I stay here tonight with you, Mrs. Shelley. I don't want to return to my own home, as you may understand."

"Of course."

She prepared a makeshift bed for him in a room close to hers. After she excused herself and returned to her bedroom, Byron could not sleep for fear he would be awakened by the deadly kisses of August and Athina Kristonosos. Only when dawn came, red and angry and hot, did he fall into an uneasy slumber.

Waking at noon, he contacted Blaquiere and said he would be leaving Genoa far sooner than originally expected, and he wished his trip conducted in as much privacy as possible. Blaquiere readily agreed.

Feverishly Byron worked all that afternoon and evening to get ready, pushing his servants without mercy. That night he sat up and did not sleep, and upon the next day, Friday, July 13, Lord Byron set sail for Greece.

CHAPTER 37

The shadow came—

—*The Vision of Judgment*

"And that is my story," Lord Byron said simply "I don't know if you believe one word of it, Mr. Early; I'm not even sure that I even care at this point. But now you have heard it, and I have fulfilled an obligation by warning you."

As he progressed in his tales, Byron's face had grown grey, his cheeks sunken like an old man's. Even his lips were a thin bloodless line now, and he resembled more a man of seventy than one half that age. With a palsied hand, he raised his glass and drained the warm wine. He leaned back and closed his eyes, his hand opening and the glass tumbling to the floor. Winston wondered for a moment if he had fallen asleep.

Some time ago, neither man remembered quite when, the candles had sputtered, then flickered out, and yet the room was not completely dark. The first faint light of dawn crept through the windows, painting the white walls with a pink tone.

Winston pressed his fingertips against his burning eyelids and shuddered. He was exhausted, yet he couldn't sleep. Byron was right. Winston didn't know if he believed it or not; and yet why would Lord Byron go to the trouble of fabricating a story like this? Too, the man seemed so earnest ... for whatever reason the poet was frightened of something or someone.

Winston stretched, heard the crack of bones still for too long. He ran a hand over his face and felt a slight stubble.

"But your story hasn't ended, my lord. I mean, you are here, safely in Greece, now more than half a year since you left Genoa."

Byron opened his eyes and Winston saw they were red-rimmed with weariness.

"You're right. Mr. Early, it's not the end yet. But the sisters are here; I cannot run away from them. No matter where I go, they will find me."

"You mentioned that they only visited at night, and that you have never seen them in the day. Why is that, my lord?"

"I do not know, Mr. Early."

For a moment they were silent. each man struggling with his own thoughts, then Byron shifted and groaned, as if in pain.

"You know, Mr. Early, when r first arrived here and saw them, I made discreet inquiries."

He was silent so long that Winston prompted him. "And?"

"The name of Kristonosos was recognized."

"Yes?"

"Recognized, I might add, Mr. Early, with a great amount of fear. But the natives wouldn't tell me anything about the family except that it was very old. My local informants were afraid—as if they suspected that once they talked about the women, they'd be visited.

"And God knows"-he rubbed his hand across his face—"they might be right." He closed his eyes, remembering the face of the dying man in the bower in Genoa. That would haunt him for the rest of his life.

"It might not have been fear."

"I saw the faces. It was fear." Suddenly he leaned forward, his face intent. "Have you been dreaming, Mr. Early?"

"A little."

"'A little.' And you don't entirely remember their content." Winston shook his head. "I thought not, sir." Byron sighed. "Perhaps it is already too late for me, for you, for all of us." He rose to pour them new wine, then stood at the grey-lit window for a few minutes. When he returned, he sank into the chair heavily.

"After what you're saying, my lord, they must be supernatural creatures."

"Yes."

"And they have powers far beyond ours."

"Yes."

"How then can we combat them? I mean, we can't sit by and let them hunt us down."

Byron's lips lifted in a curiously ironic smile. "Frankly, Mr. Early, I have no idea. I was rather hoping you might have a suggestion."

Winston Early had left some hours ago to return to the inn, and now Byron lay in his bed, attempting to sleep.

But it was useless. Thoughts roiled through his mind. Why hadn't he listened to Mary Shelley sooner? For the same reason, perhaps, that Early hadn't fully believed him until tonight.

He sighed. The boy said he would be back that evening to keep watch with Byron. But, what would they do if one of the women—or God forbid, both of them—appeared? What could be done? Nothing, he thought, wearily. They were both doomed like Shelley and his children, like Keats and his brother.

At about two in the afternoon, he fell asleep at last, but slept fitfully, starting awake, fearing that someone was in the room with him, but he was always alone. Once, late in the afternoon. he dreamed, and when he awoke, he was weeping.

He rose and put on fresh clothing, and then poured himself a stiff drink. He drank it quickly. He didn't know when he had last eaten a full meal. Days? A week Of more? Did that really matter any longer?

At sunset, Winston joined him. The artist looked little better than he, Byron noted sadly.

"Did you sleep at all today?"

"Some," Winston admitted, "but not as much as I would have liked."

"You were thinking about what I told you last night, Mr. Early?"

"Yes."

"And?"

"I Still don't know, my lord. One part of me wants to believe you wholeheartedly, but the other ... the other can't. This is all too fantastic ..."

"I understand completely. Please, Mr. Early, do not wait to believe until it is too late, as I believe that I have done."

Winston nodded.

Leaning back, Byron sipped his drink thoughtfully. "Do you know what the worst aspect of this is?" he asked, his tone ironic.

"No."

"It is; Despite what has happened to my friends and others, despite what I know about the sisters, I still desire them; perversely I long for them." He smiled grimly at the look on the artist's face. "Does that shock you?"

"No, I suppose not. Not when you say they can bewitch a man against his will."

"Yes."

For some minutes they watched the window as the blue faded, and grey sky deepened to black. Byron lit several candles and placed them about the room. They were small pools of light against a greater shadow.

Winston was still struggling not to believe. "How could Mrs. Shelley know what had happened to Keats?"

"She had his letters to her husband, and the poems, and then she wrote to Joseph Severn, and he provided much more information. Of course, we will never know all that occurred between Keats and Athina those months in London, but we can imagine what it was like."

Byron rose suddenly and went to his writing desk. He opened it, drew something out, then came back and sat once more.

"Over the past few weeks, I have written down everything that I relayed to you last night. There are many details, of course, found in this book that I didn't bother with in my retelling last night, but I think you will find them of great interest. I want you to have this book, Mr. Early, and this as well."

Reverently Winston took the two items. One was a thick cloth-bound book, tied in ribbon; the tale of the three poets. The other book was Keats's Lamia.

"I can't take these, my lord."

Byron smiled. "Yes, you can, and you must. I have no one else to leave them to."

Winston looked up sharply. "'Leave them to'? You sound as if you're about to die."

"I am."

Winston, face pale with sorrow, clasped the two books in his hands. "What are we to do?"

"It is already too late for me, dear boy. I know that now. But for you, there's still hope. Go away from here, as far away as you can, Mr. Early. Return home, if you must. for you might be somewhat safe there—perhaps they will forget about you once you are so far away. Just be careful, and never turn your back. Perhaps you will discover a way to combat these unholy creatures. I hope to God that you will."

Winston nodded, unable to speak because there was a lump in his throat.

CHAPTER 38

But her eyes were as black as death

—*Don Juan*

The days passed agonizingly slowly, and each morning Byron rose later and with deliberate care. He knew that he was powerless against the women, just as he knew they visited his dreams at night. Little by little his life was being drained from him.

It was just a matter of time.

By April, he no longer wrote poetry, nor even letters. Both proved too much an effort for him.

Winston still visited him, but Byron was trying to discourage him now. Byron wanted the boy to leave Missolonghi now, but Winston refused.

Byron knew why the artist wouldn't leave. Winston didn't want to go while Byron was still alive, and he appreciated that the boy didn't want to desert him. But he would rather have had the boy try to save his own skin and forget about Byron's. After all, his was long lost, he thought wryly.

On the fifteenth he was worse, too weak to leave his bed. His concerned servants called for Dr. Bruno, who decided to bleed Byron. Byron refused adamantly. He didn't believe in the barbaric practice.

The doctor called in a colleague, who prescribed the same. Still Byron refused, but the doctors began talking to him, one with tears in his eyes, and finally persuaded him.

Dr. Bruno drew forth a pound of the poet's blood. A little over two hours later a second pound of blood was drawn.

The remainder of that night and the next day, Byron was able to do little beyond sleep and dream. In his dreams he saw the bower from the Genoa beach once more. but instead of the Italian man lying there, it was him, and then Winston, then Shelley, then Allegra, then all the others. Sometimes the woman was Athina; sometimes it was August; sometimes both women bent over their victim.

Winston was appalled at how far his friend had slipped in the one day. He sat by the poet's bed and told him of how he planned to leave in a matter of days.

"There are still some arrangements to be made, you understand."

At first he thought Byron hadn't heard him, but finally, the poet's lips drew up into a smile. Winston knew Byron was dying, and tears came to his eyes.

"What have they said about your condition, my lord?" His voice was scarcely above a whisper.

"Consumption one said, brain fever from the other. Both are fools, and they claim consumption whenever they don't know. And all they wish to do is bleed me. Fools." The great rancor which would have been there a week earlier was now almost feeble.

Byron no longer had the strength to protest against bleeding, and so the next day the doctors managed to take a few ounces of blood from the poet. On the eighteenth, the Greek Easter Sunday, two pounds were taken from him. Then they bled him again in the evening.

Byron scarcely moved all that night or the next day, and it was late on Monday evening that he opened his eyes for the first time in over twenty-four hours. He blinked, not sure where he was, and then he remembered. He was thirsty.

"Fletcher," he called, his voice scarcely over a whisper. "Fletcher."

But he was alone in the dimly lit room. He tried raising himself up on one elbow, but could not, and he cried out in frustration.

"There, there," soothed a woman's voice.

He couldn't turn his head, either; but it didn't matter. He knew who it was.

August Kristonosos sat only a foot away on the edge of the bed.

His lips were dry as parchment.

She touched the bandage wrapped around his head, and he flinched slightly. The leeches had been applied at his temples.

"Really, my dear, the so-called doctors here are quite barbarous. Haven't they learned by now that this process of bleeding simply weakens someone? It's never improved anyone's health."

"Yes. I know." How civilized she seemed, he thought, discussing medical practice with him.

"Good evening, my lord."

Athina, too. Both here for him. He wasn't sorry, though, that his life was nearly over. He was so weary, and the pain from the bleeding was great. He just wanted it to end.

"It will end soon, my love," August said as she kissed his cheek. Her lips were cool against his fevered skin. He welcomed them.

"Why?" he struggled to ask.

"Why what?" August asked. He could only stare, not able to put into words what he meant. "Why we left you until now?"

He nodded.

"You are the greatest poet of your time, Lord Byron, and the most vital."

"You'll leave Winston alone then, won't you?" He looked at her, then at her sister. Their eyes were remote. "He hasn't done you any harm. You have me, have what you wanted all along. Please leave the boy alone. He's done nothing."

It was as if they hadn't heard him. Slowly the sisters undressed him, careful not to move him too much, and when he was naked, Athina gently kissed his lips, while August stroked his hair.

"They've cut so much," she said in a disapproving tone. "What a shame. You have lovely hair, my dear. Lovely hair."

Their hands were so soothing, he thought, and they carefully avoided touching his forehead, and he almost laughed.

Soft cool hands traveled across his chest, his stomach, caressing him, then to his groin and thighs, and he felt the prick of sharp teeth against his burning skin. Even in his weakened state, he could feel the desire rising in his body, and he smiled that his body could even respond to them now.

A full breast briefly touched his dry mouth, then was gone.

One of the sisters whispered for him to be still. He obeyed. She kissed him on the mouth, not at all harsh as in past times, then ran her tongue down his chest. The other sister stroked his arms, and thrust her tongue into his mouth and sucked greedily at his lips.

The fire that had burned so strongly in him for years now barely flickered, and yet the sensations continued racing through his body. He cried out, unfulfilled, as one woman and another teased and caressed him, bringing him close to climax, then eased away, and tempted him back, closer and closer, higher and higher.

Finally, inside him, deep, something exploded as it had never done before, and a great surge rushed through his veins, through his body, and now he saw myriad colors and sounds cart wheeling in the blackness before his eyes, and slowly the fire ebbed away.

They murmured to him, kissed his face, stroked him, and he wondered if this was how it had been for Keats, and for Shelley. Gone so long, and now …

Even as the sensations receded, so did his dreams grow pale and unimportant, and in the morning Byron did not open his eyes.

PART V
WINSTON—GREECE: 1824

CHAPTER 39

That afternoon when Winston knocked on Byron's door and a sad-faced Fletcher let him in, he knew instantly what was wrong.

"He died in the night," the servant said, then looked away. It was obvious that he had been weeping.

"I'm very sorry, Fletcher." The words sounded so flat, so unconcerned to Winston's ears. One of the age's great poets lay dead, a great man who had become his friend these past weeks, and now he could only say that he was sorry. "May I see him?"

Fletcher nodded. "Of course, Mr. Early."

He led the way to Byron's bedroom. Not knowing what to expect, Winston went at once to the bed. Byron had been washed and dressed since he was found that morning, and as Winston stared down at the pale, still face, he thought that Byron looked at peace, finally. The bandage had been removed from around his head, and he could see the terrible wounds where the leeches had been applied.

He reached over and patted the poet's hands crossed on the coverlet. They were cool, and Winston turned and fled, tears stinging in his eyes. He knew what—who—had killed Byron.

He returned to the inn and began packing. He did not sleep that night, but paced through the hours. In the morning, he visited the docks, where he booked passage on a small cramped vessel leaving with the tide. It stank of fish, but that didn't matter.

As the boat pulled away, Winston turned back for his final glimpse of Missolonghi, then he faced front again. It would be a long journey home.

That night the dreams stopped, and sleep brought him some relief. The farther away from Greece he traveled, the less inclined he was to think that the Kristonosos sisters would harm him. After all, all he had ever done was talk with them and sketch them, and in return they had been quite pleasant.

Or the sisters might well have decided it wasn't worth pursuing him. After all, what was he? Merely a beginning artist, and one who hadn't sold a single painting at that. Hardly in the league with any member of Byron or Shelley's circle.

Yet when he looked at the two books Byron gave him, he knew these thoughts were wrong; it was precisely what the women wanted him to believe, and therein lay the danger to his life.

He took a circuitous route, believing that might throw off anyone following him, and because of that he spent more time traveling than he would have liked. Several times he thought someone was watching him, but he could never see anyone, and so he figured it must be his overactive imagination.

By the time he reached France, he was somewhat refreshed, and the dreams still had not returned. Perhaps, he told himself, he had escaped them, and even at that thought a feeling of relief washed over him.

Soon to be home and safe.

He left the port of Calais, and within hours, the boat docked in London. Winston went at once to his father's office, only to find that his father had left a week ago for Royal Tunbridge Wells.

Too tired to go on, Winston went to the townhouse in Hanover Square. In the morning, he would start on his final leg of the journey, he told himself. He told the servants he had simply returned from his Grand Tour early, and that he would be spending the night there, and a room was prepared at once. He went to it and lay down, only intending to nap. Instantly he fell into a deep slumber; again no dreams disturbed him.

The next morning he got off to q much later start than he'd wanted. He selected one of his father's horses to ride, and instructed the servants to send along his trunks in a day or so. He would be bringing the most important things with him-his notebooks, and the books Byron had given him.

The air was late-summer crisp, with the sweet scent of hay and flowers drifting through the air, when he left London behind for the beautiful Kent countryside. He could hear the sound of baying hounds in the distance. The sky was a deep blue, without a single cloud in it. He was enjoying his ride.

Much better to be on a horse than a burro! he thought, amused. He hadn't realized how much he'd missed his home until he came back.

He reached Royal Tunbridge Wells late in the afternoon, and in the distance he could see the Weald, the great raised forest, and beyond that the chalk downs that almost entirely encircled the area. Home was close, very close.

Slowly Winston rode along the town's tree-lined walks and smiled at those come for the waters. He recognized some of the people, for they returned year after year; some of the older ones had been coming to the wells for twenty years or more. The iron spring here had healing qualities recognized for several centuries, reaching its zenith of popularity as a spa under Beau Nash, but then the Prince Regent, now the King, had popularized Brighton, and Royal Tunbridge Wells had grown less fashionable. Winston didn't care.

The Early estate lay south of town, no more than five miles distant, and the sun was setting as he rode up the curved sweep, lined with graceful elms, to stop before the portico.

The last rays of daylight glinted off the windows on the upper stories, then faded, leaving the massive brick building a deep shade of red. The house had been finished in 1724 by Winston's great-great-grandfather, who'd fought alongside the Duke of Marlborough at Blenheim. The house was a Palladian design with white marble columns along the portico, and imported marble statues on it.

Wide stairs, flanking the portico, led up to the double front doors, twelve-foot bronzes imported from Italy a century ago. In the back lay the exquisite gardens, a particular favorite of Winston's grandfather, who had imported many costly Dutch bulbs to his flower beds and who had spent most of his time puttering there. A maze of hedges had been planted in the previous century, but had not been tended, and when Winston was little, he'd loved wandering through the overgrown place, a large exotic jungle to his eyes.

It was a grand place, he thought fondly, and realized just how much he had missed his home, and yes, his father, too, for all that they didn't agree about much. Home. And safe now.

He jumped down, just as the front doors opened and Richard Early came down the steps. He was a tall man, like Winston, with an incredible resemblance in their faces and erect bearing, although neither man thought so. Richard's hair was the same shade as his son's, although a few streaks of silver could be seen. Still, Richard Early, in his late forties, could easily have passed for an older brother of Winston's.

"Good God, Winston, is it really you?" His father was smiling as he pumped his son's hand. "I couldn't believe it when Ramsey said he saw you. I thought the old man was having one of his spells again."

"Yessir, it is I."

"You're back early then. I hadn't thought to see you before December."

"I ... friend of mine died, you see-and so I thought it best to return, but I'll explain more fully once we're inside."

"Good, good. No luggage?"

"It's coming tomorrow."

"Good. You should have sent word ahead, you know, and I would have met you in London. Still, I'm glad to see you sooner than I'd expected. I have a great deal of news for you-and all of it good."

His father escorted him inside to the darkly paneled library, where summer or winter a fire burned in the marble fireplace. Even when hot outside, the house remained cool, and indeed damp, so that even in the height of summer, fires were kept. Only that unusual practice managed to dispel most of the coldness. Books lined two walls of the room, and in the candlelight the lettering on their spines glittered.

Richard Early poured himself a brandy, then one for his son, and urged him to sit down.

Winston was glad to be sitting on something that didn't rock or sway, and he sipped the brandy—a fine French one, as usual, for his father did not stock inferior liquor—gratefully. He wasn't sure how he would tell his father about his Grand Tour. It had been a success, in more than one way, and yet toward the end, what could he say of that terrible experience.

But before Winston could think of how he should begin his tale, his father leaped to his feet again and paced along the tiled hearth.

"I know you must have much to tell me, Winston, and I do wish to hear it-your letters, I confess, were never long enough. And there is that matter of extending your tour without my permission."

Winston shook his head. He hadn't been in the house above half an hour and already his father was criticizing him. Home, indeed.

"But before you tell me all the exciting parts that you left out of your letters, I have an important announcement to make."

Winston set his glass down. He'd rarely ever seen his father this excited. His color was high, his eyes gleaming with excitement, and Winston was reminded of a child on his birthday as he unwrapped presents. What could his father want to announce?

"This may not be easy for you, son, although I hope you will understand. While you were gone, I met a truly wonderful woman in London. As it happened, we saw one another at various parties, and then, well, one thing or another happened ... and in short"—here he took a deep breath and plunged on—"I have asked her to marry me, and she has agreed."

So, this was what the old man had been bursting at the seams about! And Winston had thought it might be something far worse! "Congratulations; Father! I daresay it's about time!" He was happy for his father, too; the old man needed companionship that faithful servants and an adult son couldn't provide.

Richard laughed; his cheeks, tinged pink, puffed out slightly. "The wedding isn't for another month. I had rather hoped that you would be home in time, and so it happens you are. But now that you're back, perhaps we can hurry matters along. I don't want to wait too long. I'm not getting any younger," he said with a slightly lascivious smile.

"Who is the lucky woman, Father?"

"You'll meet her later, Winston. She's here … on a visit." He looked beyond Winston to the outer hall, and a look of adoration appeared on his face. "Indeed, here she comes."

Winston, who had heard light footsteps while his father talked, now stood and turned to see the woman who had just descended the stairs.

Athina Kristonosos smiled at him.

CHAPTER 40

His fists clenched at his side, Winston took a step forward, almost as if he were going to leap toward her and throttle her. This was the woman, who with her sister, had killed his friend Byron! He must do something at once! Then he remembered where he was, and brought himself up short.

"My darling, this is my son Winston, about whom I've told you so much." Richard, beaming at her, then at his son, did not notice Winston's odd behavior or the fact that the color had drained from his face. "And this is Miss Athina Kristonosos, my future wife."

"How do you do?" she murmured, holding out her hand, which Winston took only briefly.

Her skin was just as cool as the first time they'd shaken hands, yet now there seemed a deadly coldness about it. He nodded curtly, but did not speak, unable to trust his voice. If he opened his mouth, he would scream and call her a murderer, and then what would his father think? And what would that creature do? Attack him then, or wait until later? No, above all he must remain calm, must think this through. It was a great blow. Here he had thought he'd escaped from them, and now, in his own house ... How she and her sister must be laughing at him!

241

Yet how beautiful she was, how alluring. She was quite exquisite in her dress of pale blue twilled sarsenet. The sleeves were short and full, arranged in festoons with four satin buttons. A broad ivory satin band circled her small waist, and the skirt had an elegant satin border of roses surmounted with leaves. At her neck she wore a necklace of sapphires and diamonds, with matching earrings and dainty bracelet. Winston recognized the jewelry: It had been his mother's. How could his father have given her those precious jewels already? It wasn't right.

He realized his father was gazing expectantly at him, still waiting for a reaction.

"Congratulations, Father." He raised his glass in silent salute.

Richard Early's face grew puzzled and Winston knew what his father must be thinking. His response had been polite, but in no way warm.

"Well now, Winston," Athina said, her eyes intent upon him, "you'll be able to do all the sketches and paintings of me and my sister—she is arriving tomorrow—that you wished earlier."

"What?" Richard raised an eyebrow.

"Oh, Richard dear, I never had a chance to tell you, but your son and I met briefly before my sister and I left Greece."

"What an amazing coincidence!" He beamed at her. "Still, with such large English colonies abroad, I'm not surprised."

"Nor I," she murmured. "Of course, at the time I did not know he was your son, for we talked little of our backgrounds. But now I can see the resemblance ... so strong, too, especially in the face." She smiled at her husband-to-be.

"And you say that you were sketching Athina and her sister, Winston? Excellent! How far did you proceed? I would like to see the drawings sometime later. Also, I would be pleased if you would paint a full portrait of Athina."

"Of course, Father." Winston was amazed at the change in his father. Richard Early actually seemed pleased with Winston's choice of occupation.

"He's such a clever, boy," Athina purred, her eyes never leaving Winston's face.

"How did you find your time spent in Greece, my boy? You and Athina must be able to compare notes. Well, don't tell me now. It can wait until after dinner, which I believe is ready. Shall we go in?" Richard offered his arm to his fiancée, and they left the library, followed by a silent Winston.

That night Richard Early was the only one of the three diners whose appetite was not adversely affected. He ate big portions, even having seconds, while for the most part Winston simply pushed his food around on the plate with his fork.

He couldn't help but glance at Athina from time to time, who sat next to his father calmly sipping red wine. That, and a few vegetables, was all she consumed during the meal, and he wondered how blind his father could be that he didn't notice something as unusual as that. Afterward, they retired to the library for coffee and brandy, and when they were settled, Richard glanced at his fiancée.

"How strange to think that you'll soon have a mother again, Winston, although really a stepmother." Richard chuckled.

"Yes."

Athina smiled, her long eyelashes swept down, giving her a coy look.

Richard licked his lips; Winston looked away, nauseated.

"Well, Winston, what was it like in that heathen land? Can't imagine why you would want to go there when they've a civil war."

"I didn't see any action, if you're worried about that. However, I never made it into the interior, but rather stayed in a village on the coast called Missolonghi." He had decided to answer any question put to him by his father, but he simply wouldn't elaborate.

"Never heard of it."

"It's rather small. Lord Byron was living there at the time of his recent death." Winston stared at Athina, but the woman was gazing with adoration at his father. Once more Winston looked away.

"That infamous poet fellow'? He died, did he? When was that, my boy?"

"In April, Father."

Richard shook his head. "I'm sorry to hear about that. I thoroughly enjoyed his poetry, although the man was an outright scoundrel."

"Yes, it is a shame," Athina murmured. "He was a very great man." Richard smiled lovingly at her, and Winston glanced down, unable to quell the sickness in the pit of his stomach. He longed to blurt out that his father's intended was the very woman who had killed Lord Byron, and Percy Bysshe Shelley, and John Keats, and countless others, but his father would laugh him out of the house. And in the end Athina and August would get what they wanted anyway. No, he had to approach this matter much more subtly.

The older man set his glass of brandy down and shifted slightly. "Now, you said you would explain why you came home early. What was it, son?" Athina rose, retired to a corner by the fireplace, and was immediately intent upon her needlework.

Winston sipped his brandy, the fiery alcohol burning all the way down his throat. If he drank enough, perhaps he would gain some courage.

"It can wait until morning, Father."

"Come, Winston, I have no secrets from Athina. I want you to know that. We're soon to be a family. Won't that be wonderful? And who knows"—there he winked at his son—"there might be the patter of little feet around the house in a short time."

Only Winston saw the look of distaste that passed across Athina's face as she bent over her canvas. He forced a smile onto his stiff lips. "Truly, this matter can wait, Father. You must forgive me but I'm tired—I've been traveling for weeks, and can hardly wait to sleep in my old bed tonight."

Richard chuckled. "Very well. Tomorrow you can tell me all about your trip—don't leave out a single detail. And I'm sure Athina will want to hear your account, because she's traveled extensively through Europe, too. Perhaps you two can compare notes."

"Perhaps, Father."

He rose, bowed slightly toward the woman, then left his father and Athina to amuse themselves. Was August really arriving tomorrow? Or was she already here ... lying in wait for him. Each recessed doorway gave him pause, thinking something would spring out at him, and more shadows than usual crowded the long silent hallways.

Reaching his old bedroom, he found it exactly as he'd left it over a year before. The massive mahogany bed, with its fine blue silk coverlet, was centered along one wall, and between the windows sat the tall dresser with brass handles where his clothes were kept. By the bed stood the low dresser with his old painted porcelain basin and ewer on it. His small desk of oak was under one window, and his easel by another.

Underfoot was the thick Oriental carpet of gold and rust and cream and black, and the long gold brocade curtains were neatly tied with black cord at the tall windows. The colors here were less subdued than below, and gave an impression of airiness. The room also received more light all day long than others in the house, which was one of the reasons he'd selected it as his room.

Wearily he eased himself onto the bed. He had seen few servants about this evening, and wondered if Athina had somehow convinced his father to dismiss some of the staff. Doubtless she and her sister would need some privacy for what they were doing. He'd seen Ramsey, his father's oldest servant, and Douglas, the young footman, and the cook, but that had been that. Surely there must yet be maids and a housekeeper. What about a groundskeeper? He knew his father wouldn't neglect the garden.

The brandy had affected him more than usual and he must be even more exhausted then he thought he was. He could scarcely keep his eyes open. He rubbed a hand across his face, then looked around the room. Where was the satchel he'd brought with him from London? He breathed with relief. Ah, there on the desk.

He leaned back against the pillows. He must think of something, some way to expose these creatures to his smitten father. And it must be done very soon. In a month or less, the wedding would be held, and he did not want Athina as his stepmother.

Tonight, though, his mind was a blank, exhaustion and liquor having taken their toll, and he could think of nothing. He undressed and crawled into bed. He thought he should stay awake, but within minutes he was soundly sleeping.

Sometime later he awoke, thinking he had heard someone. It was only a dream, and yet … hadn't he heard the rustle of material? He sat up, straining to see in the darkness. Something moved across the room, by the door, and he started.

"Who's there?" His voice sounded tremulous, and he cleared his throat and tried again. "Who's there?" His vision clearing now, he saw there was more light in the room than he'd first thought. A shaft of moonlight slipped through a crack between the draperies and gave the room an eerie silver glimmer.

A woman chuckled.

Athina.

He could see her now as she approached. She wore a filmy nightgown and he caught tantalizing glimpses of her body through the sheer material. She stopped at the foot of his bed and smiled at him, her teeth so incredibly white even in the muted light. He pushed back until he sat against the carved head of the bed, his pillow stuffed behind his back. He pulled the covers up, too, as far as they would go, as if they would afford some protection for him.

"What do you want?" he asked, not caring if he were faintly impolite. His father wasn't present, after all, to chide him.

"Is that any way to say good night to me?" she asked in sweet tones.

When he answered, his voice was gruff. "I already bid you good night earlier, Miss Kristonosos. Down in the library, if you will recall. When you were with my father." He put heavy emphasis on the last words, although why he bothered he didn't know.

"Yes, but I wish to say good night to you privately, Winston. And you needn't be so formal with me. You must call me Athina. After all, I'll soon be your own loving mother."

"You'll never be anything but a murderer to me—you and your sister."

She made a slight *tsk*ing sound, almost like a silvery laugh.

Helplessly he watched as she came nearer. He wanted to move, to call for help, but he couldn't. She was so close to him now he was enveloped in the wonderful musky perfume she wore. Then she sat down on the bed, only tantalizing inches away.

"I can't tell you how happy I am seeing you again, Winston. August and I were saddened when you left so quickly without saying good-bye. You never finished our portraits."

He kept his silence.

"Don't you think that was rude. Winston? We were such good friends, after all."

Against his will, he nodded.

"Yes, we thought it was too, and so unlike you. You were always polite to us." She ran a finger lightly down his arm. and he shivered. "So polite … so energetic, and so very talented. I can scarcely wait until you finish my portrait for your dear father."

The portrait … perhaps she would spare his life until that was done. The painting would take some weeks, and indeed, he could stretch out the sitting time so that it might be many months-perhaps even half a year-before she and her sister claimed him. As for his father … Winston shuddered.

Athina laughed lightly. "Don't worry about your father. He is a virile man in good health. I think he'll live … oh. months … yet."

Rage and terror welled within him, and he wanted to strike out at her. "Why do you want my father? He's not a poet or an artist. There's nothing very creative about him. In fact, my talent comes from my mother's side of the family, not his."

"Your father has something else that my sister and I need occasionally, Winston. Money, and lots of it." She cocked her head to one side. "Does that surprise you, my dear? Well, we have no wish to live like paupers, and our money does run out from time to time. These are unions of convenience."

"There've been others?"

"Yes, many."

"And your husbands have all died rather soon? Is that the pattern?"

"Yes, it is, you clever boy. Usually August and I find an older man, but when we discovered your father was a man of substantial means, we could not pass him by. And then of course, there was the fact that he was your father. It is so ironic, don't you think?"

He said nothing.

She slipped a cool hand across his chest, tickling him as her fingers shifted, and inside a heat started. He shivered at her touch, then opened his mouth as hers pressed down on his.

CHAPTER 41

In the morning Winston was thoroughly disgusted with himself. He stood before the mirror above the basin, shook his head at the foul creature he saw there, then without thinking, raised his hand and smashed it into the glass. Shards, small and large, exploded toward him, and he stepped back quickly.

His fist had been scratched when he slammed it against the mirror, and carefully he licked the droplets of blood from his hand, then wrapped a clean handkerchief around it. He deserved far more than a mere scratch.

He had given in to Athina far too easily, he thought angrily and with shame. Too easily. Somehow he should have fought her. But then he shook his head, because he knew he was unable to withstand her charms, no matter what he thought of her. He had had no choice, just as Byron and Keats and Shelley had had no choice in their seductions.

He knew he had some time left, a few weeks perhaps before his strength began to give out, because they wouldn't kill Winston before Athina married his father, for the death would delay the wedding. But the minute Athina and Richard were married, the sisters would arrange for him to will all of the money and the estate to Athina, his dear stepmother. And Winston and his father would die.

He had a few weeks on his side, but what did this matter, when he still didn't know how to destroy the sisters?

Just how did one kill a lamia?

He scowled momentarily at the destroyed mirror. He'd been thinking of this problem as simply ridding the world of something terrible, but it was also murder—if they were indeed human—and that was a crime. Was he then as evil as the sisters?

No. There was a great difference. They had killed wantonly; he was killing to keep them from spreading their evil. How many children had they murdered? And young men? And good men, who had given so much to the world, and who could have given so much more.

No, it was only right. The sisters must be stopped.

But, how could he accomplish this deed? Bare hands would never work—he was strong, but there were two of them, after all, and he would have to get one alone to strangle them. That might take too long, though, and doubtless the woman would struggle, perhaps even alerting the other. Too, did he have the will, the inner strength to do something like that?

And what if upon touching them, he completely surrendered to their will? He couldn't.

His father kept a number of hunting rifles and some pistols downstairs in a case along one wall of a small room just off the library. He could use one of those for the deed, he supposed.

When Winston turned eight, his father had taken him out into the fields behind the house and there taught him to shoot. Months later, they had gone hunting together for the first time, and within minutes Winston had shot a game bird. The bird had flopped about miserably until their hunting dog had retrieved it, and dropped its bloody, and still living, burden at his feet. He had stared down at the poor creature, gasping for air, as it died, and he had swallowed heavily, his face white.

Sickened, about to lose the breakfast he'd nervously wolfed down that morning, he had begged to be allowed to go home.

Disgusted, Richard had dismissed him and had never taken his son with him again.

Now, years later, who would have thought he would be grateful to his father for once teaching him this terrible skill?

True, it had been a long time since he'd used a gun, but when he was handling one regularly he had been fairly good with it. Good enough for the deed, Winston thought grimly.

And Winston would have to do it right the first time, because he suspected he would be given absolutely no second chance.

As promised August arrived the next evening, and thereafter Winston was visited regularly by either Athina or August, who would take turns seducing him. With each visit, he was less willing to act against them. Between visits he knew what he wanted to do: now if he could only get enough strength to do it.

But the days went by, and he did nothing.

"What are you?" he asked August one night when she was finished with him.

She flashed a smile back across her shoulder as she went to the door. "What do you mean, Winston? I am August Kristonosos."

"No," he said, talking taking almost too much effort, "*what* are you?"

"I thought Lord Byron told you."

"He did. But I don't understand. Not really."

"My sisters and I are your nightmares come true, Winston. That's all you need know."

"Sisters?" He tried to sit up, failed. "There are more than two of you?"

She laughed. "Yes, many more, although we are not as numerous as we once were. All of them my sisters, all of them doing precisely what Athina and I do."

He shuddered and fell back onto the bed. She left, closing the door quietly behind her, and he lay awake for the rest of the night.

CHAPTER 42

S ome days Winston forced himself to rise from the bed and get dressed, and go downstairs to eat a little breakfast or a late lunch. He was damned if he would just lie passively in bed, waiting for them to visit and sap him even further.

Since his arrival, Winston had rarely seen his father and wondered if the same terrible thing were happening to him. When nearly two weeks had passed and he'd glimpsed his father only a handful of times, Winston decided he must find him.

He did not fear to meet the sisters, because it was still afternoon, and Byron had said he had seen them only at night. Winston had never seen them in the daylight hours, either, which might prove to be his advantage—when he could finally act.

His father's bedroom was located at the opposite end of the hallway from his, and as Winston paused outside, he knocked lightly on the door. He knocked again, this time a little louder. No one answered, he opened the door and peered in.

The furniture was all on a far grander scale than that in Winston's bedroom. The cherry—wood bed was huge, fit for a king, equipped with· gauzy curtains draped in soft folds at each corner. Alongside the bed a huge fireplace with marble mantel contained a roaring fire, even though it was a warm day; Winston suspected his father was cold, as he had been since the sisters had begun visiting him.

Immense windows overlooked the gardens, and in the old days his father had often enjoyed sitting there, looking out at the display of flowers. To the right his father had hung a number of sabers across the wall, and fleetingly Winston was reminded of Byron's house in Missolonghi. He forced that unhappy memory from his mind at once.

Winston paused, but heard nothing and crossed quietly to the bed. His father lay curled up there, not quite asleep, but not entirely awake, either. No longer did Richard Early look like a young man who could pass as Winston's brother.

In the past days he had aged decades. His lined face was nearly as white as the sheets on which he lay, and his hands quaked like an old man's. His eyes shifted, and momentarily caught his son's. Winston could see fear and shame there. Richard tried to speak, his lips quivering, but he couldn't find the strength.

Winston cleared his throat. He was afraid he would cry, and then all would be lost. When he had control of himself, he bent and squeezed the trembling hand. "Don't worry, father. I'll do something."

He saw tears in his father's eyes, and he thought of all the things they hadn't said, and never would now, if the sisters were allowed to kill him. He would never get to really know his father, or his father him, and that was wrong.

He straightened. Time to act. Where was Athina now? Where did she and her sister go when night left? Because neither Byron nor he, nor anyone else for that matter, had ever seen them during the day, he had to assume the women—the *lamiae*, he corrected himself—could not, or preferred not to, move about during the daylight hours.

Which meant logically that they would be someplace where it was dark, and that perhaps his only time to kill them would be during the day. Providing, of course, that they were somehow incapacitated then.

And he wasn't so sure about that.

Quelling his rising fear, he went downstairs, found the key to the gun closet and opened it. He gazed at the rows of pistols and rifles. His father always kept them oiled and cleaned, ready at a moment's notice.

He chose a pistol which his father had purchased a few years ago from the gunsmith Elisha Haydon Collier. He hefted the flintlock revolver with its five chambers, and decided it would do. He loaded it, then slipped the revolver into his pocket.

Where to start? The cellars, first, as certainly they were the darkest part of the house. He walked through the kitchen, not even seeing the cook as he'd expected to, and let himself down into the cellars. He took a lit candle with him. The first cellar was utilized as the wine cellar. Nothing here, nor in the cellar beyond that, or the last two. Nothing but old moldering things left in storage too long. Besides, dust lay thickly upon the floor, and it hadn't been disturbed for a long time.

He returned to the first floor and searched each room there, but he suspected he wouldn't find the sisters here. And he was correct.

On to the second floor now. But even though he thoroughly searched each bedroom, he still could not find any sign of August or Athina. He was getting frustrated now, and with each passing moment, his resolve began to gradually crumble.

Only the third floor remained. No one ever went up there; in fact, he couldn't remember anyone staying in these rooms even once while he was a child. He supposed that when his mother was alive, this third floor had been opened to guests. He remembered as a child running up here and hiding, ingeniously or so he'd thought, from his father, and then wondering how his father could ever have found him. He had completely forgotten about the small tracks he'd left in the dust.

Winston quickly climbed the narrow stairs up to the third level, where he found the floors as thick with dust as those in the cellars.

He found tracks here, larger than a child's, but they were a confusing pattern because they led to every room. They must have been searching for the right place, he thought, and began looking.

The rooms were all unlocked, which was good because he didn't know where the keys were kept, and he started at the end near the staircase and began working his way down the corridor.

Nothing but nearly empty rooms, most of the furniture piled in a heap at one end, and none of it out of the ordinary.

Near the far end, however, he entered a large chamber where all the old dark red brocade draperies, still in surprisingly good condition, had been tacked carefully to the peeling window frames so that scarcely any light filtered in.

He pushed aside one curtain a few inches so that he could see more easily.

Sheets draped most of the furniture, except a great bed with a canopy of once-white satin, which was pushed against one wall. He glanced at it; empty. Next to it sat a vaguely familiar sandalwood box.

Was this his mother's? She had left so many fascinating things behind after her death, all of which he had enjoyed investigating as a child. No, this wasn't hers; and in a rush he remembered now where he'd previously seen it.

This box had been in the front room of August and Athina's home in Missolonghi. He had thought it attractive at the time, and now he still found it a beautiful object. Obviously the women had brought it with them, and perhaps the ebony box as well. He pulled out the revolver and carefully raised the lid of the sandalwood box.

He had found her at last.

Athina lay curled on a fragrant bed of dried spices, and the odor of cloves and orange and cinnamon wafted upward. He supposed she was asleep, because her eyes were closed, and she lay perfectly still. Almost like a dead woman.

He shuddered, and yet he had never seen her look so beautiful. Her cheeks had a faint blush in them, while her white skin was as pure as snow. Her blonde tresses spread across her pillow of spices, and she looked so delicate, so gentle. A sharp pain of longing stabbed through him. How could he ever have thought she was guilty of anything?

He shook his head, trying to clear it of these cobweb like thoughts. They were precisely what she wanted him to think so that he would do nothing at all. He knew the truth, though.

He raised the revolver and pulled back the hammer. But he had waited too long.

Her eyes fluttered open; she was awake. He glanced toward the window and saw that the light outside had fled. Nightfall.

And they are my nightmares, he thought.

Athina Kristonosos stared at him, her blue eyes so innocent, yet so worldly, and slowly a smile formed on her blood red lips.

"No, no!" Winston screamed aloud. He fired at her, his hand shaking, but missed by inches, and then he fired again, the bullet again just grazing the side of the box.

She sat up.

He stumbled backward, but before he could fire another shot, Athina grabbed his wrist with a grip like iron. Still smiling, she bent his hand back, farther and farther, until he dropped the revolver. She kept bending it back at an unnatural angle, until suddenly there was a loud abrupt sound as the fragile bones snapped.

Winston screamed in instant agony.

"Iron and such do not bother me or my sister," she whispered. "Now, go."

Winston needed no urging. He ran all the way down to his second-floor bedroom without pausing, and there he paced about the floor, clasping his broken wrist in his good hand. Pain and anger nearly maddened him. Why had he waited so long to act? Why had he trembled when he'd fired the gun? Why?

For a few minutes he soaked his swollen wrist in the basin of water, and when the throbbing had subsided a little, he took it out and bandaged it carefully with long strips cut from a towel.

Despite the pain that threatened to blot out all thoughts, he told himself he must think of another way to kill the sisters. He knew it was only a matter of time before they came for him, and either killed him or completely incapacitated him.

How? How? How?

What was left when you eliminated bullets? Very little, he thought bleakly.

But before he killed them, he must get his father safely out of the house. He lit a small oil lamp so that he could see in the dark and, ignoring his throbbing arm, walked quietly to his father's room.

He knocked softly.

No answer, and when he stepped into the room, he saw the sisters, August to one side of the bed, Athina straddling his father.

Both women were naked or nearly so—August wore a filmy nightshift—and their beautiful bodies were white and desirable in the candlelight. Their long hair, dark and light, trailed across his father.

One arm hung limply over the edge of the bed, and red dappled his father's chest, and Winston feared he was too late. He screamed in rage and grief, even as the women turned to face him.

Blood dripped down onto their breasts, and August ran a finger slowly down the bloody trail from mouth to nipple, then lifted her reddened finger to her lips and sucked and licked it. Athina bent over his father's groin and fed noisily.

Disgusted, he looked away. A sob escaped his throat, then he screamed wordlessly as he flung the oil lamp at the women.

August dodged to one side, and the lamp passed her without harm, but it crashed into the fireplace and managed to dislodge one of the burning logs, which rolled onto the carpet. Oil splashed onto the floor and August's nightgown, as well as the bed curtains. Tiny flames were instantly dancing across the carpet, licking at the hem of her gown and at the gauzy curtains.

Gracefully Athina slid off his father and advanced toward him. Her inner thighs glistened wetly, and her body was slick with blood and other things. For a moment he was compelled to watch her. He tore his gaze away with effort, and looked for some other weapon with which to defend himself.

One of the sabers on the wall! With his uninjured hand he grabbed the weapon down just as she threw herself at him. He fell back against the wall and tried to stab her, but he was too close to do any damage.

Her fingers, long and sharp, grabbed him and pinched deeply. He could feel himself bruising, and he twisted away. He thrust the sword at her, injured her side superficially, but still she kept after him. He raised his only good arm and slashed at her.

The sword caught her in the neck as she was moving, and sliced into her skin a few inches. He wanted to weep, to beg her forgiveness, to …

Blood and some clear liquid oozed from the wound. Her beautiful head flopped uselessly to one side, but still she wouldn't let go of him. She was smiling, the expression a hideous mockery, and he felt her lovely fingers digging deep into his arms, knew she would be pulling the meat from his arms in a minute. He wrenched away. sobbed as pain shot through him, then turned around.

"This is for Byron!" he yelled as he drove the sword into her beautiful throat. He wept as he sawed across her neck. Blood spurted out, splattering him, and she screamed, unable to stop him.

Finally, he hacked all the way through the bone, and her head dropped to the floor. He kicked her torso away, watched in horror as it flopped at his feet, then he rubbed the blood from his eyes.

August was across the room yet, but his father, somehow finding the strength, had sat up, and had clasped his arms tightly around her.

The woman was fighting him, pulling his hair, tearing his skin with her fingernails and teeth. But Richard Early never let go.

The bed was ablaze now, too; the curtains had become pillars of flame, and even as Winston watched, fire began creeping toward Richard.

"Go on," Richard cried. "Get out, Winston. It's the only way to save yourself."

"Father—"

"No, go!" he thundered.

And weeping, Winston turned and fled.

From behind he heard agonized screams. He tried to shut the horrible sounds out, but couldn't, and even as he half ran, half fell down the carriage sweep, he could still hear those inhuman screeches ringing in his ears. He paused, sobbing, to look back over his shoulder at the house now almost totally engulfed in flames, and Winston wept for his father and all that had been lost.

It took what seemed like hours, but he made his way along the road into town; and there explained a fire had started in the house, and that his father, his father's fiancée and her sister, and the servants had all perished. He had just managed to escape, and only now did the pain from his arm and the burns from the fire start hurting. Only now, he collapsed.

When Winston finally awoke, he found that he had been unconscious three days. He had been taken in by one of his father's friends, who reported that he had gone out to the house, with the fire company, but when they arrived the house was burning like a giant bonfire. They could only stand and watch helplessly. Today they had sifted through the warm ashes, but they had found no remains. The blaze had been so hot it had even burned the bones.

Winston closed his eyes, willing the tears back, but still they squeezed out from under his eyelids. He tried to rest all that day, yet could not help but think about what had happened.

That evening he answered the questions of the local authorities as best he could, and they seemed satisfied that the fire was a simple accident. Pleading that he was tired, he returned to bed.

In a week's time Winston returned to the London house, and packed what little he now owned, and then booked passage aboard a ship. His broken wrist had a splint on it and his arm was held in a sling. The pain had subsided somewhat, which was good.

The next afternoon he set sail for Greece. He had been thinking a lot during his forced convalescence, and he remembered what August had said that night in his room. That there were others besides her and her sister. And Greece was their home.

And if there were others still there, he was determined that he would hunt each one of the creatures down and destroy her before she could harm anyone else. He thought Byron would have approved.

He remembered, too, how the Kristonosos sisters had feared his bonfire that first night when he met them in Missolonghi. An important clue had been laid there, but he hadn't realized it at the time.

Winston shivered. A chill night wind had sprung up, and he hunched down into his coat and looked up at the sky. Stars sparkled like diamonds, and he breathed deeply of the salty air.

Everything was all right now; his sorrow lay behind him, and now he knew how to combat the lamiae. Slowly, Winston strolled along the railing, heading toward the stern.

Soon he would go to bed and dream no more.

Once he thought someone watched him, but he saw nothing, and shrugging slightly went below.

From the shadows behind him August Kristonosos smiled and waited.

ABOUT THE AUTHOR

Kathryn Ptacek sold her first novel, SATAN'S ANGEL, when she was just 27. Since then she has sold numerous novels, short stories, reviews, articles, and miscellaneous whatnots. She has also edited three anthologies, including the landmark WOMEN OF DARKNESS and WOMEN OF DARKNESS II.

Kathy was raised in Albuquerque, New Mexico and graduated with a degree in journalism from the University of New Mexico. While there, she was a student of bestselling authors Tony Hillerman (mysteries) and Lois Duncan (young adult). A member of the Horror Writers Association, she also edits the organization's monthly newsletter. She also has a freelance editing business, Little Bird Editorial Services.

She lives in a 128-year-old Victorian house haunted by the ghost of her late husband, writer Charles L. Grant. She shares her book-cluttered rooms with four cats, a large teapot collection, lots of Gila monster stuff, and the occasional visiting mouse. Kathy can be reached at gilaqueen@att.net or through her Facebook pages.

Book List

Horror and Suspense Novels
And No Birds Sing
Blood Autumn
Ghost Dance
Gila!
In Silence Sealed
Kachina
Looking Backwards in Darkness
Shadoweyes
The Hunted

Fantasy Novels written as Kathryn Grant

The Land of a Thousand Willows Trilogy
The Phoenix Bells
The Black Jade Road
The Willow Garden

Historical Novels written as Kathryn Atwood
Satan's Angel
Renegade Lady
The Lawless Heart
My Lady Rogue
Aurora

Historical Romance Novels written as Kathleen Maxwell
The Devil's Heart
Winter Masquerade

Curious about other Crossroad Press books? Stop by our website:
http://crossroadpress.com
We offer quality writing
in digital, audio, and print formats.

Subscribe to our newsletter on the website homepage and receive a
free eBook.

www.ingramcontent.com/pod-product-compliance
Lightning Source LLC
Chambersburg PA
CBHW030242200626
46816CB00002BA/472